The Angel of Mons

A World War I Legend

BOOKS BY JERRED METZ

Prose

The Last Eleven Days of Earl Durand

Halley's Comet, 1910:
Fire in the Sky

Drinking the Dipper Dry:
Nine Plain-Spoken Lives

Poetry

Brains, 25 ¢, Drive In

Three Legs Up, Cold as Stone:
Six Legs Down, Blood and Bone

The Temperate Voluptuary

Angels in the House

Speak Like Rain

The Angel of Mons

A World War I Legend

by

Jerred Metz

Singing Bone Press

Cover illustration (front): Alfred Pearce, with permission of the Mary Evans Library

Copy Editor: Cecile Lomer Kelly

LIBRARY AND ARCHIVES UNITED STATES CATALOGUING IN PUBLICATION

Metz, Jerred, 1943 –

    The Angel of Mons: A World War I Legend

Issued also in electronic form

ISBN 978-0-933439-02-3

First Edition

For Sarah, Zachary, Patricia, Eliana, Ravenna, Muhenned, and Sufyaan

As the opening British engagement of what was to become the Great War, (the Battle of Mons) became endowed in retrospect with every quality of greatness and was given a place in the British pantheon equal to the battles of Hastings and Agincourt. **Legends like that of the Angel of Mons settled upon it.**

Barbara Tuchman *The Guns of August*

Long after the war is over, and the facts of it have been recorded in histories, **one of the most widely known events will be the appearance of St. George and angel-warriors fighting in defense of the British (at) Mons.**

Harold Begbie, *On the Side of the Angels,* 1915

They Fought through the Hours to the End of Day: The
Retirement – Escape into the Twilight and the Night – That
Night the British Generals Marched the Exhausted BEF Thirty-
two Miles

Ahead Lay the Certainty – The Locale – From the Distance Came the
Barking of Dogs and Lantern Light – Mongo Black Disappeared into
the Gloom, The Victors Following — The Road where No Road Was –
The Cyclists – Goullet Goes Forward – The Return – Captain
Ashburner's Conversion – Report to General Smith-Dorrien: A Pawn
Offers Itself for Sacrifice – After Prolonged Silence – The Generals'
Meeting – General Smith-Dorrien's Dream – The General's
Determination – The Ride Back – Protecting the Secret

BOOK 2

DR. MALCOLM LECKIE
AND NURSE'S AIDE PHYLLIS CAMPBELL

Captain Malcolm Leckie and his Fiancée, Phyllis Campbell

After Surgery – Another Meeting – "You Saw Them?" "Yes. Clouds
Turned to Golden Angels." – In Parting

Malcolm Leckie, Wounded, Returned to British Care – Phyllis
Campbell, Nurses' Aide, Voluntary Aid Detachment, and the Hospital
Enquiry Sheets – The Angel of Mons: St. George, Intercessor and
Salvation

BOOK 3

ANGELS AT LE CATEAU AND THE VICKERS TEAMS

Without Pity or Remorse – A Lovely Place. A Deadly March – All that

Remained was to Wave the White Flag – The Quarry – To the Bottom – The
Problem of Manhandling the Gun to the Quarry Floor – Ziggy and Carmichael
down the Wall – Valley of the Shadow of Death – What Tommy Atkins Saw –
Tommy Atkins' Second Encounter with the Divine – The Ascent out of the Pit
– Let Death Rest from Toil

On this Vast Plain – Two Tethered Bosche Balloons – The Enemy Arrives –
The Air Was Still – The Germans Came up to Us – "Angels Saved us Before.
Why not Now?" – Herr Lieutenant Sardonic – A Front Row View – The Sky
of Three Suns – The Rocks Arise as Soldiers – St. George! In the Flesh! –
"Shoot an Angel of God?" – The Onslaught Halted – As Swiftly as they had
Come – Souvenirs

BOOK 4

THE ANGEL OF MONS,
CONAN DOYLE,
W. B. YEATS,
AND WINSTON CHURCHILL

Uncertainty Lay Heavy upon the Heart – Lily Loder-Symmons and
Automatic Writing – Captain Leckie's Handwriting – A Test – The
Answer – In the Library

A Heavenly Army Arose to Save Them – Yeats in Mackerson's Pub –
Yeats, the Hermetic Order of the Golden Dawn, and the Angels of the
Dark Cloud – Africanus Comes to his Aid – Arthur Machen's "The
Bowmen"

Yeats Worried – A Page Torn from a Doctor's Prescription Pad

Lady Campbell's Note – Tea – On the Way back to his Office

BOOK 5

THE LAST BRITISH SOLDIER KILLED

Acknowledgments

Many helped me in writing the book. First, Professor Leonard Unger, the University of Minnesota, who guided me through my doctoral dissertation on Yeats's poetry many years ago. Then friends who read, commented, criticized, and encouraged: Bill Froke, Howard Schwartz, Michael Castro, Bruce Hertz, Dr. Tom Barker, Alan Schwartz, and Dr. Jerry and Lois Gibson and Professor Simon MacKenzie, University of South Carolina.

Much thanks to my staunch editor, Cecile Lomer Kelly, and my final reader, Sarah Beaman-Jones.

Special thanks to M. Michel Vasko, Directeur adjoint, Office du Tourisme de la Ville de Mons, and M. Yves Bourdon, historian, specialist in World War I and expert in the Battle of Mons and the Angel of Mons, both of whom took me to sites related to the battle. Thanks to the Museum of Military History in Mons for photographs that inspired my thinking, the Bibliotech de Le Cateau for maps and accounts of the battle of Le Cateau.

I am grateful to the reference department, St. Louis Public Library, for primary source material, particularly Arthur Machen's "The Bowmen", Phyllis Campbell's article in the *Occult Review*, and other contemporaneous articles. The Joseph M. Bruccoli Great War Collection, Ernest F. Hollings Collections Library, University of South Carolina yielded useful materials. Richard Fisher, founder of The Vickers MG Collection & Research Association, helped with descriptions of the Vickers machine gun.

Thanks to Mo and Ravenna Nuaimy-Barker for their advice on cover designs and to Nicole Benson for the final book cover.

Thanks to the Sir Arthur Conan Doyle estate, for permission to use Sherlock Holmes as a character. And the Mary Evans Picture Library, London, for permission to use Alfred Pearce's illustration for the cover.

Most of all, thanks to my wife, Sarah Barker, for her encouragement, advise, good sense, and patience.

BOOK 1

THE ANGEL ST. GEORGE FROM THE CLOUD

Chapter One

The Sun Gaily Passed

Nimy Bridge, Mons-Condé Canal
23 August 1914, Mons, Belgium
8:00 P.M.

Dusk: The End of the First Day's Battle

The sun gaily passed through the morning and afternoon, falling in the west, unmindful of the suffering creatures below. The battle began that morning, slogged its way through the swelter of day.

Overhead and in the clear air a cloud took shape, towering to the heights. Light glowered through, golden, then gold-red, as the horizon beckoned the sun.

Two Vickers machine gun crews—4th Battalion, Company C, The Royal Fusiliers, Captain L.F. Ashburner commanding—craned their necks to see. Defending Nimy Bridge. Standing in the Germans' way who must cross the Mons-Condé Canal in order to attack the city. Hungry. Hot. Smoke. Sting of cordite in the nose and eyes. Exhausted. Throats dry. Water gone, except for what the Vickers gun needed.

For the moment the battlefield beyond the canal was quiet and empty. Lieutenant Maurice Dease, section leader of the company's two Vickers machine gun squads, visited the Ruffians team. He ordered them to withdraw after the next attack. The Vickers teams watched the cloud, which stood still, while inside of it, all was motion. Flames roved its contours and convolutions. Its outer edges glowed golden, the setting sun striking from behind. Shafts of sunlight pierced the cloud, brightening patches of ground. The cloud rolled, snaked, roiled like a mad sea. As suddenly as it had begun, the wild turmoil ceased. The cloud became a whirling column. With approaching dusk a haze fell.

"Steady, men. Keep your eyes out for the enemy, your mind on the gun," said Lieutenant Dease. "Watch for targets. Fire when they attack

3

the bridge."

Dease held his soldiers–the Ruffians and the Victors, as they named themselves–in high regard. Beyond being trained to obey, the machine gunners were pleased to follow him. His good sense, his crediting them with the squads' successes in training, earned their respect. That his instructors, and, most of all, Lt. Col. McMahon, held him in equally high regard, inspired him. He was younger than most of the men he commanded. A rare kind of officer.

"But what is up there, Lieutenant? It's not normal," said Gunner One, Private Sidney Godley. Always at the ready, the epitome of honor, and dependable in the heat of the battle.

Just then Company C Medical Officer, Dr. Malcolm Leckie, joined the Vickers squad. Amiable, devoted to duty, he had recently been assigned to The Fusiliers. He asked, "Lieutenant, how are you doing?"

"The Germans will make one last try before night," said Dease. "We're all right. Been at it all day. Ammo running low. We killed a vast number, more than I could ever have imagined. Once a whole company in less than than a minute. My men are full of fight. What a victory! We're ready for them to come in range again. Orderlies busy at the hospital tent?"

"Taking care for the moment. As you say, fighting will soon stop for the day. Visiting the line once more. You are my last stop." All the while the men watched the cloud.

"End of the line, that's what we are," muttered Private Paul Carmichael, Gunner Four.

Pointing to the sky, Lieutenant Dease said, "Captain, you're a man of science. What about that cloud?"

Leckie said, "In the Transvaal I saw cyclones, dust devils, sundogs, green halos around the sun, clouds of every kind. Nothing like this."

William Catchpole, Private, gunner three, spotter, said, "Across the canal. What do you say, Carmichael? Fritz is in range. I say, there's enough of them."

"Right, man." Carmichael signaled Godley. "Fire when you are ready."

Godley pulled the trigger and the gun chattered. Suddenly, the sound of British rifle fire and artillery all along the line was thick on the air.

Through a mental mist, Private Tommy Atkins, Gunner Six, Ruffians, awoke, spoke out of turn. "The cloud. How tall?"

No one answered.

After he laid a belt of bullets in its box, Catchpole looked at the cloud. "When a wee lad I played 'What I See in the Clouds.' But this is no hare or hedgehog," finding the theatrical line.

"A face! I see a face!" exclaimed Louis "Ziggy" Palmer. Catchpole's burlesque stage partner, playing stooge and dummy, he stated the obvious.

Proclaimed Catchpole. "It is a visitation from the gods of Olympus. Aeolus, no doubt."

"Who is that?" asked Palmer. "A woman you knew?"

"Dummy. Take the belt. Godley is running out."

To their left the company's second team, the Victors, let loose.

"A face," Captain Leckie said, "Looks down on us."

At that moment the cloud took the shape of a person's body. Captain Leckie thought of caryatids, the columns carved in the shape of women, their heads supporting the roofs of temples.

The gunners' neck hairs stood on end. "It's a person!" said Tommy Atkins, wide-eyed with amazement. The boy soldier, Gunner Six, Tommy Atkins, innocent and naïve, had been tempered in the fire of battle this day.

Gunner Four finished filling a belt with bullets, then looked up. "A knight in armor!" gasped Carmichael, he of the sullen disposition. "St. George. St. George, indeed! Come to save us, as the priest promised."

Up and down the British line and on the German side as well the soldiers turned their eyes skyward, watched, stunned, enthralled. Shooting ceased.

Cheers and prayers spilled from the lips of thousands, a murmur like a wind soughing through trees, mutterings of amazement. None could look away from the angel saint. The vision filled their minds.

"The saint come to Earth. Yes, as the priest proclaimed," said Dease.

A strange pattern of breathing took over the Vickers gunners, as if the breath breathed them. They were as vessels for the force of life.

Their breathing carried them to sobbing, which they gulped back.

Light streamed from St. George's face. It was so bright that the soldiers could not discern his features. Held by a leather strap, a hunting horn hung over his left shoulder. With his right hand he raised it to his lips and blared out the British call to attack. All along the line, the firing, which had stilled while the men looked on, resumed with fierce intensity.

The air brightened then gleamed. The Vickers machine gunners saw the angel in the sky and on the battlefield all at once.

Across the Canal

A cumulus cloud formed under St. George, became a fierce dragon writhing at the angel saint's feet. Thrashing rain from the cloud's under side, a torrent from the sky, curtains of blinding, cold rain buried in thick fog, drenched the Germans. Whipping wind threw rain in the eyes, stung the face. Caught in the red light of the setting sun, the rain had the color of blood.

Then the rain turned to hail the size of cricket balls, pelting, bruising and battering the Germans. Quickly covering the ground, the hail made footing treacherous. It brought the canal alive, the water erupting, a loud roar as it struck the surface. It did not cross to the British side.

Across the canal the Germans saw the angel. St. George's mighty lance flung lightning, split the heavens, blasting the battlefield north of the Mons-Condé Canal which the German army held. The air sizzled and cracked. The soldiers' faces and hands stung, as if blasted by wind-blown sand. A second bolt of lightning struck a battery of three German guns, the crews electrocuted, the guns destroyed. Then an artillery barrage of lightning. German heads ached mercilessly. Pressure pounded behind the eyes. Blindness from the intense light. In some vertigo. Others fainted. Some vomited. Others had trouble breathing. Many deaf. Many struck dead.

"Ozone and reeking sulfur, not just cordite," said a German conscript.

"I cannot hear," replied another private in General von Kluck's proud army. "Can you? I see your lips move, but cannot make out words."

6

"It is our Saint Michael, is it not?" replied the first.
"What did you say? I cannot hear."
"He would not strike us. It cannot be him."

The Judgment

The Ruffians saw all that was happening. "You see, St. George marks the Germans with his judgment. Rain. Hail! A plague on the Germans," said Paul Carmichael. "Didn't Jehovah throw hail down on the Egyptians?"

"Lightning. He saved that for the Germans. They must be worse than the Egyptians. A special plague for the Germans," said Godley.

Captain Leckie, transfixed along with the others, muttered, "When we were in the church. The priest told us. Are we not 'Messieurs de St Georges?' and 'Golden Arrows of God'? It is no mistake that I am here with you. The thirteen here and alive. We were all initiated. Took it for an honor."

"It must be more than that," said Catchpole, sobered by what he saw. "A blessing? 'Brotherhood of St. George' and there he is, saving us, saving the army. That explains, sir, doesn't it?"

Said Paul Carmichael, "Truly the plagues. Hail. Blood. The hail and lightning stop at the canal. Protected, yes, I would say."

Catchpole recalled his initiation. They had taken it as a ceremony of welcome and fraternity, not a promise of help and salvation. Several now touched the little golden arrows pinned inside their tunic collars. They each looked up at the celestial vision. St. George turned his eyes toward them. Each felt his gaze burn In the several minutes of tumult the Vickers crews held the bridge. Lieutenant Dease: "Keep the gun lively. No slacking. Look at them coming on. Bosche begging to be killed. Answer their plea. Give 'em what they want. Fill the belts quickly. We still have work to do." Meanwhile, like a retreating mist, the British line made its way to cover, then marched to safety and rest, victory theirs this first day.

Said Leckie. "To the hospital tent. God bless you." The men saluted. Captain Leckie ran off.

The machine guns the last to go.

"St. George our salvation," said Dease.

A Bullet Found Lieutenant Dease

Minutes later a bullet found Dease. Without even a groan he crawled out of view and dressed his own wound. Godley took over the gun. No sooner had Lieutenant Dease gone, than he was back. He was shot twice more in the next quarter of an hour. When the lieutenant returned to the gun the third time he was already seeing through dead eyes. He slumped over, groaned, and stirred no more. One day on the battlefield and, like many others, the lieutenant gone. All gathered about Dease, breathing his last, Dease, the first of the fallen.

Chapter Two

War will Call Us Soon

School of Musketry,
Vickers Machine Gunners' School,
Grantham, England
14 February 1914

Training

By the time the sixty soldiers–ten teams, Vickers machine gun trainees reached the training school they were first class marksmen, skilled with the Lee-Enfield rifle and the Maxim machine gun. Already they had been assigned to teams of six, the number of soldiers the Vickers gun needed to operate.

After words of welcome and introduction, Lt. Col. N.R. McMahon, the "Musketry Maniac", head of the Army's musketry school, turned to the topic of war. "Men, we do not know on what day it will happen, but those of us who serve His Majesty and his government know that war is soon to be upon us. The day will come when the pledges made among the nations a generation ago will come due. Thus, we prepare. Doctrine has it that the machine gun is a defensive weapon. All the armies of the world treat it so. Improvement over Mr. Maxim's gun lets us apply the Vickers gun to new use on the battlefield, giving us an advantage. With you we will develop strategies for offensive and defensive methods for the Vickers. You are part of the experiment."

At the close of the first morning's indoctrination Lt. Col. McMahon offered a challenge. "I will declare the team with the highest score at the end of training Vickers machine gun team One, first in the gun's history. High honor."

Captain Hill made a few remarks, followed by Sergeant Trueblood. Then the training began.

The Lectures

The Vickers machine gun trainees listened to lectures, took volumes of notes.

"Soldiers, you have been assigned your roles. You know your jobs," began Instructor Sergeant Trueblood. Then he told them what they already knew. "Gunner One, principal gunner, machine operator, swivels the gun through its mechanical arcs, fires, kills. Gunner Two guides the ammo belts into the feed-block. Three and Four haul the ammunition. Three through Six fill the belts, search for targets, watch for the enemy. And ye better be damn fast at your job, damn sharp," Sergeant Trueblood scolded. "Your life depends on it."

Private Gabriel Jessop, gunner two, Victor, thought, "Who doesn't know all that? We trained on the Maxim, for God's sake. I already know this." Jessop kept his thought to himself, ignoring the instructor. Contrary by nature, a critic and complainer, by practice, Jessop knew his work on the weapon, his role on the team, his soldier's duty. He hated waste, especially of his time. Impatient.

The sergeant drew breath, then blustered, "On the march Five and Six are in charge of gear. Six keeps track of the ammunition supply, keeps it clean, dry, in order, ready to fire. Five and Six keep an inventory of parts, a maintenance list. Thorough reports. I mean thorough! To whom does every bullet, every part belong? His Majesty!"

He looked about the hall, then, "Don't ever run out of ammo, let alone low. Caught short and you're dead." He paused, expecting a laugh. Then tried again. "The Grim Reaper takes every advantage." No one could tell that this was his humor. He turned poetic. "Like wind, Death enters the smallest crack. Like water, he seeps in wherever he can." He was angry that no one responded to his sallies of wit. So, as if the soldiers had already failed at their task, scowling, he said, "The gun misfires! While you're scratching your head wondering what's wrong with the gun your mates get killed. They won't thank you for your ignorance, I can tell you. They'll curse you! Practice! Speed! Accuracy! Give yourselves a fighting chance! Learn the whys and hows of the Vickers and how to fix it quick, or you're a goner, too." Then, "Better yet, keep it in top repair!"

Instructor Trueblood droned on for an hour. Finally, he dismissed the men.

As the Victors squad made its way across the yard to the dormitory, Gabriel Jessop loudly whispered to Private Walter Sage, Three. "Waste of time. He thinks us useless blighters and ignoramuses."

Sergeant Henry Sanders, One, overheard. "Don't talk foolishness," he said. "You were selected to train as a Vickers machine gunner. Listen to the instructor. No squirming about in your seat. No sour face like I saw you putting on. Sage, keep Jessop in line."

Before he enlisted in the army Sergeant Sanders had tried factory work. He hated the little of it he had done. He did poorly as a laborer, clerk, insurance salesman. His talents and disposition, it turned out, did not suit him for these endeavors. So he was dismissed from each position. Finally, he needed a place in life that would supply food, clothing, and shelter. As what he considered a last resort, he took the King's shilling, enlisted in the army. And, to his surprise and delight, thrived. He enjoyed the discipline, the fellowship, the ceremony. Now, five years later, he saw glory within his grasp. His gun was his lady faire for whom he wished to do honor. Vickers. Victoria. The queen, gone now, but still his Empress of the British Empire. He, a knight of modern days. He also called the gun Vixen, Vicki, gave his lady faire these names, too. Flamboyant, boastful, he went out of his way to attract attention. The team's operation and the gun's were flawless, deserving of high praise. That meant everything to Sergeant Henry Sanders.

Who will be the Top Vickers Teams?

By the fourth week of training, McMahon and his adjutant, Captain Charles Hill, who directed the training, could already rank the teams by skill, potential, morale, and fighting will. He knew which teams would represent the new gun, and apply the new way of fighting well. In the front rank, the two squads from Company C, 4th Battalion, the Royal Fusiliers.

"Fox and hounds," said McMahon.

"Fox and hounds, Sir?" said Captain Hill, not sure what his superior meant.

"Old-fashioned training. Godley's and what-s-his-name's team, the one always putting on a bit of a display? The section Lieutenant Dease directs. The foxes. The other sections, the hounds."

He said, "Sir?"

"Make the foxes think the dogs are close behind in the chase, smell

11

blood, and are catching up."

"I see. Yes."

"And make the teams closest behind think they are humiliating themselves. Tell them they are being beaten by second-rate teams, squads worse than they. Everyone will improve. Precision, speed, care of the gun. Raise all the measures, a little at a time. Toughen them. Always a little tougher."

And so it was.

McMahon saw that the leader of the Victors, Sergeant Sanders, was full of valor that would serve him and the Army well. Brains in Sidney Godley, valor in Sanders. They would, McMahon knew, lead Vickers squads One and Two, but who would be first and who second he could not yet tell. Weeks of training lay ahead.

In the Workshop

By squad and section the men from different regiments and companies gathered around workbenches in the industrial shop, training together. On each bench, a Vickers gun. The soldiers learned to take the gun apart, reassembled it, again and again, first, eyes open, then blindfolded, faster each time, less fumbling, greater accuracy, more precision. They learned the feel of each piece in the hand, each part's function, where it belonged in the gun, how to install it. Fifty-seven pieces.

Instructors went from workbench to workbench criticizing, correcting, instructing, scolding, encouraging, listening. The Ruffians and Victors worked side by side. The always-agitated mechanic, Jessop, grumbled, "Why do I have to know the name of every damn part? If we can kill Germans, get about in a fight, isn't that enough?" In the hubbub of trainees talking, it was easy to hide the conversation.

"Instructor coming. Keep Jessop quiet." To Sage, Sergeant Sanders said, "Gag him. Strangle him if you need to. We are watched and judged every minute."

"A spy listening to what I say?" asked Jessop.

Sanders continued, "What did I just say? Keep your jibes to yourself. When examined, you need to know the answers. One hundred percent for each of you. And our conduct is watched. No outbursts. No foolishness. Conduct yourself properly. I tell you, we will be Vickers team Number One gun."

Beset, Gabriel Jessop snapped, "Well, that makes no damn sense." Then mumbled, "Number One. Number One. Number One." Then, so all could hear, "Is that all you think about?"

While they spent most of their time in serious concentration, preparing for tests, readying for war, they taunted in the way of comrades, competitors. Like thunder, the grumbling rolled from the Victors' to the Ruffians' workbench. William Catchpole leaned across. "Number One? We Ruffians will put your name to shame. Victors, indeed."

Picking up the refrain, Ziggy Palmer chimed in, "You will be sorry you ever chose it. We will be Vickers Team Number One. I am certain."

Then Catchpole came after Jessop. "I will consider it a success to get out of the war alive, fulfill my term of duty. Achievement enough for me."

"I see it practical," said Sage. "The better we shoot, the more enemy we kill. The better we are, the better our chances of living."

"Enough from you," ordered Sergeant Sanders. To Jessop he said, "They are berating us, mostly you. How important is Number One? Distinction and honor. Those are important. Why bother otherwise?"

Said Hardy, humbly, "Since we will be rated, we should be the best."

"Why?" griped Jessop. "Explain why. First or third or tenth. What does it matter?"

"That's enough," said Sanders in an angry whisper. "Listen and obey, Private. You've been in the army long enough to know. I will not let you dishonor us. As much as I dislike it, I cannot let you dishonor even yourself. You must score high on the written examination. There is more to it than how good we are on the gun."

"Number One. For God's sake." Jessop grunted once more, then fell quiet.

"Talk about the gun now. Instructor coming this way," hissed Sage.

Private Walter Sage took Jessop's frequent, vociferous grousing as the man's way of venting his frustration. "The instructor reminds us how serious this is," said the laconic Sage to Jessop. "What's wrong with that?" Few words, and unperturbed, was Sage. A refugee from poverty, he found refuge in the army. Walter Sage, one of ten children.

His father, a poor laborer, could not afford to keep them all. Each child was sent into the world as soon as it was old enough to earn a shilling. Walter, the eighth. When he was selected for Vickers machine gun training sometimes he thought someone saw in him, an aptitude, a skill. At other times he thought maybe the army trained men, knowing that whatever they needed to know for a job, the instructors would teach them. Sage repeated his point. "Serious deserves repeating, my friend. Everything is serious. The more we know, the more we practice, the better soldiers we will be when it comes to the test."

"What test?" challenged Jessop.

"Don't pretend to be stupid," said Sage. "You know what test. Battle."

Angry, Jessop snapped, "Don't you teach me, child. Mind your own affairs."

In the Common Room

After the first day's lecture, the soldiers repaired to their dormitory. The two squads reflected on the instructor's lesson. "Pardon me for saying so, sir," said William Catchpole to Godley, "I heard Instructor Trueblood say Sixes are supposed to be the brains of the bunch. But look. How come they picked dim-witted Atkins for number Six?"

Godley said, "Respect, Catchpole, respect, or trouble for you. Atkins is Six when it comes to hauling and loading belts. He's the accountant, the quartermaster for parts and bullets in name only. It won't be Atkins keeping count. That will fall to the smart one among us."

"Who, you?"

"You."

Catchpole said, "I'm no good at keeping track. Not a good counter. Just curious."

"Just mean-spirited, you mean. Your life might depend on Atkins some day."

"God help me, then."

Sanders said, "Your tongue, Private! Hold your tongue if you want to keep it!"

Day by day the trainees struggled to learn what fell from Instructor Sergeant Trueblood's blistering tongue. Each day a lecture, workshop, classroom, and field exercises on the grounds about the school–two hundred fifty acres–the Ruffians and Victors. At night in the drab commons room the Vickers soldiers poured over manuals, books, notes, diagrams and maps, argued, questioned, disputed, agreed, learned.

Day by day, night after night, at first murky and random, the instructions became clear. Even so, Private Jessop returned to his complaint. "Little difference between this and the Maxim. Facts and facts about the Vickers? Isn't it enough that we can aim and shoot? How will I pass the examination? I'm no good at memorizing. Me, and good luck to Nancarrew here. "

To the assembled Catchpole said, "The truth is, Jessop's brain holds only so much," He asked, "Is that your problem? I think so."

"You're rich in the sarcasm compartment of the brain," Jessop replied.

Ziggy Palmer delivered a second thrust. "Did your brain run out of room? I would expect that of Nancarrew here, but not you. Already full, is it? Your brain?"

Always quiet, poor with words, almost silent, Private Carrew Nancarrew listened and wondered about Jessop's complaint. Was his brain different than Jessop's? The young man excelled at interpreting maps, diagrams, numbers. From youth he learned mechanics and machinery on a Welsh farm where he was a laborer. His specialty, his talent, his gift. A remarkable aptitude. A second sense. He was skilled with calculations, with the gun. He was fastest at breaking it down and reassembling. "His brains are in his fingers," Sergeant Sanders said. Nancarrew was not a thinker.

Catchpole Palmer said, "Jessop is, I am sorry to say, like indigestion, a sour stomach. Howard Lang and Alan Hardy are his antidote. Take two pills, the doctor tells old Jessop. Lang and young Hardy are the pills he needs to calm him."

"Milk of magnesia to his acid," said William Catchpole.

"Bicarbonate of soda," added Palmer.

"Alkaline to neutralize acid," continued Catchpole.

They went on. "I've got one," said Palmer. "Lang and Hardy. The cooling breath to Jessop's hot soup."

"I'll top that. Tempering cold water to Jessop's red-hot iron. We could go on." They laughed at their own humor.

"Oh, you two are too clever by half," said Sergeant Sanders. "You stir him up, laugh when he explodes."

The jibes angered Jessop. He scowled, and snapped back. "What brought you two to the army? You don't respect anything about it, or any of your comrades. What brought you here?"

Catchpole replied, "Ah, my friend, therein lies a tale. And I shall tell it to you."

Interlude:
"The Laughing Husband" and
Lord Gooseberry Tart

Adopting the speaking of a farmer said William Catchpole, "Entertainers with the King's patent, we was."

"The king of the Hottentots, yer mean," retorted Palmer. "We got no nearer the King than some lowly baronets and a duke or two."

"What do you mean? I got a baronet's dame. In plays there is always the subplot and that's where I play in life."

"We performed comic skits as Sir Edward Twaddle of Tweedledale and his valet, M. T. Head, as Stout and Sturdy, a routine about Milord's trickster gardeners, Lout and Dirty, stable muckers and lads, a bit as cheating merchants. "Sometimes we were the down-and-out flakes with sawdust in our whiskers and whiskey on our breath, as we joked about doing the naughty bit with the girl in the act, low humor, you know. Sometimes we were the doffers in the high silk hats being pesky around the wives of our betters. Cheese and Sweets. We are whatever concoction of characters we can throw together to get us on the stage and in the money."

"Mocking the aristocracy, the merchants, the ignorant poor," said Ziggy Palmer.

The same bits on three social levels. Like the clown who mimics the lion tamer, training a kitty cat, or the high wire walker with the rope on the ground."

Palmer: "We made them laugh while making them impatient for the girls, too."

The soldiers' ears pricked up when Catchpole said, "Except for the Lord whose lovely wife fancied me. He cared."

"Even so," Jessop said, "Get to what led you to take up the King's shilling?"

"My champagne and caviar was the London burlesque. My partner Palmer, Ziggy the ladies who adored him, and I did a turn, comic routines in the leg shows. Ziggy. Skinny as a chicken. Ziggy, flap your wings. Look at him. The ladies had a strange desire to kiss him and who knows what else. If he was a Jew he would be called the human mezuzah."

You'll see. "Once in a while I got to act in some dreadful theatre. Mr. Faraday bought a German musical comedy called "The Laughing Husband" that did well in Berlin, brought it to London. I got the role of Count Selztal, the nemesis and villain, the evildoer and the cause of the beautiful Hella Bruckner's downfall. When our feelings toward Germany were unfavorable, characters named Lutz Nachtigall, Ottakar Bruckner, and Hans Zimt kept patrons away. It did not sell. Even so, we got off to a roaring start. The London Times theatre critic wrote, and I remember his words, 'London's verdict upon The Laughing Husbands dainty a musical comedy as has been seen for some time.'" In disgust, he said, "A dainty musical comedy, indeed. Fluff lighter than goose down."

"Now he's reviewing a play," Gabriel Jessop said. "I asked a simple question. You are stretching out the answer."

"Enjoy the recitation. It is likely the most interesting account you will have heard in your featureless lives. Miss Gwladys Gaynor, her stage name, was an all right actress, and, like most all right actresses, she found little work on the stage. But, unlike most average actresses, she the wife of wealth. She wanted to perform on stage and her husband, Lord Gooseberry Tart I will call him, had to indulge her. He paid for the twittering musical comedy, and here we were. Milady liked the company of actors, of witty, sometimes spicy, characters.

Ziggy Palmer commented. "Now we will get to the naughty part. Listen and enjoy. Is it all right with you, Catchpole? I'll tell the plot and you tell what happened."

"That is quite good. Quite nice. Go on."

Said Palmer, "I played a minor character, so got to see what happened. In the play Ottakar Bruckner believed implicitly in his wife. With faith in her, he threw his wife into the company of the nefarious count in quest of love and dalliance, a lover of beautiful women. Even when Ottakar's best friend warned about the count's reputation, the husband did not worry. Was he not in love with his wife? Of what should he be suspicious? Meanwhile the world's tongues wagged."

"I see it coming," said Sergeant Sanders. "The lovely Mrs. Bruckner fell in love with the Lothario. Am I right?"

"Indeed, you are. But who was to blame, the play asks," Catchpole said.

Bruckner sent his wife from the home, and drowned his sorrow in Rhine wine. The friends and a divorce lawyer brings the unhappy couple back together. The count–me–was sent on his way.

Palmer said, "Silly plot, silly songs, silly dialogue. As you can guess, something about the play led to our joining the army."

Catchpole took up the story. "And if not for Miss Gaynor, I would not have enjoyed it at all. I was doing with the Lord's wife what Count Selztal was doing with Mrs. Bruckner. It tickled me, the irony. That was half the fun. Lord Gooseberry Tart was Ottakar Bruckner. I played Count Selztal on stage and in Miss Gaynor's dressing room and boudoir. My downfall. Milord found me charming, offered me cigars, brandy, evenings of dullish conversation, never suspecting. Though our play did not end the way "The Laughing Husband" did. Yes, Lord Gooseberry Tart sent his wife from his door. But unlike the Count, who was only banned from this small slice of society, the Lord threatened to charge me with alienating his wife's affections. Not him directly, of course, but his solicitor. "

Ziggy Palmer took up the tale. "We were surprised. We thought the cuckold wouldn't want his name sullied. I think that is the word. Milord gave Catchpole a choice."

"Believing that war would come soon and hoping I would suffer a miserable death, the Lord would permit me to enlist in the Army. Or I could go to jail. So off Palmer and I footed it to join the Territorials. Why'd he come? We are brothers of the spirit, drinking pals since the beginning. No work, no eat. We've seen the formula operate without fail. So we stick together, starve together, eat together. We wouldn't be any good, one without the other. We tooted out of there and here we are, training for war. That's how we ended up here, me having a bit of the naughty with Milord Gooseberry's wife."

"Ah, I recall the day. And those were the days," sarcastic Palmer chortled. "Might as well go out laughing. When we go home to jolly England we'll return to perform in the finest leg shows in London, or at least Liverpool."

"Why are you here? Were you accused of anything?" asked Godley.

"Accessory, they call it. I was a decoy, a distraction, and lookout. My fun with so many of the ladies kept old Gooseberry's attention on me. I was the topic of much gossip. He though I was the one he had to watch out for. I didn't want to break up the act. I really didn't have anything else to do. We were a team and that was that."

Gunners Godley and Sanders Report to the Section Leader

Each evening the two top gunners reported to section leader Dease to evaluate the soldiers' progress, problems, solutions. "Sanders," he asked, "What about your two, fresh from the varsity?"

"Hardy and the Lang fellow?" replied the Sergeant Sanders. "They still have the schoolboy's enthusiasm for things new and well ordered. They consider army life an adventure. One fills his head with pictures, the other, with stories and words. One scratches words in a notebook, the other scratches lines, sketches. Dream of being an artist, the one, a writer, the other."

Hardy hoped to follow the path of a distant relative, Thomas Hardy, novelist and poet. The young Alan Hardy read his many books, met the author twice.

"They have no idea what's coming, do they?" remarked Lieutenant Dease.

"I try to teach them, prepare them. They still have many schoolboy fantasies. On the team, on the gun they are fine. Eager, proficient, calm, steady. They are made of good stuff. They'll hold up."

"And Sage?" Lieutenant Dease asked.

Sergeant Sander's opinion: "If you listen to him he is either equal minded, or indecisive. He can't tell which he is himself."

"Does it matter?"

"He is not the stuff of leadership."

"That's not what you need him for."

"Sage can handle his job. He steadies the men. That he does well."

"Good enough, then, Sanders," replied Dease. "In any case, they need more toughening, more grit. Take care you give it to them. They all need more."

"That's what I'm telling them. But that Jessop. . . . I hope he straightens out."

Dease said, "Enough for one day. Tomorrow, work them harder. None of us have been to war. But I think it will take more toughness than the recruits have to put up a good fight, to win."

On the Firing Range and Fields at Hythe and Grantham

The soldiers trained. The squads practiced maneuvering in open country, ranging through every kind of terrain. They raced in full service kits. Calisthenics. Stamina, dexterity, speed. Built their bodies. And minds. Among the recent recruits–six months in training boys and men became soldiers. The veterans, who had a natural contempt for recruits, overcame it, and even came to like them. Those new to His Majesty's army grew accustomed to the routines and rigors of army life. Their fear of their instructors and the veterans diminished. They knew they could depend on each other.

Catchpole complained, "I've been drilled to death. I dream about the weapon's parts. They dance before me, singing and cavorting. They replace the lovely girls of my dreams, the delights of the dancehall, much to my regret."

His colleague in mischief, Palmer said, "Drilled to distraction. I have forgotten everything else about life. I will kill Germans just to get even for the torments I have already endured. If not for them, I would be living a life of ease, posted to some sweet place in the colonies, eating well, playing cricket, better yet, polo, going to parties, romancing the ladies, lazing in the tropical sun."

On the firing range the instructors timed each action, scored each shot, each man, each team, for speed and accuracy always needing improvement.

In the field the soldiers practiced sighting, elevating mechanisms, searching fire, distribution of fire, searching with distribution, fixed fire, correcting measurement error fire, volume of fire, accuracy of fire, sustained, indirect, overhead, and plunging fire. The Vickers trainees rehearsed enfilade and frontal fire, known distance, field, and combat fire, extended drill order firing, and control. The gunners fired in formation and at formations. They fired by squad, platoon, and company. They practiced as squad and platoon skirmishers, squad in column and platoon in column, platoon advancing in thin lines, squad and platoon rushes. Fired at every formation in every likely terrain. Mastered spotting hidden and lurking targets. Their eyes sharpening, their senses awakening to signs of enemy presence and movements.

Knackers Hauled a Dozen Dead Horses

The Vickers company officials and engineers and the school staff needed to see what the guns would do when bullets struck flesh and bone at long range. Knackers hauled a dozen dead horses onto the firing range instead of taking them off to grind into animal feed. The two teams, the Ruffians and the Victors, helped the knackers prop them up across the firing range one thousand yards from the guns. The teams fired off several short bursts, a few longer, then joined the officials examining the remains. The stench arising from the blasted organs, digestive system, and blood sickened all but the knackers.

To the school staff and Vickers Company executives and engineers Lt. Col. McMahon observed, "Devastation at long range. Greater power than the Maxim." Captain George Hill, adjutant, took up the refrain. "The bullet's work when it hits the target. Splendid."

Among themselves the soldiers commented. "Is this how the dead will smell?" asked Tommy Atkins.

Tommy Atkins, a boy from London, held his breath against the smell. There he lived with his father and mother in the back of his father's cobbler's shop. The smell of the dead horses brought back the smell of leather, polishes, dyes, rubber, machine oil. The smells sickened him. One reason he joined the army. He thought, is this what dead men will smell like? He felt queasy, a little faint, but kept his composure. As the men drew closer for a look, in his mind's eye Atkins saw the mess as what would be left of a man. A shiver ran through his body. He broke out in a sweat.

"The blasted dead," announced Gabriel Jessop. "Lived near a slaughterhouse when I was a boy. Same stink." Even as they examined the remains, a handful of flies settled on the flesh to lay their eggs.

Victor Alan Hardy, said, "Pieces barely big enough to recognize as horseflesh."

"Bone shards, splinters," added Private Lang.

Young Carrew Nancarrew, a boy from the Welsh farm country, aspired to escape the cow byre and the hayfield. Here he was, quiet, little to say, willing to do what he was ordered. He muttered, "Hardly enough meat for the knackers to haul off. Can't leave it to rot. Horrid stink soon enough." He was accustomed to the stench of dead animals. Some butchered, some just dead.

Holding up a bullet, Private Lang remarked, "When one of these bullets strikes a man. . . ." and did not finish the sentence.

"When the bullet strikes a man," Jessop said, taking up Lang's refrain, "His earthly woes are over."

Said Walter Sage, "The wounded? His woes have just begun."

Ruffian Catchpole said, "Hate to be on the other end of one of these bullets."

"We will leave many Germans wounded on the field of battle," said Lieutenant Dease. "The wounded more an obstruction than the dead. The litter carriers have to haul them through gunfire and artillery. Make lovely targets."

Gunner Godley countered, "The dead can wait for the cease fire."

Ziggy Palmer offered his opinion. "The Vickers does the nasty on everything it hits."

The Tournament

Stingy with praise, little by little the instructors brought the teams to mastery in everything about the Vickers gun. In time everything smooth, fast, proficient, the gunners interchangeable parts of the Vickers machine gun. Everything became second nature. The same held true for field maneuvers and tactical matters.

In the final days the instructors tested, ranked, graded them. All around sounded the staccato barking and belching of the guns, encouraging shouts of the men, and curses, ridicule, chastisement, taunts from the instructors.

Training done, Captain Hill announced, "Tomorrow a contest. The top four teams, a spectacle of marksmanship and teamwork. More than a test. A celebration after the morning's passing out parade. The prizes: the two top guns will represent all of you trained Vickers machine gunners and tour the Vickers manufactory. Meet the workers who built your weapon. The winning teams will receive extra soup tickets."

To his fellow Victors Jessop quietly griped, "Some prizes. Not worth much, I say."

"About wagers. . . ." Captain Hill did not finish the sentence. The men knew what would follow. No wagering. But the soldiers would have a stake in the contest. That evening natural touts and bookies emerged from the class. The next day a punter's holiday. Even bets. Pick your team. Bet on your man. Every kind of proposition and combination.

The four squads assembled on the firing range. Captain Hill explained, pointing left and right, he said, "Two posts. Fields of fire in opposite directions." The captain mustered a feeble joke. "We do not want you to shoot each other. We need all the soldiers we have." The men gave the obligatory laugh.

"First test: marksmanship. Single shots at hidden targets rising." He instructed the four teams, then said, "The test will determine the victor. High team score wins."

"Instructions clear?" said Captain Hill.

"Yes, sir," replied Godley and Sanders and the other two squad leaders.

"The rest?"

Murmured "yes, sirs" and "all rights" from the rest signaled assent.

"Good. The honor of your weapon is at stake."

The first two teams finished their salvos in fewer than three minutes. Two squads ran forward, took the targets down from their frames, inserted fresh ones, and deposited the ones they retrieved on the umpire's table.

Then Hill said, "Ruffians, as you call yourselves, fire to the west, Victors, to the east. The range is ready."

Exclaimed Henry Sanders, "The Victors will be victorious. What do you say, Godley?"

"Your name does not predict your winning," said Godley. "We will rub your noses in defeat."

Gunners Two removed the bullet from every other pouch in the belt, enough for the thirty-six rounds that would be fired. Each soldier had to depress the trigger twice to fire a bullet.

Each field hid six targets. The Ruffians and Victors took their places. The umpire ordered, "Target! Fire!" Six shots, ten seconds. Then, "Halt fire!" Ten seconds' pause. The next gunner in line took the place of the one before. Two fed the belt for One, Three for Two, and so on. A new target—high, low, near, far, left, right, back and forth—rose. Again, "Fire!" The targets came up in a different order for each gunner, though after the first few fired the others knew where the targets were.

The observers cheered the gunners on, a free-for-all of expressions of encouragement mingled with threat, taunt, elation, jeer, mockery, ejaculations, a thorough lack of decorum.

The soldiers drew a folded slip of paper with a number on it from a cap to determine the order in which they would fire.

The pair drawn to fire last were the rustic Nancarrew, Number Four, Victors, and his city cousin and counterpart in timidity and meekness, Number Six, Ruffian Tommy Atkins, as un-ruffian a lad as could be. Mum throughout the trial, they took their turns. Atkins was the least skilled, the least proficient of the Ruffians. While waiting his turn, the naïve Tommy Atkins whispered to Sidney Godley, "Is it possible to score below zero? I mean, if enough bullets miss the target."

"Possible? Yes," said Godley. "Do not frighten yourself. You will shoot admirably. We are Vickers Team One. Calm yourself. Winning is our way."

Victor Carrew Nancarrew, a much better gunner than Atkins, was ready, the index fingers of both hands on the two triggers, already feeling triumphant. Bound in friendship by their timidity and shyness, the two were now antagonists. They looked at each other across the few yards that separated them. Nancarrew glowered to rattle his comrade. Atkins' already taut nerves and tense muscles tightened even further, constricting his breathing. Even so, he had the good sense to reply, thinned his eyes to a piercing gaze.

Though all in a sweat, atremble with worry before grasping the triggers, Atkins took a slow, deep breath, became a different man. His fellow Ruffians saw him calm himself, become attentive, focused. "A spirit must have grabbed him by the soul and given him a new life," said Catchpole to Sidney Godley.

After their round, Nancarrew, impatient and nervous, asked, "Who won?"

"Wait," said Captain Hill. "Give the counters time and quiet."

Four soldiers marked the holes in the target rings, tallied the score.

Then the umpire posted individual and team scores. The Victors and Ruffians scored highest, ahead of the other two teams by a hair's breadth. The Ruffians slipped by the Victors, a consequence of the Victors' mistakes rather than by their skill. Tommy Atkins scored higher than Nancarrew. None could explain how, least of all Tommy himself, though poor shooting on Nancarrew's part contributed to his triumph.

"I'm as surprised as anyone," Atkins said.

Shaking Atkins hand in congratulation, Sidney Godley said, "We were so close to Sanders' men in score. Who would have thought that you would make the difference? But you did."

Up spoke Catchpole. "And in our favor. That is the amazing part."

At the Victors disgusted, Sergeant Sanders growled, "You cost us Number One."

Nancarrew lowered his head. "Sorry, sir. Very sorry."

Hardy came to the berated Nancarrew's defense. "It's not his fault that we were not far enough ahead so that his few points did not keep us far enough ahead to win. It could have been that way as well. Don't put all the blame on him."

"Oh, they beat us. And by the slimmest of margins. That's what I hate. And it does not seem to matter one way or the other to Godley. What a waste." Sanders stomped off, angry.

Tommy Atkins approached. "Carrew, can I talk with you?" They stepped out of hearing. "Still friends? And hope we are. Your men will be all on you. I don't know how it happened. Just got lucky, I expect."

Ruffian William Catchpole went to Sergeant Sanders, shook his hand, said, "You so-called Victors won."

"Won? We lost." said Sanders.

"You won my pity for coming in second."

Said Catchpole, "Oh, yes indeed. We are Vickers One in skill, rating, spirit, humor, valor, and intelligence. QED."

"QE what?" said Palmer.

."QED, 'Quod Erat Demonstrandum.' 'Which was to be

demonstrated.'

Or 'thus I have proved.' In this case, quite easily done," said Catchpole. "Quite easily indeed, thanks to the Victors losing."

The soldiers had received their pay chits the day before. After the contest large sums of wagered money exchanged hands.

The winners' prizes–a medal, a letter of commendation, and a soup ticket–a blue linen card:

> Your Commanding Officer and Brigade Commander have informed me that you have distinguished yourself by your conduct in the field. I read their report with much pleasure.
>
> Signed,
>
> _____
>
> Major-General

"He didn't even sign," said Catchpole. "The line is blank."

"I hope it's official. I'd hate to miss out on the soup," scoffed Palmer. "And a trip to the Vickers manufactory."

Lt. Colonel Norman R. McMahon
Congratulates the Winners

Dease whispered loud enough for the squad to hear, "Staff Officer McMahon coming. Salute, give your name and position on the gun. Nothing more. Do not bark. This isn't roll call." Chief Instructor Lt. Colonel Norman McMahon stepped before Godley who stiffened in salute. "Private Sidney Godley Gunner One, sir."

"Congratulations to you and your section, Lieutenant. Your scores combined are the highest of all the sections."

"Thank you, sir," said Dease. "Private Godley is in charge of the winning squad, sir. He deserves the congratulations, sir."

McMahon turned to Godley, "Consequently, you are Vickers Team One, sir."

Godley saluted, "Thank you, sir." Dease ordered, "Next."

Ever the master of ceremonies and stage performer, William Catchpole imagined himself introducing Palmer. "Number Three readies a stack of belts for Number Two. Three and Four watch out for the men firing and feeding the belts, spot targets and trouble, keep their eyes on everything that goes on." His thoughts went on. "We spotters have the eyes of hawks, the vigilance of mother wolves. We will find the Bosche, wherever they are, then call out their location for Gunner One."

Catchpole's internal monologue went on, more flamboyantly. "And I proudly introduce Number Two, Louis–we call him Ziggy Palmer." In his mind's eye he saw Palmer offer a crisp salute and smile broadly, as if to say this man Catchpole makes me jolly. And pleased to meet you. Private Catchpole was proud of his speech.

"Palmer, sir. Gunner Two."

So caught up in his imagining was Catchpole that he did not see Lt. Col. McMahon standing in front of him, awaiting a salute.

"Name and post," ordered Dease in a gruff, peremptory whisper. The abrupt voice startled Catchpole out of his reverie. Catchpole saluted. "William Catchpole, Gunner Three, sir."

Then in quick order, "Carmichael, Number Four, Ruffians, sir."

Hoping for a more settled and honorable life than roustabout and sideshow performer than the circus and the tabor had given him, Paul Carmichael had thrown in his chances with a post in the army. Scrapes with a circus strong man over the affections of a trapeze artist convinced him that he stood a better chance of success in life with a gun in his hand than a bare-fisted encounter he was certain to lose. And so here he was, saluting and uttering a few uncalled for words.

"Ruffians are you?" said McMahon. "I should hope so, private. Indeed, I hope so."

"Five, Wigston. Private Wigston."

In a voice barely audible, "Number Six, Private Atkins, sir."

Then McMahon inspected the Victors. Sergeant Sanders ordered, "Salute!" and broke into speech. "We are the Victors, keepers of the gun we name Vixen, Vicki, the angry huntress, mother fox. I am Sergeant Henry Sanders, Number One."

Privates Alan Hardy and Howard Lang cringed in embarrassment and disbelief that their leader should speak in such a way.

"Victors is it? Good. May victory be ours, and swiftly," replied McMahon.

"Gunner Two, Private Jessop, Sir."

Sanders added, "Already grey at the temples, family left behind."

Hardy and Lang recoiled again. Sanders was stepping beyond proper bounds.

"Three, Walter Sage, mechanic."

Nervously, up spoke Number Four, Private Carrew Nancarrew, the short, stocky country boy.

Next the friends, eager for adventure, subjects for their arts. "Hardy, Private. Number Five, sir." He had already written accounts and reflections on his training, his friends, speculations about the future. Soon, he hoped, war would give him stories of adventure, derring-do, mishaps, miraculous escapes, bravery, and victory. After the war, which all expected to be brief, he planned to turn his material into writing in the manner of H.G. Wells and Arnold Bennett.

Private Howard Lang, Number Six, nephew of the recently deceased Andrew Lang, collector and editor of fairy tales, poet, critic, essayist, recently President of the British Psychical Society–saluted crisply and introduced himself. An aspiring painter, he had already sketched enough pictures of training exercises to fill a small gallery with his work.

McMahon raised his eyebrows, asked, "Hardy, is it? Lang?"

"Relatives of the famous, sir," said Lang.

"You are good at the gun. That is what counts here. I see from your records that you are. That is why you are at gun Number Two."

McMahon addressed the Ruffians and Victors. "Captain Hill told you that the best two teams would visit the Vickers manufactory. A gesture of good will. Cooperation. Important for morale. Take proper care. Follow your leader's instructions–Lieutenant Dease."

Jessop quietly grumbled, "Good will? Public relations, he means."

McMahon overheard, but replied as if he was merely moving to his next point. "We need more guns, and quickly. We depend on the workers' craft. They want to make guns, many, and soon. Mutual effort. They are your brothers in battle. They serve on the home front."

The men saluted again, the Lieutenant Colonel turning on his heels and moving off.

Passing out Parade

Before commissioning and awards- and medal-giving, the instructors spoke. Then Lt. Col. McMahon. He ended his address, saying, "As you have learned much from your instructors, we have learned much from you. The Vickers machine gun is a grand experiment. You are proving the gun's worth–a weapon not only for defense, but, as we have proved, offense. We have surprises for the Germans when the time comes. One gun has the fire-power of ten rifles."

In the ranks the surly Jessop whispered to Nancarrew, standing next to him, "But it takes six men to operate it. Six-tenths, or three-fifths improvement if measured by manpower, not ten times. Right, numbers expert?"

Overhearing, Sergeant Sanders angrily shushed him.

The Ruffians and Victors Plan their Tableau

For the closing ceremonies each squad was to put on a patriotic tableau vivant, the production mounted on limbers and paraded in review that late afternoon to catch the splendor of the setting sun. In the manner of memorials from the 1870 Franco-Prussian War, one team wrapped themselves in sheets as togas, reproduced scenes from ancient Greece or Rome. Bare arms and left breast. Brass circlets about their biceps. Laurel wreaths crowning their heads. Others took on poses associated with the battles of Malplaquet and Crécy in France, where Britain won important victories in the past.

At Lieutenant Dease's section up spoke Atkins. "May we honor our nation's patron, Saint George?"

"Saint, indeed! Who needs a saint?" chided Jessop.

"He's a warrior, you fool. We need his help and protection. The boy has a thought!" said Palmer. "He's come alive! He's vivant himself. Let us honor our little thinker and our saint."

"Atkins is innocent, all right. But no saint," said Carmichael. "Nothing has tempted him yet."

"He's angelic, putting up with your taunts and insults," said Victor Private Hardy.

"I don't mean Atkins is a saint," said Ziggy Palmer. "I mean Saint

29

George."

Lang said, "Let's do what Atkins says. Do the boy some good."

"Here! Here! For Tommy Atkins," the men cheered.

Atkins' cheeks flushed. He wished he hadn't spoken. Even more, he wished they had rejected his idea. The men saw that the young man was mortified. What he mumbled in reply no one could decipher.

"In *tableaux vivants* there is no movement. And silent. Much too respectful, I say," William Catchpole observed. "But I have an idea!"

"That's how they're supposed to be," said Alan Hardy.

"St. George and the dragon! In our tableau will be a wriggling, squawking dragon, surrounded by squalling imps, devils dressed in red. All along the way St. George fights the dragon, wards off the imps. Kills the dragon in front of the reviewing stand. Plum jam for blood."

The soldiers brightened at the idea, chiming in all at once.

"Put life into the vivant." said Alan Hardy.

"Exactly. Play on the word. Clever bloke, you are," said Catchpole. Ever the impresario, Catchpole took charge of the proceedings. "Atkins will be our St. George. He will kill the dragon, the Anti-Christ."

Godley patted Atkins on a back. "Consider yourself honored. You are a soldier."

Quietly, humbly, "Thank you."

By nature, Carmichael, suspicious, hung back. Bruised by circus life–roustabout and side show performer–he now found himself in an element that called on his talents and treated him honorably. Said Carmichael, "I'm in with the armorers. I've shown them some stunts. Swallowed bayonets and ceremonial swords from their supply. Bent steel and ate fire. They liked it. And they'll appreciate the plan. I'll get them to fashion sheet metal into armor and helmet for Atkins. Fit him out."

Jessop said, "I will borrow a lance from the cavalry."

"In what sense do you mean 'borrow'?" asked Sergeant Sanders. "We'll not violate regulations."

"Return it after the parade," said Jessop. "We've no need of lances. Leave them to the cavalry."

The teams decided what needed to be done. Some ran off to gather discarded canvas, cut it up, sew it into a tube that would Carmichael and Nancarrew fit inside of, they the crude dragon's body. Walter Sage said to Atkins, "If they don't move about enough prod them with your lance."

"Be respectful. Don't insult him. Don't make the saint a cartoon character. We may need his divine help in the days to come," said Tommy Atkins.

"You think one of his statues would come alive and punish us?" joked Palmer.

Added William Catchpole, "If you have a guinea he might come alive in your pocket and bite your pecker."

Celebration

An evening's feast and entertainment followed passing out parade. Comic skits, pantomimes, parodies of songs and poems, imitations of officers and staff, mockery of the Kaiser and Fritz, all in jolly humor. A fencing competition, a boxing match, judo.

A festive air permeated the celebration.

Catchpole and Palmer, until recently actors in the world of the London leg-show, burlesque, and cheap comic drama, fashioned several skits for the Ruffians and the Victors. "The Beaux Belles" dressed as seductive chorus girls, in falsetto they sang the love melodies of the day replacing the innocent expressions of romantic love with ribald lyrics they had written. In addition, the two perfected a skit for themselves of the oafish private and the officious colonel–Private Timorous and Colonel Bravado–pungent with witty sarcasm.

Paul Carmichael performed some of his sideshow feats. He tied cloth patches for swabbing the gun's and rifle's barrels to a stick, soaked it in petrol, lit the cloth with a lucifer, ate fire. He swallowed his bayonet, attached to his rifle. The men loved it, hooted and applauded.

The Ruffians and Victors took first prize for the entertainment–another meal-ticket–but lost for the tableau. The team representing the battle of Malplaquet won that prize.

Next Day, at the Manufactory

The Ruffians and Victors visited parallel workstations, machinists intently at their work. Hum of motors driving drill presses, grinders, lathes. The squealing and grinding of drills on steel. Metallic smell of steel filings, the sweet aroma of hot cutting oil. Clank and the resounding ping of hammer on anvil. Hiss of escaping steam. Mechanics measuring, tightening, adjusting, testing–each man a part of the machine. Tool and die maker, lathe operator, forgery worker, engineer, blacksmith. Men of brawn, men of brain. Meticulous to a fault. Seamstresses sewed the canvas belts that will hold the bullets, punched in the heavy rivets to hold the brass strips that separate the bullets. Gunsmiths, packers, chemists, engineers.

Beside the factory was the firing range where engineers, mechanics, and technicians tested the Vickers. On this day the workers came out to watch the Vickers guns in the hands of trained gunners. As if choreographed to a cadence, a rhythm, the drills and exercises were carried out with grace and precision. The workers saw the teams work in unison, no orders being signaled. They cheered each feat of marksmanship. For the finale the Gunners One broke down and reassembled the guns blindfolded.

"It's like magic," a worker exclaimed.

"They are machines themselves," commented another.

Alan Hardy spoke, "Private Howard Lang, related to the late Andrew Lang"–a murmur of recognition rippled through the hall–"wrote a poem when we finished our tour of your factory. Wrote it a few minutes ago, in praise of your work and what we learned today. 'Our Weapon' he calls it." Hardy read,

> "Twin sisters, born of the same mind,
> the same metal, parts cast
> from the same pouring of molten steel,
> same billet, milled by the same hands,
> their tripods, cast of the same
> cupola-load of iron, same ingot.
> Like the English people,
> cast in the fire of history."

The workers applauded politely. Paul Carmichael spoke up. "Private Lang calls it a poem of sorts, but of what sort I have no idea."

They laughed.

Before they left the manufactory a machinist etched the poem in the two guns' stocks. A gift to the soldiers, a bond. Dease spoke. "We shall remember you and what you do for Britain. We will fight for you and, our government tells us, for civilization. All for England and King George. Thank you," he said.

"Hear, hear," the workers responded.

Then the company officers addressed the workers and the soldiers–a quiet ceremony of congratulation. The chairman of the Vickers Sons board of directors presented the two teams with their battle-ready Vickers guns. The teams saluted the workers with a last firing of the guns. A wild cheer went up. The workers made their way back to their tasks, talking about what they had seen. The soldiers drove back to school.

Comments, Congratulations, Salutations, and Wishes for Success

The next day Lieutenant General Sir James Montcrieff Grierson, General Commanding Officer of the Eastern Command of England, Commanding Officer of II Corps, British Expeditionary Force, reviewed the class. He was well known to the Corps, well liked, and respected. "Soldiers," he said, "You have learned much and you have taught us much about the value of the Vickers machine gun. Lt. Col. McMahon reports that we will use the gun to great advantage, when the time comes." He went on, offering comments, congratulations, salutations, and wishes for success in the coming war. "You are now prepared to serve his Majesty and his government, the people of England, the British Empire, and any who need our aid in time of war." Then General Grierson dismissed them to await orders.

Chapter Three

To Mons

King Leopold I Infantry Gunners Training Grounds,
Outskirts of Mons, Belgium
15 August, 1914

These Vickers Machine Gun Squads Went on Ahead

Along the coast of France, advanced groups were disembarking from England to ready for the war King George V had declared on 4 August. The two Vickers machine gun crews from Company C, the 4th Royal Fusiliers, British Expeditionary Force, the Ruffians and the Victors, landed at Calais. French vans transported them in secret over country roads and through the towns of Hédin, Saint-Pol-Sur-Ternoise, Houdain, Bully-les-Mines west, turning north and crossing the French-Belgian border at Camphin-en-Pévèle. There the crews pushed and hauled their limber and the two guns aboard two Belgian Army lorries. Captain Henri Lambert, Belgian army, liaison and host, introduced himself to Lieutenant Dease and Sergeant Sanders. He said, "I am pleased to meet you."

Lieutenant Dease said, "Greetings to you, sir, on behalf of our teams."

Captain Lambert continued. "Our army eagerly awaits the British in the field. King Albert, the Belgian army, and the people, we have done more than any expected us capable of. The Germans found us an able foe. But soon, in who knows how many days the Germans will be here upon us and across the border into France. Now is the time for the British to take our place."

The lieutenant and the sergeant rode in the cab with Captain Lambert. He said, "Of the soldiers you will meet today only I speak English. Have you any who can translate? I could do it, but it would be difficult, no? Better if someone else."

"Privates Alan Hardy and Howard Lang, speak French," replied Sanders. "They can translate."

Lieutenant Dease said, "Captain Lambert, the horse transport is to arrive in four days. Might you have a team to haul the limber until our stock arrives?"

"Our horses are on the battlefield already. We've lost many."

"We had to load and unload the limbers three times already. We cannot haul them ourselves. What about the farmers here about?"

"As you see, harvest is underway. The horses are at work. You have money to buy? While the peasants are loyal Belgians, they are farmers first. We will help you haul until we find horses."

The road snaked around slag heaps and the detritus of mining and smelting. In the heart of the mining and foundry region the outskirts of Mons there were ditches, pits, coal mounds, coke piles all about. The smell of chemicals and industrial waste, smoke from foundries and factories, was strong in the air.

Captain Lambert said, "Ahead. The Mons-Condé canal. Like a moat surrounding a castle, the canal protects one avenue of advance to the city. The most vulnerable entry is this bridge." He said, "As you see, it is exposed on three sides. A salient, you call it in English. Nimy. The road through the town across leads directly to Mons. North and south of it the German army will infiltrate the farm fields and villages."

"Being first and second guns, we have the choice of position. We shall claim the honor of defending the bridge," said Lieutenant Dease. "What do you say?" he asked Sergeant Sanders.

"Greatest risk, greatest honor," said Sanders. "We claim it as our post."

"May fortune favor you," said Captain Lambert. He went on. "We are passing over the ground right now. Attend to the lay of the land. This is where the enemy will come from. Swells and depressions. You do not get a good view until they come over this ridge, a thousand yards away. We cross the Nimy bridge just ahead. See the abutments? I recommend placing a gun there and one below, close to the canal."

The lorry reached Mons, passed through the gates of a military compound. "Here are your barracks for the moment, our armory," said Lambert. The rest of the British soldiers climbed down from the back of the lorry. Two Belgian Maxim machine gun crews marched out from a long low, drop-sided indoor firing range to meet their British counterparts. The Vickers crews lined up in order of gunner number, One through Six, first the Ruffians, then the Victors. Dease said,

"Salute, give your name and position on the gun."

When they reached Gunner Four, Private Carrew Nancarrew spoke up. The odd succession of sounds bewildered the Belgians. Was this a bird call? A Congo chant?

"Alan Hardy, Private. Gunner five. I am pleased to meet you." Then in French. "Heureux de faire votre connaissance."

"Areillement. Je suis Private Howard Lang. Gunner Six."

The Belgian Maxim teams then introduced themselves.

The twelve British gunners and the dozen Belgians lined up and, one by one, the lines passed each other, each man shaking the hand of each new ally. The first links between allies being forged, now the pledges made seventy-five years ago called for honoring with action.

Unloading the Limbers

Joined by the Maxim teams, the teams rolled the limbers down two rough planks, hauled them through the armory doors.

Dease ordered, "Haul out the tripod, Atkins. Hurry, now."

To Private Lang, Sanders said, "Check the water hose connection. The last time we practiced it leaked."

Up spoke Gabriel Jessop, Gunner Two, Victor, mechanic, perpetual oil and grease in his fingerprints and under his nails. Years ago and in anticipation of war the Army recruited men from the mechanical trades–machinists, toolmakers, mechanics. Lathe and pressmen, men skilled at grinding valves, cutting internal and external threads, work on arm-atures, wiring, truing and boring, drilling, designing, welding, all kinds of mechanical work. Griping, Jessop said, "They told me the Army needed mechanics."

To Hardy and Lang Sergeant Sanders said, "Do not translate. You know what is coming. Our new friends do not need to hear it."

Jessop went on. "I'm thinkin' more pay than what I was earning at the time. Armory four blocks away from home. Closer than where I worked at the time. Walk to work. I'll keep the Army's lorries in running order. Keep the engines tuned. Keep the motorcycles in running order. A good job. Close to the kids and wife. Home for dinner and a nap. So I join. I didn't ask what I'd mechanic on or where. Turns out I'm a machine gun mechanic. Basic training first. Then machine gun school. Now off to war. "

"Not happy he's in the army," Hardy said in French.

The Belgians smiled and nodded.

Willard Catchpole observed, "I could recite his complaints."

"They are etched in our minds like grooves in a lithographic plate," Howard Lang said. "We cannot forget them even though we want to."

"It is a form of mental torture," said Walter Sage. To Jessop he said, "As much as I like you."

Now, the British soldiers nodded their agreement.

Our Ladies

While the teams worked at laying in the guns Sergeant Sanders said, "Even though nothing is more manly than a machine gun, we give them women's names. Ships the same. From Vickers we get Vixen, Vicki, Victoria—word-play. Honors to the old queen gone many years."

Howard Lang said, "Queen of the world's greatest empire. Sovereign of the world. The sun never sets, and all that. Vicki, as if she was a tramp or strumpet, like most Vickis. Queen and whore. Supposed to be how men see women."

"Vicious the gun is, surely. We call ourselves the Victors. I say, word-play all around," said Hardy, as if reciting a report to a school class. "Rhetoric. "

Said Catchpole, "Our ladies are sweet to those who serve them. Smooth action. Quite and gentle."

"But heartless, brutal to her enemies," added Jessop. "Bullets 2,450 feet a second. How many meters is that?"

"Our ladies," Sidney Godley said, "Will reap Death's own ripe harvest."

Patting the gun affectionately, Sage said, "Her bite is worse than her bark, to turn about an old saying. And her bark is quieter than the old Maxim. Muted recoil. You can hear the difference."

"A better field gun," Godley said. "It will prove itself well suited for mobile action."

Following this line of thought, Sanders said, "The Army's doctrine is that the machine gun is good only for defense. True, the limber hobbles us. The generals have not discovered the tactical benefits the Vickers' lighter weight gives. Often doctrines live long past their utility. His Majesty's Navy knew how to cure and prevent scurvy and rickets and early death four decades before ordering limes and lemons on all its vessels. Same thing here. Though I don't think they will wait forty years before letting loose our guns."

Catchpole: "Sadly, the Vickers is not well thought of in military circles." He wiggled his index and middle fingers of both hands— quotation marks—around "military circles" to signify his opinion of the opinion of those who denigrate his weapon. Dease: "Except for our General McMahon. He knows its value. Preaches it. We are his acolytes, his disciples, his demonstration and proof. Someday he, and we, will prove the Vickers' value to His Majesty's government. Wait and see."

Out of nowhere arose the dour voice of Paul Carmichael. "Forget His Majesty's government. The Germans will learn soon enough. They'll see what the machine gun does, properly handled. The infantry fires fifteen dead-on shots a minute. One every two seconds among the best. Thirty a minute. One Vickers does the work of ten rifles, they say," Paul Carmichael offered. "The gun will tear the Bosche to shreds."

Catchpole: "Dead gun, dead gunners. All of which the Maxim gunners already know."

The Briefing

Captain Lambert said, "Before we celebrate our meeting I must brief you." The men adjourned to the indoor firing range. Lambert called his men to attention, and the British followed. "If you please, gentlemen, sit down, all. Soldiers, these British are here to help us ready Mons for inevitable battle. The Germans will attack France, the border not twenty kilometers to the south. For two weeks there is war in Belgium and in the west of France. We saw. Day and night the German army marched through Brussels. Foot soldiers, cavalry, artillery, impedimenta. We estimate a quarter million. Perhaps more passed through since we left and before they disbursed to destroy villages along the way. How many casualties they suffered–may there be many–as they crossed Belgium, how many they left behind to occupy our towns, and how thinly their line spreads I do not know. Never enough intelligence," he explained.

"These soldiers and I have already been fighting thirty miles to the north, just south of Brussels. We were sent on to prepare Mons."

"The Germans did not expect resistance. The Kaiser expected his cousin, our King Albert, to grant him free passage so he could attack France from the west. Of course, Belgium would not let Germany violate our nation's sovereignty without a fight. The Germans miscalculated our will. Their propaganda convinced them we are a weak people. They were surprised."

Sidney Godley said, "The press published the English version of the German communiqué and demands. The Kaiser's tone was cynical, mocking."

Captain Lambert replied, "For our fighting them, harassing and delaying their progress, they treat our citizens as enemy belligerents, destroying towns, and villages. They kill, burn, rape, pillage."

"Begging your pardon, Captain," said Sanders, Howard Lang translating, "I see it a bit different. It is not retribution. Cynical Private Godley called it. This was planned. They were ready for resistance."

"We will never know for certain. For now it does not matter. They are here and we must fight them," said the captain. "They tried to break the people's will. Force the government to surrender. They failed. They left destruction behind, occupy much of our country."

Captain Lambert went to two maps tacked to the wall, one of Mons and immediate vicinity, the other of the whole country. With his baton he pointed out the cities as he named them. "The enemy is on its way to strike Mons, Maubeuge, Charleroi, Namur, Cambrai, Caudry. You see these towns are close to the border. Namur is well fortified, but it is not enough to hold the enemy off. They can easily by-pass Namur. I predict that the Bosche have enough soldiers to strike all the towns at the same time. Then they will cross en masse into France. As I say, ready Mons."

Captain Lambert continued, "You will aid us in preparing the city for battle. Our citizens will help. Mons is their home. Many families have been here for generations, some since antiquity." Pointing to the map of Mons again, he said, "The Mons-Condé canal is our line of defense. Sixty feet wide, seven feet deep, eighteen miles long. A strong barrier. The Germans will have to cross the few bridges, which we will stoutly defend. They may have boats, or their engineers may lay pontoon bridges. Though no one has seen any. In any case, they will approach from that direction. There is no other way."

The Belgian captain described the general plan. "When the Germans draw close factories will shut so the workers can help prepare our defense. Miners, foundry workers, barge men, farmers will come, too. On the east side of the canal with axes, hatchets, saws cut trees and saplings. With scythes and sickles clear brush. Make the Bosche clear targets. Businesses will close, too. The workers will prepare the city streets for defense. The police, of course, will direct much of the work. On the west side you will want trenches for cover, for, I am sure, that is where you will deploy your troops. Half a meter deep, the earth dug out, packed hard in front, gives a meter's protection."

"There are few of us here to plan. We will use your eyes to select the work most being needed and where you will deploy the British force. With good fortune, the French and British armies will reach here in time to defend the city. We hope that the Belgian army's gallant resistance, which delayed–and surely surprised–the Germans, drained them of energy and enthusiasm."

Up spoke Carmichael. "I was with a circus. Sword swallower, ate fire, walked on glass, stuck needles through my cheeks. A German owned the circus. The clowns, almost everyone was German. The trapeze artists, 'The Flying Assholes' I call them. I know the Germans. Arrogant. Vindictive when crossed. Vengeful. Hate the British. Lie. I suspect they were spies, traveling about England. We set up not far from military bases. My point is, the Bosche are not like us. I can predict what they will do."

Replied Captain Lambert. "In any case they have soldiers, armaments, equipment, the ammunition to fight. You are young men and eager. This will be your first battle. You are well trained. Many who fought the Boers instructed you. If those who come after you are stout and brave, we have every hope of success."

Private Godley said, "We've the expression, 'trial by fire.' The phrase refers to other sad matters. In this instance we and the guns will undergo a real trial by fire–gun-fire–in the days to come."

Said Dease. "We hope to do honor to our nation, our king, and you who we come to defend."

A Belgian soldier spoke up. Hardy and Lang translated. "Those are brave words. They must be followed by brave deeds. The barbarity the

Bosche are inflicting on our people fills me with anger and sadness." The mood became sober, the soldiers now thinking about the days ahead.

Through the briefing the Belgians heard what the British soldiers had said in translation. They understood much of what was being said through gestures and facial expressions. Beyond the information, these conveyed the ribaldry, the camaraderie, the off hand manner of the British squads. The Belgians saw that among these dozen men there was little regard for rank or station. The Belgians admired these qualities in their new comrades.

Said Captain Lambert, "Now champagne and camaraderie." Toasts, wishes for good fortune in French and English warmed the hearts of all. Confidence, abounding good will, pervaded the group.

Thus ended the busman's holiday before the busman's hell.

"Mons Shares St. George with You British"

Before leaving the Vickers teams Lambert said, "You are not under my command. Nevertheless, I have instructions for you. Consider them a request, if you please."

"What do you need us to do?" asked Lieutenant Dease.

"Tomorrow morning, Sunday, we will escort you to St. Waudru Church. In his sermon the priest will explain to the congregation who you are and why you are here. I know that, whatever your religious persuasion, each of you will conduct yourself respectfully. The truth is, Mons's founding and history have not merely the religious about it, but the sacred as well, if you can see the difference." He fell silent for a moment. Then, "I am a native of Mons. I hold the city close to my heart. That is one reason I was sent here to prepare it. The city shares St. George with you British as patron saint. We venerate the saint, probably more actively than you do. On many occasions he has aided us, chased the aggressors from our land. The saying goes, 'as above, so below.'"

"What do you mean, sir?" asked the Victor, Walter Sage.

"There is eternal warfare between the forces of good and evil for the hearts of men, for souls. Satan never rests. His minions are ever at work. Once again the dragon is among us. Many times the war comes to earth. Many times our beloved city has been conquered. The Spanish, the

Dutch, Austria, France, even the English. Each time the good Saint George came to our salvation. Prayer, penitence, blood, and death. Each time he redeemed us. Between us and the Evil One stands the saint. We are told that he shall redeem us once again. As far as you are concerned, know that tomorrow you and your squads will be initiated, honorary members in a fraternal order, the 'Brotherhood of Dieu and Monseigneur Saint Georges.' St. George chose you."

"Really? Saint George picked us, Dease," snickered Sergeant Sanders.

"Please take this with seriousness and respect. You will learn more tomorrow," said Lambert.

"That is not much of an instruction," said Henry Sanders.

Ignoring the sarcasm, Captain Lambert continued. "In addition to the dozen of you, your medical officer will join you in Mons. He, too will be initiated."

Added Dease, "We shall be pleased to comply. We will convey the information to our men."

Captain Henri Lambert continued, "After the church service and a ceremony welcoming you, we will examine the canal and all the crossing points."

That evening the two Vickers teams and Captain Malcolm Leckie, chief medical officer of Company C, the Royal Fusiliers, were feted at Restaurant Les Gribaumontes, the second floor reserved for dignitaries and the meetings of civic, religious, and fraternal organizations. Fine Belgian beer, wine, a dinner of local delicacies and special dishes, coffee, liquor—a convivial evening ended the day.

Chapter Four

The Priest's Sermon:
St. George and Mons

16 August 1914
St. Waudru Church
Mons, Belgium

"God and Monseigneur Saint Georges"

Next morning the burgomaster of Mons, along with Captain Lambert, the Maxim gunners, church and municipal officials, escorted Vickers teams and Captain Leckie to the church.

Seated, the soldiers watched and heard the priest and the acolytes conduct the rites. Accompanied by a sonorous organ, the choir sang hymns in French and Latin. Like a stage show, Catchpole thought, and well performed. The Vickers teams and Captain Leckie sat patiently, reverently, only Captain Leckie, Hardy, and Lang understanding what was spoken in French.

After the reading of scripture and a homily, the congregation joined the choir in more hymns. Instead of a sermon, the priest spoke to the matter at hand–the war to come. He paused after each sentence so a military attaché could translate for the guests.

The priest addressed the British soldiers. "Friends from across the sea, amongst us members of the 'Fellowship of God and Monseigneur Saint Georges' listen, along with you. When you leave the church, turn and look back. You will see the fellowship's name carved in the stone lintel above the door. Its office is on the Grande Place. Its chambers share a wall with the Burgomaster's office."

"Last month St. George's foretold that the first battle between Germany and Britain will be fought in Mons. The blood the British will spill on our soil will sanctify their sacrifice and honor the Saint."

"Twelve hundred years ago the good abbess Waudru founded a monastery and the community of Mons on this very spot. Declared a saint, her sacred relics we lovingly venerate. She taught that St. George in heaven protects us. In the year of our Lord and Savior 1380 clerics and professors–in reality alchemists, magi, and mystics–the scientist-philosophers of their day–founded the "Brotherhood of God and Monseigneur Saint Georges." The priest paused in reverential thought then said, "In the precincts of this holy church we venerate the warrior saint. Our ancient books teach that by1440 the Lumecon was already an ancient ceremony."

Pointing to the crossbeam above the middle isle, he said, "On Trinity Sunday the saint's relics parade in this gilded coach you see above. Down a steep cobbled hill the coach makes a sharp turn at the end. Top heavy. Imagine." The Vickers teams looked up, grateful to have their attention momentarily called to something novel. The priest turned his hands, the top to the bottom, the coach overturning. "Much store is set in how well the men bring the coach back into the church. It's turning over brings bad tidings. So legend has it."

He paused. The next words changed the subject. "Two ceremonies in one day. The afternoon of Trinity Sunday the Master of the Brotherhood engages in 'The Game of St. Georges,' you would call it in English. Dressed in mail and armor and on horseback, the Master chases and fights a wickerwork and canvas dragon, decorated with ribbons and charms."

The Vickers teams recalled their own enactment of the slaying of the dragon, Tommy Atkins, their St. George, with shame, Catchpole and Palmer, the comedy they put on. How strange, Alan Hardy thought, that the priest should describe the same scene. Sage and Jessop gave one another a knowing glance. The priest went on. "Members within the wickerwork propel it down the streets. Others garbed as devil's imps and the forces of evil flit about the monster. The crowd surges forward, taunting the dragon, snatching charms from its tail. At the climax, in the Grande Place St. George slays the monster. There is an uproar and cheering. The demons shed their costumes and disappear into the crowd as if by magic and so quickly that you cannot tell who they are." Lang knew that he was hearing the enactment of a local fairy tale with which his uncle was familiar. Again and again Howard read Andrew Lang's fantasies and fairy tales–the Blue, Red, Green–a dozen books, a dozen colors–Books. Even now he carried one in his knapsack.

The evening before, at dinner Howard Lang was introduced to M.

Michel Tallent, schoolteacher, member of the municipal council, who was eager to meet him. A student of folk literature and fairy tales himself, Mr. Tallent was thrilled to meet a relative of Andrew Lang, a luminary in the field. The teacher and the private had spoken then with delight of the uncle's work. The two sat beside each other in church. Lang leaned over and whispered, "Is this a story you particularly favor? I suppose you know a great deal about the good saint."

M. Tallent replied, in a whisper also, "Our beloved protector proclaims us his blessed children. You are his, also–the English. The citizens of Mons, and all Belgians, say St. George slew the dragon here on our sacred mount. Always St. George scourged the oppressor, returned the city to the people of Mons."

Then, the priest addressed the British soldiers directly. "The good saint sent you, his English, to be our bulwark. May he find us worthy, and bless and aid us in the coming days. For we know the Germans, the devil's workers, are eager to subjugate and destroy us."

The service over, the priest gave the benediction and hurried down from the pulpit, detaining Captain Leckie by the arm. In labored English he said, "Gentlemen, stay a moment." Captain Lambert translated the rest of what he said. "You endured a long-winded speech. I appreciate your patience. You needed to hear our history. But come."

The priest pointed out the bas-relief sculptures, scenes of St. George's holy life to the soldiers. Decorum required them to attend to what he was saying. Lambert translated. "Here St. George, a tribune in the Roman Army, pleads with Emperor Diocletian to stop persecuting Christians." At the next, "In the Emperor's presence the good saint is beheaded." In the third, "Here, resurrected, he leads the Crusaders' Army at the Battle of Antioch in 1098." They moved to the last of the sculptures. He said, "As you can see, this depicts the very church we are in. Can you tell what is taking place?" St. George astride his horse and the dragon lying dead on the ground. He concluded, "The dragon represents the Emperor Diocletian and Satan." The priest gave this talk many times to tourists.

The translator said, "Beyond the celebration and festivities even now every year the people of Mons and St. George solemnize a pledge. The people promise to conduct themselves honorably and deal justly, as the Brotherhood and our Christian faith instructs. In return, the saint protects his city from Satan's forces in the coming year. Thus, our good people believe our warrior saint in heaven will stand for us in the battle to come."

Then, the priest said, "I know you have important duties yet to attend to." He said, "But a few minutes' delay will do no harm," and, with a sweep of his arm, he directed them to a low oaken door. Lieutenant Dease replied, "No, sir. A small delay. It is as you say."

"Please, gentlemen." He opened the door and followed behind.

Accompanying them down narrow spiral stone steps, Captain Lambert said, "The story and our ceremonies must strike you as quaint, hardly appropriate to the occasion. Our people cherish the story of our saint. To us it is sacred text, a hymn all know by heart." Lambert knocked in a distinct pattern on a narrow wooden door. He said, "We are twenty feet directly beneath the church altar, the church's heart." The door opened. From inside a voice said, "Enter the inner sanctum." The men ducked low and passed into a tiny chapel. Lambert concluded, "We will explain the story's importance to us and England. And you personally. Each of you."

"The Golden Arrows of God"

As ornate as the sanctuary was–statues, carved marble graves of knights and ladies, the rococo carriage suspended from the ceiling by thick ropes–the chapel was as bare. Naked, rough stone walls, stone floor, windowless, like a penitent's cell, the furnishings, a library table and a straight-backed chair. Dim flickering light from tapers in sconces on the walls mingled shadows and darkness with light.

A dozen men had slipped into a room ahead of the Vickers squads, taken up posts behind stone pillars which held up the massive altar. These witnesses and auditors were silent. Hoping that this was a ceremony of welcome, the soldiers thought a drop of sherry or, better, a draft of good Belgian beer awaited. All felt cold seeping up from the floor through their boots.

The priest spoke again, Captain Lambert translating. "These men, whose faces you cannot see, are here to testify to the truth of what happens between us now. You will keep what is said and done in the strictest confidence. Being gentlemen, officers, and soldiers pledged to your King, you needn't take a spoken vow."

A man cloaked in a bearskin fringed with sable and ermine, stepped out of the shadows. A hood masked his face in the flickering light. His right hand held a lance. Over his left shoulder hung a bow, a sheaf of arrows in a quiver over his right. Slowly he spoke, deliberately weighing each phrase. His English was tinged with accent. His voice rose and fell in volume like the waves of the sea. "Gentlemen, I identify myself by station, not by name. I am master of the 'Brotherhood of God and Monseigneur Saint Georges', of which our good priest spoke. What he did not say–within the brotherhood is a secret order, without record, official name, or evidence of its existence. Nonetheless, the dozen members, whose identity is secret, meet once a year in conclave to practice the highest order of prayer, meditation, ceremony, and rites St. George has taught us. We are of many denominations, our practices mystical, universal. We draw on many traditions.

The two Vickers teams and Captain Leckie, especially the captain and Howard Lang, were intrigued by what they heard. A mystical order. Both realized that, being told the order's secrets, they were inducted into the order, initiates.

The speaker went on. "We dozen gathered in this room–'The Golden Arrows of God'–are sworn protectors of the people of Mons and the ancient Belgium, the Belgium before 1831when the European powers established the state. In yearly gathering St. George communicates directly with us. He pledges to defend his devoted vassals, thanes, knights, esquires, and servants. Such a time has come. The blessed saint instructed us to initiate a dozen plus one British soldiers into the brotherhood. You are those soldiers. St. George gave us signs to identify you by. Your roles in the coming war will be extraordinary. What these roles will be, the good saint did not say. He called you to serve the cause of freedom and victory, opposed by the devil's devices. This is not for choosing. Step forward and receive the signs, acts, and tokens of your election."

Captain Leckie and the others, and finally, reluctant, mystified young Tommy Atkins stepped forward. Most considered this an act of good will, like joining a civic or fraternal organization.

The master solemnly pricked each man's thumb with the tip of an arrow he took from the quiver. Each affixed his blooded print to a sheet of parchment and wrote his name, also in his own blood.

When all had signed, the master of the "Golden Arrows of God" spoke. "Secrecy. Devotion. It is as if you swore to the saint himself with your blood. You are now 'Golden Arrows of God.' Handing each an inch-long gold arrow, he said, "This symbol signifies your bond with St. George. Gentlemen, wear this pin behind a lapel, inside a pocket. Keep it with you always. The saint will call upon you to serve the good people of the world."

"Bow your heads, gentlemen." The priest uttered another benediction. "We ask God and St. George for blessings upon you in this time of testing and tribulation."

The master of the order spoke once more. "I remind you. Silence about all that transpired here."

Captain Henri Lambert led the soldiers up the stairs and to the vestibule. In parting, he said, "You will meet with our civil and military authorities. Already work is underway. Our citizens will help fortify our city. Even now they are barricading streets. Breaking out bricks from buildings that face the approaches, sad to say."

Chapter Five

The Angel St. George of Mons

Mons, Belgium
Nimy Bridge
23 August 1914
8:00 a.m.

A small town, an insignificant fort, owing to a series of strategic movements, suddenly becomes a point of the highest value. It represents the key to a position which the assailing part is bound at any cost to carry, the defending party at any cost to hold.

The Schools of Charles the Great
J. Bass Mullinger

Shortly after this the enemy started to advance in mass down the railroad cutting, about 800 yards off, and Maurice Dease fired his two machine-guns into them and absolutely mowed them down. I should judge without exaggeration that he killed at least 500 in the two minutes. The whole cutting was full of bodies and this cheered up all up.

Voices and Images of the Great War
Lyn Macdonald

Preparation

In the few days before, many businesses in Mons closed. Horses and mules hauled scrap lumber and waste wood, stone, and brick on carts into the city. Under the gendarmes' direction, tradesmen, clerks, merchants piled the debris into rough barricades. When the Germans

49

drew close, were a day away, factories around Mons shut. Miners, foundry and factory workers, laborers, farmers from the countryside, bargemen came with axes and saws, lopping shears, clippers, pruning hooks, scythes, sickles, hatchets, rope, bare hands to cut and haul away trees, saplings, osiers, reeds, brush on the canal's west bank. Make the Bosche easy targets for the British, a feast spread for Death. On the east side men of Mons dug shallow trenches with picks and spades. Half a meter of earth dug out, packed hard in front. On the British side of the canal all the vegetation stood, screened the army from the Germans.

Sunday Morning

Church bells throughout the city rang the call to worship. On their way to church, families walked, latecomers scurrying, stragglers putting themselves together. The citizens at prayer, listening to sermons and homilies, singing hymns.

At the same time the, sixty thousand soldiers of the British Expeditionary Force–four infantry divisions and one of cavalry–occupied the canal's south side, deployed along eighteen miles, a long expanse, thinly covered.

The Mons-Condé canal was sixty-four feet wide, seven feet deep. On the far side of the Nimy Bridge, a levee retained the north side, a paved road built on an old towpath. The Germans had to cross the few bridges to attack the city.

The Vickers teams arrived at their posts–the south end of the Nimy Bridge, the salient, before daybreak. They knew that today they would fire to kill and be the targets of German fire. The day before, the first British shots had been fired, the first cavalry chase, the first casualties. The Ruffians finished laying in sandbags. "Assemble the gun," ordered Lieutenant Dease. "Ready for fire."

Godley and Catchpole went to work.

"Hand me the range finder," said Dease.

"I see four good targets," said Palmer.

They set the gun and sighted. "Eight hundred yards beyond the bridge for raking fire," Dease said. "Fire as soon as there are enough Germans to make it worth spending the bullets."

"Set for the bridge's foot for concentrated fire," Carmichael added.

"Those three tall slag heaps. Germans will climb to fire on us. Shot over the abutment. The Jerrys need to clean out our little nest before they can get across."

"We stand between them and Mons. Site for a thousand yards away and further up the hill," said Ziggy Palmer. "They will come up out of that swale after the drop down from the hill. Come up out of the cut. Let them advance close so they can't turn and run."

"They won't do that," Lieutenant Dease said. "Their officers would shoot them."

"What about the concentration, the formation?" said Catchpole, "How they will attack?"

"The infantry will do its work. They will fire when the Bosche crest the rise," said Sidney Godley. "We'll clean any that get through. Then go for them further away. Keep the Germans off."

"No idea how many will pour over the ridge. How many we will kill, how many belts we will fire," said Paul Carmichael.

"The first action in battle," Lieutenant Maurice Dease said. "First bullets."

"First wounds," Godley said.

Catchpole added, "First deaths."

"Many firsts," Carmichael concluded.

After the gun was set and the range and settings recorded the Ruffians came down from the emplacement and walked about on the bridge, patrolling and studying the targets.

Burdened with four wicker baskets, one in each hand, a canvas sack slung over the boy's shoulder clanking as he walked, a boy, six or seven, and a little girl, stumbled and staggered toward them from across the canal.

Godley called out, "Easy, boy. Don't fall."

Catchpole said, "I think he's bringing us bloody good Belgian beer."

The girl, in her going-to-church dress, opened the baskets, and offered, wrapped in linen, two dozen freshly baked rolls, a jar of wild strawberry jam, poppy seed tarts, jugs of coffee nicely dosed with cognac, two dozen bottles of beer. Delicious treats. The last for a long time. "Vive L'Angleterre! Velcum Wallonia. Eat!" he said. "Eat!" pointing to the food.

To the children Palmer said, "Mina kinder. That's German, ain't it?"

He asked, "Who talks Frog? Maybe call over Hardy or Lang. I could drink a dozen bottles of Belgian beer and be well satisfied." Turning from the children he said, "I hope there's treats all around in the bars in town when we get there, us saving them from the Huns."

Boy's name, Albert, after the king. Girl's, Helena, after the queen. The Ruffians had a jolly chat with the children, pointing and nodding and smiling and mangled French. The gunners spread the feast of tasty morsels on the top of the bridge abutment.

Fifty yards to the east and at the canal's edge, the Victors, hearing the voices and the clinking of bottles and seeing the food, left their gun. Reaching the bridge on the run and out of breath, Henry Sanders huffed, "Don't you bloody tourists leave us out! Give up to the soldiers!"

Number Two alongside, Gabriel Jessop said, "I'll tell you what's going on. Belgian beer! We'll all have a taste."

Followed close behind, the other four Victors. Number Three, Hardy, howled, "Our fair share! And more!"

Like boys on holiday, the Victors mingled with the Ruffians. "Didn't we recently part? Welcome back, brothers," said Catchpole.

Grabbing a bottle in each hand from the canvas sack, said Jessop, "One for now, one for later. Pass the bottle opener."

"There may not be a later. I'm drinking mine now," said Hardy.

To salvage some beer for himself, Godley said, "These poor children didn't come to provision the British Expeditionary Force. Take one, you greedy bastards, and leave the rest for others more deserving."

Springing to his feet, fists raised Jessop said, "More deserving, says who? If we wasn't getting ready to fight the Germans, I'd show you who's more deserving."

"Calm yourself, Jessop," said Catchpole. "Have some coffee. Laced, you might say, with cognac. "

Said Sidney Godley, "Let us salute each another. We are the first Vickers teams whose bullets will taste blood!"

The cheer went up, "Hear! Hear!" and the men drank.

Palmer cried, "Three cheers for old Mr. Vickers. Hip! Hip! Hurray!"

They cheered and raised the bottles, drank again.

Catchpole chimed in, "And to old Maxim before him. Take another swig, if you didn't gulp the whole bottle all at once, you gluttons."

"I say, can we pray? Before battle." Tommy Atkins asked.

"For another beer? That don't sound like you, Atkins. Has the drink gone to your empty head already?" asked William Catchpole.

"Turning chaplain on us, are you?" asked Palmer.

Dropping to his knees, hands clasped, eyes closed, head turned skyward, Catchpole prayed in mock reverence, "Fight beside us, St. George. May we kill many and all of us live."

Henry Sanders seconded, "Every soldier's prayer."

As if a parishioner had interrupted the parson in prayer, Catchpole indignantly complained, "You didn't hear me say 'amen' yet."

Up piped Hardy. "Hurry. Battle awaits."

"I'm with Private Atkins," said Dease. "At least a moment of silent prayer now. Show him a little respect. He's worked hard, come along. He deserves it."

Spoke up Atkins, "Also the Lord and Jesus. They deserve it most."

The men fell silent for a moment.

"Might as well add St. George," goaded Catchpole. "Got your little arrow? Might use it to poke a Bosche in the eye if it comes to hand-to-hand."

Disgusted, Godley said, "Turn prayer into sacrilege. God forgive you."

Palmer said, "So sanctimonious. Joke or cry? Like William says, kill or be killed." Kneeling in imitation of prayer, he said, "God, keep the terrors from us in our moment of battle." He asked Private Godley, "Is that more like it?"

"No, not more like it," Godley angrily retorted.

"God bless the children and the beer and damn the Huns. Amen," said Catchpole. "Ready to eat?"

Sage clasped his hands in prayer, closed his eyes, "After we beat the Huns today, please, Lord, let us strip off these wool uniforms and go for a nice swim in the canal. It is so hot."

Said Gabriel Jessop, "The canal will be running red when we finish. Swim in blood, want to?"

Tommy Atkins ate his rolls and looked dejectedly at the water in the canal. "I had no idea what I was starting," he said.

By Tonight We Will be Victorious

Medical Officer Captain Malcolm Leckie, Royal Army Medical Corps, strolled onto the bridge and over to the men. "Good morning, gentlemen. What's the commotion?" Nodding toward the children, the baskets, the linen cloth, he said, "A gift of friendship, I take it."

"We aren't thieves," said Gabriel Jessop.

"Here comes Doctor," Dease said. "Welcome, sir. Smell the coffee and cognac? Join us."

Said Palmer, "Welcome, indeed, sir. The good deacon from Mons church would approve. Here's the thirteenth initiate. Sign from heaven? Wearing your gold pin?"

"Indeed. And you?"

"Wouldn't dress without it, not me, for luck's sake. I am full of superstitions," said Palmer. "Come join us, sir, for a morsel. The children brought treats."

Dease continued, "Thirteen gathered at table. Well, on sandbags anyway. Almost the Lord's supper. 'God's Golden Arrows', didn't the priest call us?"

Said Sergeant Sanders, "Very poetical."

Walter Sage piped up, "Captain, I th ink the boys is celebratin' victory, that's what I think. It ain't come yet, but they expect it. Don't deprive yerself, Captain, sir. Indulge. Some for all. Remember who fed you when it comes time for patching us up. Vickers teams first, please, sir."

"I must give you preference," joked the doctor.

"God's Golden Arrows," said Sage.

"You have me there."

"We'll know by tonight that we are victorious," mused Jessop. "From what the priest said, the good saint is always busy at work. But he takes a long time to get the work done. All those wars and occupations of Mons lasted many years."

Catchpole said, "There is an old joke."

"What joke is that?" asked Carmichael.

"Priest tells his congregation to God a million pounds is like a farthing, a million years passes in just a second. Wanting to get a fortune a parishioner prays, 'Dear Lord, I want a million pounds.' God answers, 'Just a second.' Maybe the same with St. George."

"We will see how long this takes," said Dease.

Said Paul Carmichael, "I'll bet the Germans have their own saints. Maybe the saints and their angels fight it out in heaven. Who knows?"

Henry Sanders tapped the captain's shoulder. "You'll have to use my drink tin and plate, sir." And to no one in particular, "Fill the captain's cup. Give him some of this fine beer, men."

Pouring some of his beer into the tin cup, Dease said, "Here, Captain, some of mine. To your good health."

"To yours, too, Lieutenant. To you all. Long life," said Captain Leckie.

"See where we are, Captain? War," said Catchpole.

Said Palmer. "Exposed, but hopeful nonetheless."

"Not hopeless," echoed Catchpole.

"It's a wish, my friend. A hope," said Leckie.

"I'm not much for beer. Take some of mine, too," said Nancarrew, kind-hearted private. The others stepped forward to offer some of their beer.

"More than enough, men. I need to be clear-minded," said Leckie.

Godley gestured to the little girl, and said, "Give the captain a bun." Helena spoke to the boy, their gestures showing that they did not understand.

Leckie said, "Si vous plait, un petit pain."

The girl opened the napkin, displaying the empty inside. She said, "Excusez-moi, monsieur, il n'y en a plus."

"Too late for pastries, captain. All ate up," said Catchpole. To his comrades, in mock-anger: "Shame on you." Wiping crumbs and custard from his mouth, he said, "These gluttons been shoveling it down right before our very eyes. No thought for others."

The soldiers ate, joked, planned, still patrolling the bridge.

Palmer added, "I blame the children. I'll bet they snuck off, sat, their backs against the bridge railing, nibbling buns they kept for themselves. Naughty children."

Henry Sanders chimed in, "Little buggers, stealing from us like that."

"This might be their last treat, too. You heard what the Germans do," Captain Leckie said, "When they 'invest' a city. Arrest the civil authorities, declare martial law, and run the town, enslave the residents. They shoot people outright for no reason. Barbarians, they are."

Said Sanders, "Burn whole villages."

"Who says?" asked Walter Sage.

"Captain Lambert. He saw it. He told us," said Sergeant Sanders.

"True. They call them reprisals for the Belgians not letting them march through the country. Arrogant bastards they are," exclaimed Hardy. "Haven't you talked with the Belgian gunners?"

"Can you parlez vous? How could I talk with them?" asked Sanders.

"The Belgian soldiers told of horrid things the Bosche did to the innocent Belgian citizens," replied Lang. "Sacked and burned towns and cities. Belgians murdered for being Belgians. Girls and wives ravished. People killed in every manner of atrocious act. As if Belgium had attacked Germany and now Germany was getting its just revenge. Belgians resisted the Germans' violating their sovereignty. Held up their progress. Interfered with their plans."

"From here on things can only get worse, I say," Gabriel Jessop joked. "We drank the beer. You kissed the girls. Quit while you're ahead, I say. What do you say we head for home?"

"Nerves getting to you?" asked Carmichael.

"Things can't get any better," said Allan Hardy. "I believe this is as peaceful as life will be for quite a while. Ever hear of Thomas Hardy? I read his books and poems. Arch-pessimist. Distant relative. Things will get worse. Much worse."

Looking at his wristwatch, Dease said, "Back to your posts. What do you say, Sergeant Sanders?"

"We are here to fight and win. We will give all we have," said Sanders.

Patting and stroking the little girl's hair, Jessop said, "I braided my little girl's hair just like this sweet girl's. She preferred having me do it over her mother. Memories. Well. I wonder why the children aren't in church?"

Having finished his beer, Carmichael came awake. "Maybe fear kept people home."

The churchly Atkins spoke up, "And many in church for the same reason."

Carmichael: "Same prospect, different responses."

The Vickers squad packed up the children's baskets then they shooed them off the bridge.

Sage said "Mercy buckets" to the children.

"Pour les treats, les beer," said Jessop. "Scat, now. Get home safe. Thank yer mum! Thank yer da."

The children scurried off back across the bridge chattering away about their great adventure.

"We should have given them a memento," said Tommy Atkins sadly. "But what, I don't know. It is too late now anyway."

Carrying out orders, the Vickers squads closed Nimy Bridge to carts, lorries, and cars, let townspeople walking and riding bicycles cross. "Warn everyone to take shelter," said Dease. Hardy taught the men what to say to the citizens. Finally, none could cross.

The Ruffians and the Victors shook hands all around, separated, made their way back to their emplacements, took their positions, checked the guns a last time.

The last they saw of peace. Battle near at hand.

The Cloud of Dust

Private Godley has laid out the tool pouch for repairs, key alongside in case he should be shot or captured. Tommy Atkins checked to make sure the water canister was full. The others were caught up in idle conversation.

Godley called out, "What kind of lookouts are you? See that dust cloud rising in the north? Either the Jerrys are far away and many, or close at hand and few. No telling which from here. You better be ready."

Piped up Gunner Six, Atkins, "We'll know how many when they come in sight."

"The lad is wise, he is. Dust in the distance. They are coming," echoed Ziggy Palmer.

Godley observed, "They are coming on fast."

"Won't be long," remarked Carmichael. "Cavalry first. Reconnoiter from the edges, just beyond range. Infantry behind. Slower. Then they have to set range for machine-guns and artillery. By now they know where we are."

"Might, might not," said Catchpole. "Us hidden in the willows and reeds."

"If they've got a brain, they know we're here," Atkins ventured.

"How would you know, you brainless creature?" retorted Palmer.

"Leave off the poor boy," said Godley.

"We've kept out of sight, quiet. If we haven't seen or smelled them, chances are they haven't seen or smelled us. They have a surprise coming," said sword swallower Carmichael. "They might think they are going to cross the bridge and march into the city. That would be to my liking."

"They have to know we won't let them cross if we're here," said Catchpole.

Atkins piped up, "Sure, we'll hold onto this position hard."

Godley said to Six, "You are coming alive. Good for you."

Catchpole said, "Him growing up. Wouldn't that be something wonderful!"

"They think we won't fight," Atkins went on." We'll show 'em."

"Listen to the boy," said William Catchpole. "Keep it up and you'll be shaving before long. Don't cut yourself with your razor. They don't give medals for wounds not received in battle." He laughed at his own jest.

Where the Canal Makes a Sharp Turn

In any formation there are always better and worse places on the line. The two Vickers squads occupied the furthest bulge on the Nimy salient, the western edge, exposed to Hun fire from three directions. They picked it themselves when they first made their way to Mons eight days before. Honor, pride. Top Vickers teams. The Ruffians were behind an abutment on the bridge's south edge, their targets beyond the bridge on the opposite bank.

The braggadocio went on, the raising of courage. Carmichael said, "Surely they don't think we are going to waste this position."

In his schoolboy wisdom Tommy Atkins said, "They think we're cowards. They think we won't fight."

Said Palmer, "Not fight! I'll give 'em 'not fight!'"

Finally the dust cloud, the German infantry, swarmed over the ridge, marched straight down the hill, waves rushing upon a shore. Dease shouted from a distance, "Here they come. Hold steady, ready to fire." Godley and all the men took their positions. When they came in sight of the bridge the Bosche massed together, funneled, like tide rushing into a narrow inlet. The Fusiliers along the canal let loose their "mad minutes", each soldier firing at least a round every four seconds—fifteen wounded or dead Germans every minute for each British infantryman. When the first German soldiers were eight hundred yards from the bridge Dease shouted, "Fire!" loud enough for both teams to hear. "Vicki and Vixen send their greetings."

"And farewell," said Carmichael.

William Catchpole said, "Give 'em a murdering fusillade. Fill the line with hot lead."

When the shooting began there was barely a square yard across the canal where a living person could stand for a half a minute and not be in a bullet's path, let alone pass through the depth and width of the range the firing spanned. The Germans' action, disorganized in the face of first fire, confirmed the wild hope that they did not know where the British Army was, how situated, nor how many opposed them. Nor did the German generals know British musketry. They committed their troops to storm Mons–the city unprotected, they thought. Take the city without resistance.

The Ruffians and Victors kept up their fire. Up leapt Paul Carmichael. "God help us!" he bellowed. "But we're bloomin' marvels! D'ye see 'em? The Jerrys ain't going down in dozens, it's hundreds, it is. Look! Look! There's a bloody company cut down while I'm talking!"

The fever of battle inflamed the Vickers squads. Mortal combat, slay or be slain. Between bursts of gunfire they heard what sounded like the howling and wailing of wild beasts, and a phrase or two of German shouted from across the canal. It seemed that time stood still. There was only the present moment. "We've dished up a stew of fresh meat and Bosche blood for gravy to the gods of war," shouted Paul Carmichael.

On the Slag Heaps

Two dozen German snipers appeared just over the edges of three slagheaps closest to the canal–hot slag, acrid smoke curling from fissures–heaps tall enough so the snipers could fire over the sand-bagged emplacement on the Ruffians. Clear shots. But the acrid smoke and sulfur and putrid hydrogen sulfide stung the snipers' noses, burned their throats. They coughed. Their eyes teared. Terrible conditions for a sniper, standing out, exposed.

"Christ, why are they coming out like that?" said Paul Carmichael.

"Don't they know that they can stand behind the edge, use it for a brace, expose only the head, a miniscule target? Not the whole body," replied Dease.

Catchpole added, "What kind of training do they have?"

"More like, who's shouting the orders? In Germany the officer gives orders and the soldier obeys," remarked Palmer.

"Same with us," said Catchpole.

"But our officers respect us."

"Some do. Some do not," retorted Carmichael.

"The German conscript. The civilian obeys his superior. The arist-ocrat officers are the same superiors, now in uniform—insignia, braids, ribbons, boots, crop, and all," said Palmer.

"That's what I said. Weren't you listening?" said Carmichael.

"But look at that. Silhouetted. They stand out like iron soldiers at a Brighton Pier shooting gallery," said Dease. "Call out the settings."

Number Two Gunner read them off and Godley said, "I'll pick them off right to left. Send the Bosche a gift on behalf of our Belgian friends and St. George." He turned the angry Vixen on them. In an instant the snipers were gone.

Another dozen crawled onto the slag pile's face and into crevices. "Even worse. Watch this," Private Godley said. Instead of shooting the soldiers where they stood with a few bursts he got the slag sliding below their feet. He picked them off as they slipped and tumbled. "More honor in hitting a moving target than a still," he joked.

Said Private Palmer, "Good work."

"Not so fast," Catchpole said, a hint of the jibe in his voice. "It wouldn't surprise me if they shot one another, flopping about so, shooting all the while."

The gunner said, "I got the slag sliding and they did the rest?"

"It is possible," eyebrows raised, arms expressing his own disbelief,

Palmer added. "Some could have even died of broken necks. Not been shot at all."

With a laugh Catchpole said, "He's kidding you, Private. Good show. Good plan. Good work. Hip, hip."

Busy being slaughtered, the Huns lost the spirit of attack. An hour of withering fire changed the Germans' minds entirely about fighting the British. They were anything but the easy prey the Germans convinced themselves they were. The Kaiser boasted that he could send his police after the British and arrest them like the trespassers. The Territorial Army had learned a great deal about warfare fighting the Boers, sprouted modern ideas, new tactics, strategies, improved weapons.

The British Expeditionary Force, soldiers by profession, was eager to teach the Bosche a stern lesson.

At the same time, the British command did not know and did not believe that the German generals sent soldiers by the hundred thousand.

The field of battle the Germans occupied filled with the wounded and dead. The Bosche stepped around the bodies of their comrades. The blood, the viscera turned them squeamish. Consequently, they paid less attention to the British than they should have. This doubly benefited the British. The Germans, being less attentive to the attack, made easier targets, the British less likely to get shot.

No time for rest or food. A tin of cold tea. A dry biscuit. Only a moment to strike a lucifer and light a cigarette, take a few puffs, and back to fighting. Cigarettes were new to Atkins, a novelty that went with soldiering. He developed a taste for the things, the flame, the tip of red smolder, the curling smoke when the air was still.

Tommy Atkins' First Death

Bombs exploded all around the Ruffians and Victors, many close by, fragments flying about, ear-shattering noise. The German gunners refined their aim. Sandbags protected the Ruffians before and behind. Tommy Atkins rose and ran toward the limber to get water for the canister. A shell exploded overhead, sprayed shrapnel. A piece pierced his throat. He was prostrate on the ground. Gurgling, breath arrested, his face turning purple. Tommy Atkins was the first to die on this first day of battle.

Implored Palmer, "Where's the doctor? Sure, he was here for the beer. Where is he now? We were not taught how to pull shrapnel from a man's neck."

Catchpole stuck his index finger inside the wound, probed about. "It is in a funny way, lodged. It needs something to grasp it. The bullet extractor?

"I'll give it a try," said Sidney Godley. With the pliers he tried to reach inside the wound. "This isn't working. Pry his mouth open. See if you can get it from inside." Peering in and probing with his fingers he said, "No sign of it. I hate to see the boy go. No doctor, no help. Gone."

"Step aside," Carmichael said. "I swallow swords. I know the inside of the throat even better than a doctor. I think I can push the metal through the rest of the way. It's worth trying, if he is going to die anyway." After a few moment's pressing he said, "I've done it. Now, each of you grab a leg. Hoist him up so his head is a foot above the ground. Shake him," said Paul Carmichael. "Give him the up and down. Don't mash his skull on the cobbles. I'll pound his back. Palmer, pummel his chest hard. Use your fists. Dislodge the fragment. Don't let it fall down his throat." Catchpole and Godley each took a leg and lifted. The others did as Private Carmichael directed.

Tommy Atkins spit out the iron shard. He began to breathe.

"Put me down, put me down!" he said hoarsely. "The doctor said it wasn't time."

"The doctor was not here," said Dease.

Tommy said, "The doctor. St. George. In hospital."

"What hospital? St. George? You are blabbering. You were here the whole time. Everything over in two minutes," said Carmichael. "We saved yer bloomin' life. Ain't you got a 'thank you' for us? Didn't need to bother with you, except we'd be another hand short."

"Besides, we didn't know what we'd write to your dear mother, so we saved your life," said Ziggy Palmer.

"What happened, then? I was in a hospital set up in a school. Empty cots. I told the doctor in my tunic's lining a letter for my parents. Can you mail it? Says he, 'You don't need a letter yet. You are too early. Your time will come when the army fights again at Mons.' I don't know what he meant. He spoke. I mean he spoke in my mind. I heard his voice inside. The doctor, I saw when he turned away, had wings on his back.

Are you an angel, I thought? But I couldn't ask, my throat stuck. When he turned to me he was St. George, full battle array. It was him. Same as we saw on the wall in the church. My heart filled with joy. I feel like a different person. A man." Tears filled his eyes. He rubbed them away with his tunic's sleeve.

"Listen to the boy. Such deep thoughts. He sounds like a philosopher," said William Catchpole.

"Quite. Do listen to him," said Dease.

Atkins continued. "What I saw, heard, even felt was more real than anything of this world. In religion I only know Bible stories. Even so, I sense that I touched the divine. Or it touched me. "

"Your brain was overactive, was all. We brought you back. You have the sword swallower to thank," said William Catchpole.

Nervous with this kind of talk, Palmer joked, "Aw, Atkins, too bad you didn't go."

"Why do you say that, you lout?" shot Sidney Godley.

"It's best to die among the first. Dead the first day of war's more glory than dead later. People's grief runs thin," said Palmer.

Atkins said, "Nothing I could do. I was sent back and that's all there is to it. I'm glad to be alive. Blessed by the saint. What did 'when the army fights again at Mons mean'?"

"Aw, you fools! Maudlin philosophy. Me, I'm for long life and plenty of it!" said Catchpole.

"Ye picked the wrong profession, my friend, if long life's what you're craving," said Carmichael. "You should have stayed where you were if you wanted a long life."

"Ah," said Catchpole. "But that's a story for another day. A stay in prison was the choice. Get iodine and bandages and fix this soldier up. Hurry. Don't want infection to set in."

"No pain," said Atkins.

"Shock. It will wear off. I'll give you a dose of morphine," said Dease.

"Take a look, will you?" Atkins asked. "Squeamish, are you?" There was a change in Atkins' tone, his outlook.

Lieutenant Dease leaned over. "Turn your head if you can. I can't see that side." He exclaimed, "I'll be blessed! No sign of a wound. Flesh as good as before! I've heard such tales, but took them for story.

Report this to the doctor?"

"A miracle," shouted Palmer.

"He'll think you're crazy. Keep this among ourselves," said Catchpole. "Happy to have our little soldier back. Might be something to this 'Golden Arrows of God.' I thought it was a ceremony. If they threw you back from the dead it must mean the rest of us will live through what is to come."

"Let us hope," said Dease.

"Being there was nothing extraordinary," Tommy Atkins said.

"Being where?" asked Dease.

"Heaven. If that was heaven it isn't worth dying for. Just an ordinary hospital ward."

"Probably the antechamber. Not heaven itself," said Palmer.

"What do you know about heaven?" said his partner, Catchpole. "You old drunk and fornicator, you should know about hell." Turning to Dease, Catchpole said, "Should we report Atkins dead and resurrected?"

"Always the joker. In your heart, you are happy to have Atkins back. Moved by what happened. I can tell."

Atkins thought, "Am I a Lazarus?" He said, "Ready for duty, sir. I'm off to get water." Atkins rose unsteadily, saluted, and went off.

At the Victors:
St. George and his Horde of Angels Descends
8:00 p.m.

Just then a barrage of lightning struck the battlefield. Angel St. George descended from the sky, materialized on the German side of the canal, a knight astride a horse. His myriad angels, foot soldiers and cavalry, circled down from the sky, like a flock of ravens. A roar arose from the invisible heavenly host. The Vickers teams saw tumult and confusion, a collapse of order among the Bosche. The German cavalry horses shied, wheeled, whinnied in piteous terror, and threw their mounts to the ground. The Vickers teams could not comprehend what they saw. Thoughts of their initiation returned. Hardy and Lang instinctively touched the pins at the back of their tunics' lapels. At the same time, it seemed that their bodies were weightless, as if they floated a few inches above the ground. The others experienced the same sensations.

They heard the sound of carillons ringing out an old church anthem though there was no church in view.

With the viciousness of ravening wolves, the divine troops circled then attacked the German soldiers with swords and pikes. The Bosche soldiers froze, stunned, confused, and in terror. A fog, impenetrable, accompanied the thrashing rain, enveloped the Germans in darkness. A wind came up, throwing piercing sand, then pebbles, then gravel into their faces. Then stones the size of fists fell from the sky upon the German infantry.

Silence descended on the Germans, their artillery, rifle, and machine guns unfired.

Sergeant Sanders and his men saw commotion on the German side, the soldiers looking skyward, pointing, animated in talk. They saw the sky brighten.

"A Bible story sky," exclaimed Jessop, "Heavenly rays shooting out of the clouds. I saw in Bible picture books. Looked just like this."

They stayed to watch the slaughter and tumult the angels wrought on the canal's far side.

Even so, some of the Germans advanced. The Victors turned to the gun in time to stop them before they reached the bridge. Then, with transecting fire, the Ruffians and Victors pushed the German soldiers farther from the bridge, the Bosche thoroughly exposed.

Chapter Six

Across the Canal the Germans
Saw the Phenomenon in the Heavens

Nimy Bridge, Mons Canal
23 August 1914, Mons Belgium
8:15 p.m.

And So They Saw

The German soldiers closest to the canal faced east, the cloud being
to the west of them. But those pressing up from the rear saw. Before
they reached the crest of the rise before it slopes down to the canal, the
soldiers in small bands widely scattered, saw the cloud swirl, glimmer,
take form–a warrior angel. An artillery squad took up position right
behind the rise. Their horses pulled the caisson, the carriage groaning,
harnesses straining. The angel turned in the sky as if upon a revolving
pedestal, sometimes facing them, sometimes in profile, then back and
wings toward them. The soldiers whispered speculation among themselves.

"I must be crazed from exhaustion," exclaimed artilleryman
Wilhelm Werkmeister.

"Crazed? No. It is an angel from heaven," the churchly Klaus Egon
argued.

Private Dieter Luebke asked, "When did we last eat?"

"A day since," said Werkmeister. "Iron rations only."

"Too much marching. Three weeks," groused Franz Spies.

"Be reasonable," said Egon. "How could all of us see it if was not
there? It could not be. Surely divine will guides and directs the
changes," said Egon. "It is a sign from heaven, proclaiming that we will
destroy the British today, march on to swift victory over vile France."

"Nonsense. Too much fighting," said Werkmeister. "Those
Belgians. They would run like frightened women, we were told, as soon
as we came in sight. Would not even leave their houses. Like
policemen, we could arrest the whole Belgian army. So why did it take
three weeks to get here when we should already have France's surrender

66

in hand?"

"You are speaking treason," said Egon. "You will be reported."

"Then tell me where I am wrong and I will apologize to the Kaiser himself."

"You will soon lose your tongue and your life," said Franz Spies. "Shut your mouth."

Turning the conversation, Luebke saved his comrade. "And drink?" he catechized.

Conscript Spies replied, "Since my canteen ran out."

"When was that?" asked Julius Werkmeister.

"Yesterday morning."

Said Oskar Traugott, glorifier of the ways of the Kaiser and General von Kluck, "Dry now. No need to stop and piss. Saves time. A good thing. Brings us that much closer to victory."

"A point in our favor, surely," said Conscript Spies, now sarcastic.

"Drank from a muddy pond this morning," said Conscript Max Luebke. "I don't feel sick yet. Three weeks fighting and not yet in France."

"So you said," grumbled Traugott, tired of talk, watching the angel overhead as he marched forward.

Werkmeister continued, "Such heat. I say what we see isn't there. I tell you, as soon as we fill our bellies it will disappear. Nothing out of the ordinary in seeing angels when you are in starved and thirsty."

Spies whispered, "Shush. The sergeant is nearby."

"It is odd, this cloud," said Luebke.

Said Egon. "A sign from God. We will be victorious. We will squash the British like insects. They are few and feeble. We are many and strong. Our generals are wise."

"I hope Egon is correct. We shall see," proclaimed Traugott. "Who do you think the angel is? Gabriel? Michael? One of our own?"

Said Klaus Egon, "One of our warrior saints. Come to fight, bring us victory."

"Do the English have saints?" asked Werkmeister. "Maybe this angel, this warrior, appears to them as one of theirs. The English have their own prayers and priests and blessings."

"And we have curses for them," said Klaus Egon.

As they crested the rise they saw the field strewn with dead and wounded soldiers, their fellows. They saw the monstrous angel, now glowering down upon them.

From Drunk with Gladness to Sober with Grief

The two Vickers teams and Captain Leckie knew Saint George saved them in their moment of peril.

Three times Lieutenant Dease left his observation post to guide his men at their guns, twice to the Victors, the last time, the Ruffians. On each visit he was shot. The first time, without even a groan, he crawled out of view and dressed his own wound. No sooner had Lieutenant Dease returned to his post than he saw trouble below. This time a bullet struck him when he was making his way back to his post. When the lieutenant reached the Ruffians on his third trip he was already seeing through dead eyes. He slumped over, groaned, and stirred no more. One day on the battlefield and, like many others, the lieutenant gone. All gathered about Dease, breathing his last, Dease, fallen.

From drunk with gladness, the Ruffians were sober with grief, spirits crushed.

"Poor Dease. Poor boy," Godley moaned. "Move his body out of the way. Protect it. Atkins, take hold of his arms. Carmichael, pick him up by his legs." Atkins fell faint. Godley said, "The lieutenant was your friend, your protector. Do him this last service. Gently lift his body. Careful of his dangling head. Set him behind the sandbags, where he will be safe for now. A sweet soul," said Godley. "Carry him. Months of training, getting to know one another, joking, become brothers. He was innocence and enthusiasm, the willing comrade."

Even those who mocked everything–even their own sorry plight– Catchpole and Palmer behaved with decorum. They had always ex- empted Dease from their jibes and sallies of wit. "It is good to see sincerity in a young man, in a fellow being. He commanded men older, more worldly than himself," said William Catchpole. "It was not only that he was the best gunner. There was something angelic about the lad. A man I would follow in faith and devotion. No one of his stature to take his place. Our hope for glory fades with him."

Godley said, "We will make do, all right. Lay him on his back.

Close his eyes. Rest his cap over his face."

As the Ruffians stepped toward their fallen brother, a formless glow rose over his stomach, took the shape of an orb, overlaid him from head to foot, stood upright on Dease's chest. The men hastened out of the way. The form drifted upward like a weather balloon lifted by a gentle breeze. As it rose, the speed of its ascent increased. It was the same lieutenant whose body lay at their feet, but shimmering, wispy, a golden Lieutenant Maurice Dease.

The farther up he rose, the smaller he became until he was a glimmering speck of light. Suddenly the spark became a streak of gold like a comet's head, and stopped at St. George's right hand. The speck grew into Lieutenant Dease, half the size of the angel, aglow in angelic light. His features were again distinct, but fixed now, stern.

Gasped Catchpole, "In uniform and full kit."

Barely able to contain his tears, his voice quavering, Tommy Atkins said, "The first comrade I lost. He protected me. Taught me. Part of me is gone with him."

"A cynic all my life, and now I see this," said Carmichael.

They looked from the angel in the sky to Dease lying before them and back again to the spectacle above. How could this be, they thought.

Then all the gunners–Ruffians and Victors–heard Dease's voice. "God is no mere onlooker. He casts his lot with the righteous when the way is imperiled." Then, "The unseen world helps the living visible world."

The voice seemed to come from the very air itself. Yet what was happening seemed at the moment in the way of a dream.

Palmer, the arch-skeptic, said, "There's no explaining. St. George? Dease turned angel?" He went on. "A mad man's hallucinations make sense to him. None of this makes sense to a sane person."

"We seem to be receiving what the church would call a dispensation," said William Catchpole.

Palmer said, "Who knows? Maybe other soldiers are being sent back from death to life. Like Atkins was. Who knows what's going on down the line and across the canal?"

Paul Carmichael entered the conversation. "What about Golden Arrows? I haven't seen Germans getting up after they go down."

With a sharp reply, Palmer: "What about the wounded who hobble away or just lay on the ground?"

"You and your quibbles. The angel I see alongside St. George is Lieutenant Dease. That's good enough for me. It points to a special place for us. As I said, Golden Arrows. Believe it or not."

"Time to cut the jabber. Pay attention," said Godley. "Bosche artillery is finding its range. Shells falling all about. We must avenge our dead companion."

Lieutenant Dease's Ascent and Transfiguration

(Dease's Thoughts)

When the third bullet pierced my right thigh I shuddered, as if electricity had passed through my body. My heart, a burning coal, the next instant was a clod of ice. I had bled too much.

Between consciousness and a faint, I prayed, "God, take me."

A voice within, the voice of St. George, answered my irreverent summons. "Prepare yourself, Arrow of God. You are Britain's first sacrifice of uncountable sacrifices the nations will make."

I thought I'd rather do without the honor and live, but our fates are beyond our rathers and hopes. Then I parted from my body. It was as if I was ascending in an observation balloon. Looking down, I saw the ground rush away. Was the "I" my soul, I wondered? The vastness of space before me, the earth below. The sounds of the battlefield faded into silent. I entered the realm of the dead.

A shout from far below reached my ears. "God save us!" Beside the bridge I saw Company C, Royal Fusiliers, far below, the soldiers the size of fleas. They were looking up. The cry was theirs. "Dease!" I heard them shout. "Lieutenant Dease, God has blessed you! Golden Arrows of God. For St. George and England!"

Then I looked into the countenance of St. George, who stood alongside. I felt the supernal presence as tremors in my flesh, my sinews, quakings down to the bones and marrow. Kneeling, I said, "Sweet saint, I worship at your feet!"

"Stand, sir! You shall serve at my side. Now is time to fight, not worship."

For an instant or an eon I knew the saint's mind, his very thoughts.

Through his eyes I saw all time and all of eternity–from creation to annihilation. At the saint's side I witnessed horrors that mankind has never yet experienced, hell come to earth. I saw my comrades below, my body lying on the ground.

I cried. My tears fell to earth. Caught in the setting sun's rays they looked like droplets of molten gold. The voice's words and the vision became an exultation, a movement of the spirit ministers preach about.

Even German Officers and Staff in the Field Saw the Angel

His adjutant, Dieter Friedrich, coaxed Captain Maximillian Mueller. "Overhead. But you see them, Herr Captain? Now there are two. What do you say, Captain? A second rose up from the ground and stands alongside. Smaller, like the ranking of angels and apostles in our churches."

"Of course I see, Corporal. But I don't have to believe what I see. A skilled illusionist can make you see anything he wants–a lady disappear, a bird fly from a handkerchief. In Munich I saw Houdini do many tricks. As real as they seemed, all was fake, illusion. An alienist would say what we've been through, seeing angels in the clouds is no surprise. That's all it is, I tell you."

"But we all see them," the adjutant retorted. "Seeing is believing."

"Sometimes it is not. Such a thing is mass hallucination. Or mass hypnosis. The British are capable of such things," argued Captain Mueller.

"Do they have magicians in their war department?"

"Maybe Houdini himself, for all I know. This is nothing. We are here to fight. When we invest this city I will command the prisoners of war and the hospitals. Prepare yourself to work. Our orders are to stay in this city, put the Belgians to work. Forget about clouds and angels, my friend."

They Fought through the Hours to the End of Day: The Retirement

Company C, the Royal Fusiliers, and the whole of the BEF, was ordered to withdraw when circumstances permitted. Suddenly the battle-field fell silent, as if the sky had swallowed up all the sound. All along the canal the German rifle triggers clicked and lanyards snapped on German artillery, but not a rifle or gun fired.

In the pause, the British along the canal withdrew to the safety of the town and then along roads to the south of Mons. Some took up defensive positions and ambushes in Nimy and Mons to harass and kill unsuspecting Germans when they breeched the salient, which they inevitably would. Infantry around Nimy Bridge had a nasty run to make, two hundred yards across open fields, a gradual, exposed slope all the way to the first cover the town beyond could give.

While the thin line of troops withdrew, the Victors and Ruffians held their positions, crossfire transecting the bridge, the Vixen and Vicki pouring blistering fire, keeping up their farewells to the falling Germans. The clatter of the Ruffians' own gun was deafening.

The silence lasted for a quarter of an hour, causing consternation among the Germans. Then the whistle and howl, the groaning air and thump of Bosche bombs leaving the cannons' mouths, began again with increased ferocity.

Said Sanders, "The bloody Germans will attack any bloody second now. This is no hallucination, no vision, no séance. This is bloody war."

As he ran back to the gun, Lang asked, "What's the sky got to do with us? Golden Arrows, that's what."

Sanders exclaimed, "But clouds won't protect us from bullets, bombs, bayonets. God gave us the gun to kill Germans. Get to it!"

Nancarrew said, "But the angel. Will he fight? God bless me!"

"The show is over," ordered Sanders. "The angel gave us a respite and time for our men to withdraw. But the angel won't hold the bridge. We must. We've fighting to do."

Gabriel, giddy with explanation, cried, "The angel out of clouds. I've become a believer."

The Ruffians and Victors fired prolonged bursts into the flood of Bosche running across the fields toward the bridge.

Godley asked Atkins, "How's the ammunition? We've been firing all day."

"Little left. A dozen belts' worth. One fresh barrel."

The Germans came on, wave after wave, shooting wildly. They did not aim, fired from the waist. The attack become frantic, Germans shouting encouragement, fear, pain, exultation. Just then German artillery began firing from over and beyond the ridge. The air filled with the roar, the booming and whistling of bombs, a crescendo reached. Finally the Bosche mass of Germans overwhelmed the British defense, crossed the bridge, breeched the salient.

At the last the Vickers teams were to break the guns down, throw the parts in the canal, and run off. Sergeant Sanders, now leading both teams, told the men, "Captain Ashburner promised us new guns when we reach the new line of defense. But we won't part with them. I'll carry the tripod. Godley, carry yours. Have someone haul the gun. They are hot. Be careful." As heavy as the parts were, Carmichael and Walter Sage hoisted them on their shoulders. "Lift and tie Lieutenant Dease atop the ammunition cart. We are taking him with us, too. Catchpole and Palmer, haul the cart and run like hell. It is a conspicuous target, but it will protect you." To the rest, he said, "Spread out, keep low, run in spurts, zigzag, get behind anything that sticks above the ground, get inside the town." The cart slowed Catchpole and Palmer, trudging up the rise. The rest of the men resist the temptation to bunch up in front of the cart. Making their way across the field, the Vickers squads passed British dead and maimed. Four medical orderlies carried the wounded on litters in the midst of German gunfire. Passing, one asked, "Taking your man to the medical tent?"

"He is beyond help," said Sidney Godley.

The orderly said, "We are without a doctor. Captain Leckie got one in the neck. Shrapnel. He's alive. Serious wound. " The men went on, the orderlies going one way, the gunners another.

Captain Horace Ashburner's plan called for sappers' explosives to destroy the bridge, but they did not go off.

Having mowed down Germans all day, the Vickers teams and all the British were elated, proud of their work. The British Expeditionary Force won a fair victory and was eager to fight the next day, ready to give the Huns more of the same.

Escape into the Twilight and the Night

When the Germans finally crossed the bridges the British were nowhere to be found. The entire British force escaped into the dusk. The Germans took revenge on the innocent citizens of Nimy, who, to the

German way of thinking, were collaborators, saboteurs. The soldiers roused everyone from their houses, shops, and businesses–men, women, and children–that lined both sides of the Rue de Nimy. The Huns mixed them among the soldiers and forced them to march. The Germans knew that if the British were still about they would not shoot for fear of hitting the poor Belgians. While the Germans had no such scruples, they knew anyone not on their side was an enemy to be treated with hatred and malice. German logic.

More German soldiers came behind along the Rue de Nimy, pried cobbles from the roadways, used them to smash the windows of every building. Armed with bottles filled with petrol and stoppered with cloth, other soldiers threw the incendiaries, setting the buildings ablaze. Looking back, the fleeing townspeople saw their homes and shops burning, saw the flames and smoke, adding to their woe and fear. The Germans marched the poor people all the way to Mons, where they added the Burgomaster and city council, the priest, and other officials to the throng. In short order, General Somebody-or-Other installed himself as governor, imposing strict rule and restrictive regulations on the people, to humiliate and control.

That Night the British Generals
Marched the Exhausted BEF Thirty-two Miles

Instead of their expected reward for a day's good fighting, a night in the *estaminets* and congratulations in kisses and hugs and more from the girls of the town, the British soldiers got nothing. They were disgusted. Why leave Mons, they wanted to know. They had whipped the Bosche and wanted to do it again tomorrow. The higher-ups didn't bother telling them why the army withdrew. By the next evening the two Vickers teams were beyond Belgium's border and at the foot of the Forest of Mormal.

Chapter Seven

Jeanne d'Arc and the Road Through

The Forét de Mormal
24 August, 1914

> *When the British reached the Forest of Mormal in Northern France they had to break into two corps and passed on either side. Each corps was more vulnerable than it would have been if they had been able to move en masse. Moving en masse would slow the passage, giving the German First and Second Armies coming from the northwest time to trap them, where battle was unwelcome, terrain, time, and fatigue, considered. Better at Le Cateau, the British could reach the town and fortify it.*

> *Heroes and Legends of World War I*
> Arch Whitehouse

Ahead Lay the Certainty

The plan: divide the army in half to skirt the vast Forest of Mormal—the First Corps, 1st and 2nd Divisions along the eastern side of the forest, the 2nd Corps, 3rd and 5th Divisions along the west.

Ahead lay the certainty of refugees clogging the way–carts, barrows, wagons, buggies, baggage, children, the aged, cripples and the infirm, all in shock and grief, terrified. Ahead miscalculations, misunderstandings, bad directions, hunger, thirst, fatigue. Pack-laden soldiers, baggage, guns, horses, mules, provisions. The unforeseen could arise at any moment. The smallest mishap could have disastrous consequences.

Marching through pleasant countryside. Gentle hills and valleys, church spires, villages, forests, fields. A hot day. The soldiers did not

75

know when they passed from Belgium into France.

The day before the British held off the German onslaught at Mons, back-peddling–the hardest kind of soldiering. The British had no food after the battle at Mons began, no water after their canteens ran dry. The Germans were fatigued with marching and fierce fighting that had gone on for three weeks.

The Locale

The Forét de Mormal: an ancient forest dense with beech and oak. Streams and rivers ran through. Springs gurgled from the roots of monstrous trees forming isolated marshes and miniature meadows. Nine miles long and three to five wide. Sometimes the preserve of a king or prince, sometimes a wilderness untouched by any but the charcoal burner, the fisherman, the trapper, the hunter, the interior rarely visited even by them. Forbidding to any but those who lived on its outskirts, it was believed to be a dwelling of malevolent forces easily provoked when disturbed.

Reaching the northern point of the Forest of Mormal Captain Ashburner told his adjutant, Mungo Black, "Entrench here. Strike the lines east to west. Two lines, one twenty yards out from the edge of the brambles and brush, the other farther forward. There's barely light to see. Get the men digging. Two hundred feet long. The Vickers guns for cross-fire, at the flanks." The captain asked, "Where are the gun crews? The Germans are in a hurry to catch us with the forest at our backs. Move fast."

The Victors dug far from the Captain, who placed himself at the center of the line. Private Hardy ran off into the brambles, cut four beech saplings, cut each into four stakes, hacked to a point at one end. Gabriel Jessop pounded them into the ground, one every twenty-five feet. Right behind, Walter Sage tied fifty-foot lengths of yellow cord to the stakes, marking off the two hundred feet. "Dig behind the cord," he repeated as he passed along the line of troops. "Get your grubbers out. Foot and a half deep. Pile and pack the dirt in front."

The dirt thrown up and the trenching were the soldiers' protection, prone and squatting, from rifle bullets, but from nothing else in the German arsenal. Prone shooting only. They could not rise to shoot. They did not intend to stay long. A shallow trench was all they needed.

The Victors held the eastern end of the line.

The gentle rise and fall of the fields caught the darkening shadows the trees threw across the land, the shadows themselves faded into the forest before the falling darkness. The peasants had brought in a second harvest of hay, the haycocks dotting the fields–places where soldiers could hide and shoot the enemy, and isolated islands easily overrun in an assault.

"Promise of a third cutting, the grass being calf-high already," said country-bred Nancarrew. "The crops about will be trampled to dust. Like the work of locusts. Every blade crushed. No harvest."

In mock grief Hardy said, "Bad luck, ain't it?"

"But ain't this a pretty wood?" tossing a spade full of dirt, said Jessop. "In merrie England this would be a lord's estate."

"Demesne, they called it. Beautiful word," added Howard Lang.

"Probably was here, too," said Sidney Godley. "Someone planted these trees in ancient days. I'm striking stone and roots."

"And here we are digging rifle pits," Sage claimed, "We'd be flushing grouse for milord and his noble guests."

"To the hounds! Yoikes! Yoikes!" his friend Gabriel cheered.

The thick, deep roots of alfalfa and clover made digging the forward line difficult. In the line close to the forest, the digging was even tougher. The men used their inadequate shovels to chop through heavy roots, thick brush, and bramble, vines, briars, weeds, saplings between the field and the forest. Underneath the topsoil was heavy clay, brick-hard in this dry month of summer.

Up and down the line was heard the thud, shush, and scraping of shovels in dirt, the sharp ping of steel on rock. In a gabble of voices, loudly whispered irritations and complaints in the growing dark. Up and down the line. Disgruntled grumbling, and invective toward the nasty German whose horrid behavior pulled them from cozy barracks and comfortable messes across the Channel.

"Hard work after a hard night and day's march."

"Train us as gunners and we dig ditches."

"Engineering they call it."

"You want to sit out in the open, numbskull? Keep digging."

Alan Hardy threw in his ha'penny's worth, called back, " 'Ditch digging' lacks dignity, don't you know? 'Engineers,' top of the line. That's the difference. Engineers of the Royal Fusiliers are we."

Down the line the theme was picked up. "Engineers don't grow blisters and calluses."

"Hell, they don't. Can we get this done quick?"

"Where are we?" asked Jessop.

"Somewhere hereabouts Belgium turns into France, doesn't it?" asked Walter Sage.

"The map says Forêt de Mormal is in France," answered Sanders. "But who knows? They always jiggle the borders after a war."

"Ain't that the point of going to war?" said Sage. "More land, less land, my land, your land."

Said Walter Jessop, "Yer quite the poet."

"We are not in France," argued Lang. "We stand on Belgian soil, not French."

"France? Belgium? What's the bloody difference? Wherever we are, we are digging a bloody rifle pit," complained Hardy. To Nancarrew, he said, "What do you think, you mum bird?"

"Never talks, he don't," Jessop offered. "Just digs, the mum bird."

Adjutant Mungo Black reached the Victors' position, said in a loud whisper, "Cut the prattle. No time for jokes. Keep digging. You need to protect yourselves."

Chided Howard Lang, "We'll be marching soon."

"The German's are coming. Every minute is precious. Dig, you devils. Mind your work, men." Black walked back to the center of the line, took up his post.

From across the Field Came the Barking of Dogs and Lantern Light

The sound of barking traveled from dog to dog, farm to farm, field to field, coming ever closer.

The men dug on. Walter Sage caught a glint of light beyond the line and to the south. "Something's astir," he whispered. "Coming across the field." He asked, "Peasant with a lantern?"

"Where?" Jessop asked. "German spy?"

"Back the way we marched," Hardy said. "Someone's coming.

Maybe the peasants don't know massed armies are on the way, right in this bloody fool of a Frenchman's path."

"I say he's Belgian," said Jessop.

"Belgian, French. Leave it behind, you irritation," groused Sage.

"Farmer coming to look after his fields, see who's stealing his crops. Probably carrying a club, ready to strike," observed Lang. "Heard our digging. After his buried treasure, his francs and gold. We'll call to him when he gets near."

"Maybe he can show us the way, lead us to the French gals with the wiggle-waggle in their walk," said the lascivious Henry. "Or the way to the nearest *estaminet*. I could use a pint of ale, bottle of wine. I'm parched."

Taking up the strain, William Sage said, "Maybe this is the enchanted forest where the water tastes like wine. But shouldn't we shout the farmer a warning. Who speaks French?"

"Vous-les vous!" said Jessop.

"That's no warning," said Sage.

"At least he knows somebody's here," said Gabriel. "That's all we need him to know." Then, putting on a fake French accent, he continued, "The Germans are coming this way. There is a war. Hide your family and flocks in the forest, if you know it well enough."

"Look at that, will ye?" said Walter Sage.

"He's coming right toward us," Jessop said.

Walter whispered, " It ain't a man. It's a shepherdess. Her dress? See her crook?"

"Looking for her lost sheep," said Gabriel.

"Or turnips for her dinner. We passed a vegetable patch a while back," Nancarrew said.

"Little Bo Peep, she lost her sheep and didn't know where to find them," recited Howard Lang.

"Leave them alone, and they'll come home, something, something, something behind them," added Hardy.

Objects Jessop, "Wagging their tails. Nursery rhymes. My God! Have we come to infancy and the nursery?"

"A will-o-the-wisp it is," hissed Walter Sage. "Do they have elves in France, too?"

"Pixies? They are small. She is human size."

"She's coming fast, must be running!" exclaimed private Godley.

Alan Hardy observed, "But the lamp holds steady. No up and down. No swaying side to side."

The men stopped digging and stood dumbfounded, jaws agape, eyes wide.

"Faster than we can run!" Hardy said. Clearly a woman, the figure passed to the left of the trenching line, not ten yards from the men, toward the forest. "She doesn't notice us, with all the scraping, shoveling, dirt flying about. And our voices," he concluded.

Suddenly the light from the lantern flared, encircling the woman in fire.

"She's ablaze. Skirt must 'a' caught from the lantern!" said Jessop in a loud whisper.

"A French peasant nothing! Look at 'er. Wings, by God! Look at 'er close. She's a bloody angel!" said Walter Sage.

In an instant the light became bright as lightning, she within a shell of light, the light obscuring her features. The angel, or spirit, substantial as an actress on a limelight lit stage.

"She's real, God bless us!" said Jessop.

"Bloody funny to me," said Walter Sage. "Looks like a Gibson girl with wings."

"When did you ever see a picture of a Gibson girl, you bloody codger?"

Before Sage answered, Howard Lang rubbed his eyes. "I see her, too!"

Sage: "No white gown. No sandals. She's in armor. Sword in scabbard, shield on left arm, steel helmet under her right, the lantern in her right hand. No gold band around her hair. Blimey."

"I see the white wings, too. Jeanne d'Arc!" exclaimed Henry Sanders, amazed.

"John Dark? Who's that?" asked Jessop.

"You old mechanic, its Joan of Arc," said Sergeant Sanders.

"You're going daft. No sleep, no drink, no food, no brains left to think with," said Jessop. "You should know better."

The angel turned toward them, her features drowned in the light's intensity. She passed beyond them into the scrub, swinging her lantern her shield pointing toward the forest, signaling them forward. "She wants us to follow," said Sergeant Sanders.

"It's like in school books. Joan of Arc leading the French to battle," said Alan Hardy. Rubbing his eyes, he said, "Wake me. I'm dreaming."

"You ain't dreamin'," said Walter Sage. "She's here. We all see her. Another angel come."

"Keep digging or you'll be arguing when the Germans arrive," a voice called from down the line.

"She's beckoning us," Walter Sage repeated. "With a wave of her arm."

"Like old Hamlet's ghost calling on the watch," whispered Lang to himself. "Twilight. Time bewitched."

Walter Sage: "The brambles and briars aren't stopping her at all. She's passing over them, floating in the air." The men stopped shoveling, pointing their grubbers at what they saw, or holding them at their sides. They turned away from the trench and faced the forest.

Corporal Mungo Black–a jackal. The men called him Black-Heart, but never to his face. Black had a sense for things out of order, always appeared at the right moment to catch a soldier in a dereliction. He crept up between the forest and the trench, saw the Victors gabbing, not digging, worst of all, facing in the wrong direction. "Keep digging, you lazy louts!" he ordered. His correcting faults always ended with the reminded that their lack of diligence would be their deaths and the deaths of others.

He barked, "Nothing for you in the forest. Face about and dig!" His nostrils flared, as if to draw in more air to feed his fires.

In those few moments the light flickered, faded, flared brightly, and went out.

"No sign of the angel." Said Walter Sage, "Where is she? Gone. Can't see her."

Black: "Angel! What are you talking about!"

Sage foolishly ventured the words: "Corporal, we saw an angel. Right behind where you are."

The corporal unsnapped his holstered, grabbed the pistol grip. "What are you up to?"

Godley turned about and began digging furiously. "Digging, sir." The Victors joined him, shoveling.

Hands on his hips, Mungo Black looked on. He said. "No more

foolishness, you hear? Back to the work. Eyes on the ground."

The Victors could not help glancing back into the woods, not all at the same time, but like hens in a hen yard, each taking a turn, each following the other dumbly.

"Disobey me, will you! Keep yer eyes ahead, yer mugs."

Sage, the last to look, said, "It is back."

"What are you pulling? You are relieved of duty. Go to the. . . ."

All heads turned except the corporal's. "Look, Corporal," Sergeant Sander said.

"Strike me dumb!" he whispered when he turned and saw, at first a mist, then a glow.

Above the scrub and saplings the light blossomed again, hung in air, became an eagle, then Joan of Arc.

She overwhelmed the Victors' senses, kindled fire in their brains.

The angel floated ahead, suspended ten feet above the ground, still beckoning them onward.

Transfixed, pistol in hand, Black exclaimed, "Strike me dumb!"

At first the Victors thought that somehow the German artillery had made its way around the forest from the south and discovered a BEF contingent. Did a night battle rage? "None of our troops came through before us," said Hardy. "We are at the head. God knows where the French are, but I doubt they're in front of us."

"They could not get here," added Sergeant Sanders.

When the angel passed out of sight light showered the darkening sky with threads of gold the blessed artists of earlier ages used to paint Jesus' halo, and those of the saints and angels. Said mechanic Nancarrew, "This light–too bright for the eyes. Like welding without wearing a mask. You'll come away with blind spots in your eyes that won't go away. Too much, burn you blind." They had to cover their eyes.

The ground rumbled, shook, and trembled. As if the Titans, huge as mountains, wrenched themselves out of the earth. As if the Hebrew God's Behemoth trampled the earth as prophesy promised for the end of days. The Victors heard the sound of limbs cracking, branches crashing, wrenched and ripped from trees, entire trunks topping as if a tornado ravaged the forest ahead. Then followed the sharp smell of fresh-cut timber, raw wood, humus, and just-plowed earth. Battle and storm.

Mungo Black Disappeared into the Gloom, The Victors Following

Corporal Black put his pistol back in its holster, hurrying to the head of the line.

One by one the Victors folded their trenching shovels, strapped on their packs, shouldered their rifles, left their post. Of their own accord, their feet drew the soldiers into the woods behind the corporal. The Victors hacked their way through the thick belt of brush, thorns, and bush, scratched and scraped. Corporal Black discovered an opening small animals and deer traveled to reach the farmers' fields and grasses and grains.

"A passage, and the light ahead," said Mungo Black. "Briars all about. Rifles on safety. Don't snag your triggers."

Gabriel Jessop: "This must be one of them angels militant the Bible talks of, knows to hide the entrance to the passageway."

"Warrior! What do you think Joan of Arc is? Soldier! General!" replied Sanders.

A dozen yards into the wood they found a ditch. Covering the lens, Hardy turned on his electric torch, pointed it to the ground letting only light through the flesh of his fingers. "Clean of vegetation," the writer said. He knelt and scraped up a handful of dirt, worked it through his fingers then called Nancarrew over. ""You know dirt, farm boy. Smell."

Gunner Nancarrew held the dirt to his nose and breathed in short sniffs. "Not top soil or humus. Fresh, pure clay. You could make bricks from it. Moist enough, too."

Lang, the artist, looked at it. "Red as a French lady's rouge. Fine enough for a potter to work."

Sanders came over and looked into the dark expanse. "What have we here? Shine more light. Someone digging a foundation for a shed, a storage bin? What's this?"

Nancarrew got on his hands and knees, crawled the width of the ditch and came back. "Ten yards edge to edge. The vegetation clear gone. Not a tree or a rock or a root or twig in it. Dirt compact, like compressed by weighted rollers they ready roadbeds with. This is no foundation. A road, sunk a foot below the forest floor."

The Angel of Mons

"That's what all the tumult and commotion was, by God," said Sage.

The men could see only as far as the light from the electric torches reached. Beyond the light were signs that the road went on.

"I must tell the captain," said Black.

"How will you convince him, sir?" asked Sergeant Sanders.

"Surely he and those along the line heard the noise, saw the lights. He must now be looking to find out what happened."

The Ruffians, too, had heard the sounds, but saw no light, being at the other end of the line and, at that moment, looking off in a different direction. The Golden Arrows of God, the Victors and the Ruffians, heard the tumult that produced the road, showed up at the same spot to investigate.

The Road where No Road Was

A quarter of an hour arguing and swearing on the Bible and examination by the Captain passed before Black and Sergeant Sanders persuaded him to leave his inspection of the trenching work and go with them into the forest.

Said Captain Ashburner, "Our engineers studied the maps. Cavalry found bridle paths and wagon paths that end at cabins, or charcoal burners' huts. Ruts and paths peter out after one hundred yards. We looked for just such a road. Prayed for one. The natives say no road goes through. This morning our aeroplanes flew over for a last look. Thick stands of beech and oak. I'll take a look, but you are wasting time."

At first he saw the clay bed as far as the electric torchlight reached. He ran fifty yards along it with Gunner One, Sanders and his adjutant, as astounded as the others had been. Captain Ashburner said, "The cavalry, the people who live about say no road. How did you find it? For now, Black, send the cyclists quick. Find out what this is, where it goes. No reason, yet, as you say, here it is."

Minutes later five scouts met him behind the trenching, each pushing his bicycle, rifle and kit attached.

The Cyclists

Captain Ashburner raced for the Army throughout Europe and the

British Empire. Beat all opponents. He was among the best in bike racing–stage, circuit, point-to-point–and their superior in rank. The only soldier who knew what cyclists could really do. Ashburner trained the crew in their roles as military scouts and couriers. They were cyclists first, soldiers after.

They squatted in a huddle, their bikes parked in a straight row.

Alfred Goullet, Australia's champion, came to England to join his friend and rival, Sergeant Harry Bailey, English bike racing champion. They thought they would tour Europe at the Army's expense, race against the Europeans. Have a grand time. Their friend, Willie Spencer, was along, too. They were the elite of the cyclists' corps. The others were policemen recruited to the corps. No postmen, no delivery boys.

Ashburner said, "Tonight you are my intelligence officers."

He described signs of a road. The men would ride in a wedge creating lower pressure in the center, save the one going farthest from having to push against the air. On the outward run Goullet, top rider, would go the farthest. As far as the road goes, each cyclist would drop off every two miles, catch his wind, go ahead a mile slowly, wait for the one ahead to return with Goullet's message. Four minutes a mile going and coming, if the road went the full nine miles of the forest–a little more than an hour.

The captain assigned each cyclist his place. Going the farthest: Goullet, second, Bailey, next, Spencer, then Mandrake, and Leslie. Ashburner said, "I doubt the road goes very far, but I need to know. Explore and report. Watch out for Bosche. They might have something to do with this. Note the compass, distance. Map the road as you go. What it is composed of. If it goes the nine miles you will report in over an hour. Meanwhile we proceed with the trenching."

Spoke up Bailey, "Captain, we have motorbikes. Why not one of those? Cut the time to practically nothing."

"Use your head," the Captain replied.

"Oh, I see, sir. Quiet as she goes."

With mocking dismay, hitting his forehead with his open fist, Ashburner: "Oh, my God."

Goullet Goes Forward

The men rode off. The road went on. Man by man, the cyclists dropped off. Already fatigued by riding in clay when he left Bailey behind, Goullet thought the last three miles, the two ahead and the one back, would wear him out. He planned to stretch his legs, catch his wind, and stretch his cramped back when he met Bailey on the ride back. Yet, no sooner had he left Bailey than he felt renewed, a second wind. But it was more than that. When Goullet passed Bailey's sight, he saw a glow, then a pillar of light. The light concentrated itself, became an angel in armor. The pedals spun without resistance. The spokes hummed with the wind they made. He was transported in minutes to the end of the forest. Ahead he saw by the angel's light a farm field. The light grew smaller and smaller, shrunk to the size of a lantern. In its glow Bailey saw it was in a peasant's hand, a shepherdess, crook in one hand, walking across the rough field, the light dimming and disappearing. Then, in an instant he was back at Bailey's side. Yet to Bailey it seemed that his friend had been gone a quarter of an hour. "The road goes all the way through! Hard packed clay all the way. The road will support the wagons and carts, if that's what the army wants to send. I'll scratch a note for the captain. No need for the details."

The Return

Rider five, Leslie, panting, perspiring, his face beet-red, dropped his bike, ran up, saluted Captain Ashburner, who was studying a map with Corporal Black and a couple of sergeants.

Saluting, Leslie said, "Reporting to the Captain."

Frowning mild disappointment, Ashburner said, "I won't slay the messenger." The captain looked at his watch. "The road ended after a mile? Where are the rest? You could have all come back together. Why isn't Goullet making the report?"

"Beg pardon, sir?"

Captain Ashburner looked at his watch in the lantern light. "I put him in charge. He should report."

"I'm sure he's a long way back, sir?"

"What do you mean?"

"The road goes all the way through. He will be a long time coming, sir. Eighteen miles cycling on clay."

"What do you mean? You were gone a quarter of an hour."

"Fifteen minutes, sir?"

"Don't repeat me. Look," he said, pointing to his wristwatch's face. "It's 21:30. You left at 21:15."

"Begging your pardon, sir. Nearly two hours the ride took us. I rode half an hour myself, a little more coming and going." Private Leslie looked at his own watch. "Captain, mine says 23:30."

"Your watch is wrong by two hours."

"All I know is I waited a long time for Mandrake. The road goes through, sir. Begging your pardon."

The captain said, "Time within the forest different from time outside? Is it possible?"

"The message says the road goes through. My stint of the run was straight south, no obstructions." Leslie looked at his watch again.

Leslie handed the captain the envelope.

Captain Ashburner's Conversion

Horace Ashburner opened the envelope, unfolded the paper and read. "Road goes straight through. South. No deviation. Same quality of surface, undersurface, varied grade, but nothing too steep, uniform width." There was also a map–one line south to north–distance and one compass reading at the margin.

Flashed in the captain's mind the cover of a beloved childhood book, Land of Sweet Surprises, a revolving picture book he cherished when a babe. Each left-hand page had a simple poem. The right-hand page contained two circular pictures, one behind the other, on a rivet. To go from one picture and reveal the other the child Horace moved a ribbon tab back and forth from left to right along the circle's bottom with great care. Finally, the pictures rubbed to dullness, the tabs torn, Ashburner now, too old for childish toys, abandoned the book. The poem that introduced this world of wonders, arose, sweet, every word fresh in his memory:

Far away and yet among us
Lies a country all have seen,
Cloudless skies and golden woodlands,

Silver waters, meadows green;
And the voices of the city,
And the sounds of toil and strife
Never reach this lovely country,
Never spoil its happy life;
And its roses bloom forever,
And its gold has no alloy,
For the Land of Sweet Surprises
Is the children's world of joy.

The child Horace Ashburner kept the book at his grandmother's country cottage, being of farm folk, in a box of treasures to read and enjoy when he visited. Horace Ashburner, Captain, Royal Fusiliers, smelled his grandmother's old-fashioned roses in full bloom on a warm summer's day.

Tears arose unbidden and streamed down his cheeks. In the darkness none could see. He wiped his face with his handkerchief. Joyful memories of the most pleasant scents and scenes.

Then a woman's voice whispered to the captain, "What you saw in the forest came from nowhere but goes somewhere." Ashburner was mystified, worried. He had a company to command, must be in the best form, mind and body. The voice spoke again, this time more loudly. "I am Jeanne d'Arc. All the angels and saints of heaven, Jesus Christ, and God himself heard my petition and prayer. Angels built the road for the Army's salvation. Save France. Save Belgium. Defeat Satan."

"In your time the road seemed to have been built in an instant. In heavenly time the work took an eon to finish."

Though Leslie gave no sign, he was certain the cyclist must have heard the voice.

Convinced of the truth of Goulett's report and of what Leslie had said, he asked, "What did you see?"

"It was too dark. I rode the first two miles then loped along a mile further, waiting for Mandrake to come back. As you instructed. Captain, an engineering battalion with teams of horses pulling graders and rollers couldn't have done a better job in a quarter-year's work. Smooth, flat it was, just like where we started. Mandrake behind me said the road was the same where he rode. He went to the fifth mile."

"This road wasn't here when we reconnoitered. I led the patrol."

"I was with you, sir."

"So you were." He paused and thought. "Good work, Leslie. Dismissed."

"This morning, no road. By night, a well-engineered route," the captain thought. "A blessing. Like Mons."

Report to General Smith-Dorrien:
A Pawn Offers Itself for Sacrifice

Horace Ashburner knew that he must bring the strange intelligence to General Smith-Dorrien.

His mind spoke to him with the voice of reason and objection. "No way for your report to reach the general. General Horace Smith-Dorrien has been in command for five days. He has to move the entire Corps, exhausted and pursued. He is detail-perfect. By the Regulations."

Yet his mind answered, "Ye must go and tell him."

One voice said, "You tell him angels made a road tonight."

A cacophony of internal voices:

"Horace Ashburner, a fool."

"Declare you a traitor. Saboteur."

"Yet I will go."

"Or judge you lunatic. A coward. Unfit for duty. Shirking your duty."

Yet with each reason for why he should not go, an affirming voice replied, "I will go. Even so, I will go."

One voice consuls: "If General Smith-Dorrien knows of no road, the Corps will be no worse off than it is now. The original plan might do, get the army through."

Ashburner's thought began with "If the General doesn't heed. . ." but a sardonic voice interrupted: "General heed you? Folly!"

Ashburner's thought: "But the work of the angels shall not go to waste."

"You a prophet? You a lunatic."

His resolve still strong, he thought, "I shall go."

"The Army may already be on the march."

Ashburner thought, "Lose the battle, lose the war. Win the battle, win the war."

The skeptical voice replied, "Stay where you are. The war belongs to the generals."

Ashburner knew the engineers would see the imbecility of the idea. His report a mark of his ignorance. Pilots flew over the forest that very morning, reported what they saw.

Another voice said, "Hard-earned rank. Stripped." A chorus of voices: "Home you go. Blighty. Career caput."

"Court martial. Drummed out. Pity."

"A dozen reasons against, zero for."

Yet a voice resolved "I go! I will go." In his mind's eye he saw the wagons, guns, and impedimenta trundling along a straight road. He murmured, "They will reach Le Cateau, the soldiers fresh with easy marching. The horses fresh. All the impedimenta. Time to ready. Give the Germans a raking."

And so he went.

After Prolonged Silence

Finally, Ashburner spoke to Black, as if his adjutant had overheard the conversation that had taken place in the captain's mind. "I'll go." Hershel Grimley, Ashburner's companion, his batman, personal servant, would drive. Having long served together, they were like brothers, one caring for the other.

Black asked, "Go where, sir?"

"The General will listen. The road."

"Of course," said Black. "I hope he will. I pray he will. You put your career at hazard. Chance requires it. May the angel open the general's ear. The men are done with trenching. Nothing to do but wait."

The Generals' Meeting

Field Marshal General John Denton Pinkstone French, Commander-in-Chief, the British Expeditionary Force, split the army in half, Corps I and II, each group having to circumvent the Forest of Mormal as the fastest, though not the safest, way to put the British Expeditionary Force in position at Le Cateau.

That evening, planning for II Corps maneuvers for later that night with his officers, General Horace Smith-Dorrien pointed to the tip of the Mormal forest. He was in the thrall to the map before him. It drew General Smith-Dorrien into itself. He saw the map itself change–now with parallel broken lines signifying an unpaved road, running the length of the forest. He knew that no one else saw what he had seen. As if suspended in air, his body parallel to the ground, he was a thousand feet above, looking down on the forest. Ahead a flock of birds circled, swirling in bands and rings, forming a halo just beyond his reach. In museums he had seen paintings of such birds, and bird-like creatures, and cherubim-winged, ruddy-faced plump children–stringing ribbons of lapis lazuli blue and gold about the Virgin's head, and angels in the shape of birds. He recalled Fra Angelico's painting, the blessed Virgin and the holy child, and this phantasmagoria of beings.

Even now he heard in the birds' loud chirping, the hymning of angels in an unearthly language. Then, just above and beyond arm's reach flew an eagle, crying its kill call. Talons extended, it gripped the General's shoulder blades. Instantly Smith-Dorrien was the eagle in every bone and muscle. Floating in air, more tipping and turning as he fancied. His mind became its mind, empty of word, of thought, instantly filled with wisdom, sensation, and feeling. Four words, loudly uttered in a terrifying voice from within, penetrated his mind: "Golden Arrows of God." Rather than sensing light and image coming toward him, his seeing went outward, a rapid and endless succession of golden arrows shot forth from his golden eyes. Below he saw a wide, straight roadway, free of obstacle from one end of the forest to the other. The colors of rosin and rust, amber and straw, its clay stood out starkly in the midst of the forest's greens and browns. Then filmy clouds formed beneath him, thickened, became billows of cloud, obliterated the ground.

Inside his eyelids was darkness the color of pitch. He had the sensation of standing at the edge of an abyss, at the rim of the void, the nothing before creation, the nothing after destruction.

He regained a sense of the room, of his body, of self. From the fading mist of the vision, he spoke. "A bit faint. Had a bite this morning, a biscuit at noon. Get me a chair."

Instantly, Chief-of-Staff Forestier-Walker brought him a chair. The general sat, closing his eyes, rubbing his forehead. "Give me a moment."

Before dismissing the council General Smith-Dorrien gave his final instructions for the plan of march and the next day's battle. For as long as the council lasted the markings on the map remained, then faded, disappeared. Once again he saw an impenetrable, trackless forest.

The general stood, went to the map, tapped the star marking the town of Le Cateau and drew a line along the ancient Roman road with his riding crop where the two corps were to meet next day. He said, "Here we will stand and fight."

Although his vision moved General Smith-Dorrien profoundly, he kept his composure. No one showed any sign of having seen what the General saw, noticed anything out of the ordinary.

His experience mystified him. Having soldiered in South Africa against the Zulus and in India he had heard of witch doctors and shamans whose patients see and sense what wasn't there to see, hear what wasn't to be heard. He knew of hypnotists who could control an audience's will, mediums, and mind readers whose fakery fooled even scientists and scholars. He knew what had happened was different from any of these.

Said General Smith-Dorrien to Sergeant-at-Arms Boyd, "I will lie down for a few minutes' rest. Restore myself for the night that lies ahead. It is now 17:30. Wake me in half an hour. The men will push off at midnight. I can rest now."

General Smith-Dorrien's Dream

Tension drained from his body, he fell into a profound sleep. In the last minutes of sleep came and went a dream, a wisp only remaining. His alarm clock rang. As relaxed and at peace as he had been when he drifted into sleep, he awoke filled with dread and foreboding. The smell of cordite and blood filled the room. Had battle arrived? Of the dream he recalled sitting at the table in this tent, issuing the same orders he had given for the plan of battle before he rested. In the dream he heard the voice of Sergeant-at-Arms Boyd: "The very idea! You've no right here. Back to your post." He heard a reply, caught only the words "Royal Fusiliers." Awake, Smith-Dorrien sensed that the dream foresaw a battle, a bungle, a rout, France and England defeated, Germany triumphant.

The general rose from his cot, crossed the sparsely furnished room, and took his jacket from a chair back. Just then he heard a commotion outside his door. He heard an unfamiliar voice say "Royal Fusiliers". His aide-de-camp's voice, rising in volume, repeated the reply he heard in his dream, "No, sir. The very idea! You've no right here. Back to your post."

"Lieutenant Boyle, let him in," the General ordered.

Saluting, at rigid attention, the captain introduced himself, "Sir, Company C, Royal Fusiliers, Captain Horace Ashburner, commanding, and reporting."

"Come in, Captain. You insist on seeing me in private at this crucial moment. Why? The Army is about to march. You have left your post."

"I have, sir. But for good reason."

"If you haven't come for good reason, sir, it's the stockade and drummed from the Army for you."

"Sir, you may well court martial me after I report." Nervous, Ashburner licked his dry lips, then as quickly as he could get the words out, the captain said, "There is a road through the Mormal Forest wide enough to carry a good portion of the force through."

Smith-Dorrian rose from his desk, walked around to the front, and sat on the edge. "Reconnaissance said there is no such road. Cavalry, aeroplanes. Can you account for this mistake?"

"You will think me mad, sir, but the road was not there when the cavalry reconnoitered."

"And now it is? Where did this road come from? Lunacy accounts for the road's sudden appearance." So the General spoke, but he already believed what the captain said.

"Makes no sense, sir. A miracle wrought by angels."

"It must be."

Then Captain Ashburner recounted the events briefly.

"Sent scouts by bicycle. A nine-mile road extends the length of the forest. Suitable for infantry, baggage, and cavalry. If you arrest me, do not worry. My men are entrenched and ready to harass and delay the Germans. Their orders have not changed. It is only that. . ."

"Enough, sir. I need not tell you, you violated regulations. You are officer enough to know that. You risk your career. I take that into account, both for and against you. How many soldiers would swear that they have seen your road?"

"At least a dozen, maybe more. Five cyclists rode it. All sworn to secrecy. We said nothing to the rest of the men, not even the officers."

"How do you know they told the truth?"

"No reason for them to lie. They are honest men. I know them personally."

"I take your word as a soldier in the King's army that you have given me a true account of what you discovered. You did right to come." He resumed his seat behind his desk. "That is all, sir. Return to your post. You've done your duty."

Captain Ashburner saluted crisply, turned on his heel, and walked toward the door.

On impulse Smith-Dorrian said, "One moment. 'Golden Arrows of God.' Does it mean anything to you?"

"Sir, heard the phrase. Rumors. Something to do with the company's Vickers crews and our doctor, Captain Leckie, wounded and a prisoner. Symbolic sort of stuff, I figure. One of the teams spotted the road, sir."

"'Golden Arrows of God,'" muttered General Smith-Dorrien. "There is more to this than you know, sir. Dismissed."

The General's Determination

The Commander-in-Chief's plan called for I and II Corps to meet the next day along a line from Le Cateau to Cambrai. The General considered. II Corps will outrun the Germans and entrench properly at the next line of defense at Le Cateau. Save the horses and mules. Save the men. Fewer miles. Easier going. Undetected. II Corps will be fresh and ready, the Germans, worn. They've marched and fought to exhaustion. Their communication line, thin. Short on supplies. They are in the enemy's country, we among friends, allies. Von Kluck will take an outer path around the forest. Will he calculate that I and II Corps will separate? German aeroplanes have flown over the forest. Saw what we had seen. No way through. Von Kluck will time his movements so he can harass and attack us from the rear. When he reaches that point where he expects to find us, we will be gone and away, he having miles yet to go to find us.

General Smith-Dorrien thought, I cannot tell anyone what I plan to do. Under the circumstances there is time to give the men extra rest and food. We will steal the march on the Germans by splitting into two groups, the group passing through the forest taking Joan of Arc's road.

The Ride Back

Ashburner got back in the car. "Start 'er up. Let's go."

"Surprised to see you. Did they kick you out? Are we making a run for it?"

"I think he's issuing new orders."

"For your arrest? Don't joke."

"I'm not."

"You saw the general? I don't believe you. I'm afraid he'll send you to Blighty. The brig. Put you in mental, that's what."

"If he was going to, he would have done it then. I tell you, he called me in."

"Weren't you challenged at the door?"

"Yes, but Smith-Dorrian called me in. I did not dare ask why. A clue. Before I left he asked me about the words 'Golden Arrows of God'. I told him the little I know. That was odd, now that I think about it."

"And if we're wrong, the General's career will be over. I still don't believe what you think he's going to do. "

"He took my word."

"We'll see if there's a change in orders, but there won't be. Listening to you is one thing. Sending troops into the forest is entirely different. How will he tell the staff? They'll think he's daft, remove him on the spot. That would be reasonable, don't you agree? They'll think he dove off the deep end. End his career."

"He'll be one for decoration if he takes the road through."

"Says you. We'd better get out of here as quick as we can."

A motorcycle courier caught up and signaled the car to pull off the road.

"Told you. Off to the brig."

The courier dismounted. "Open the window, sir. Orders from the General. Open and read them. I'm to report your response."

"Response? Orders is orders. I don't understand." To Hershel

Ashburner said, "Turn on the electric torch." The captain opened the envelope and read. "Cut brush on both sides of the trenches wide enough for wagons and supplies to pass in." To the courier he said, "I'll carry out the General's orders." He punched Grimsley's shoulder and shouted, "There you have it. Who'd have thought?"

Hershel turned off the light.

The courier said, "Two more documents."

Horace Ashburner, loyal to Majesty and country, reached in and took out another envelope. "Turn the torch on again," he said to his driver. The front had the typed message "Unseal and read when you reach the Royal Fusiliers at the Mormal Forest."

"Nothing to read in this yet."

"One more," the courier said. A note card, the general's insignia on the front. "I am to stay with you until you have read the note and watch you burn it."

The captain read. "If I wasn't seeing this with my own eyes I'd never believe it."

He read and whispered, "'Though I would like to, sorry I will not commend you or mention you in a dispatch. Thank you heartily for bringing me the report.' It is unsigned. Got a lucifer?"

"May I burn it for you, sir?" Realizing that this was to be treated as a sacred act, Ashburner said, with the tone of comradely affection, "Please."

Grimley lit the match and burned the paper, dropping it to the ground when the flame licked his fingers. "Ouch!"

"Hate to part with it. Better than a commendation."

The courier started his motorcycle, saluted, turned back to the compound. Grimley turned on the ignition and pressed the starter. Off they drove.

"I'd love to be inside his brain to know what he thought. What made him believe me?"

"It's yer honest face done it."

"Not likely."

Horace Ashburner's heart swelled. He thought, a little child shall lead you. He thought himself a child again, the storybook with revolving pictures. A child filled with wonder and curiosity. Nothing more surprising than a road where hours ago there had been none.

Protecting the Secret

After II Corps had passed through, the Royal Fusiliers had to, as best they could, mask the way to the road. It being night, and the Germans a few hours behind, the soldiers had to do the job well enough to deceive. They feverishly dug holes for putting the bigger saplings upright in the ground, scattered brush and brambles about so it looked like natural growth. Beyond this, though they had now the advantage over the Germans they had to keep enough in the trenches to keep up the ruse. When the first of the Germans in their tens of thousands reached the northern tip of the Forét de Mormal, one hundred British soldiers let loose with all they had, creating the impression of an army making a stand, pushing the Germans to the extreme east of the ancient Roman road. Some died in keeping up the deception, among them Mungo Black, who led the ruse.

The last vestiges of night left them as the last of the British force passed out of the forest's southern edge. Scouts were posted to signal the battle line when they had signs of the Germans advancing.

Last through the forest were the Royal Fusiliers, the last of those being the two Vickers crews, the Ruffians and the Victors.

BOOK 2

DR. MALCOLM LECKIE AND
NURSE'S AIDE PHYLLIS CAMPBELL

Chapter Eight

The Engagement

Country Seat of the Archibalds
Date: 14 February, 1914

Dr. Malcolm Leckie, Battalion, Royal Fusiliers. Royal Army Medical Corps. Supernumerary Captain, Restored to the establish-ment. Returned in February.

The Daily Chronicle

Captain Malcolm Leckie and his Fiancée, Phyllis Campbell

Invitations went forth, the acceptances quickly returned.

"Mr. and Mrs. James Campbell are honoured to announce the engagement,"

et cetera, et cetera.

Saturday evening, St. Valentine's Day. A day for expressions and declarations of love. A gentleman, dressed in tails and white tie, evening wear, not his military uniform, bore the marks of privilege: Malcolm Leckie, Captain, R.A.M.C. An athlete's trim physique, clean-shaven except for a neat moustache, stiff with military habit. The attention of all who were first meeting him this evening fell upon the Captain, followed Leckie as he was introduced to the guests. Phyllis Campbell's fiancé, everyone knew.

Lissome, a dancer, Phyllis was lovely in her gown, her hair fixed in the fashion of the day. Flushed with the excitement of the evening, and thrilled with the prospect of marriage to her handsome medical officer, she was gay and vivacious.

Long before Captain Leckie's ship docked at Southampton from Alexandria he and Phyllis Campbell had met and courted in France at parties and weekends at the estates of the nobility. Though separated in years and experience, they fell in love. Delighted, ecstatic, Phyllis gladly accepted Malcolm's proposal.

A week after arriving in London from Alexandria Captain Leckie asked Phyllis Campbell's father for her hand in marriage. Though a mere army doctor and brother in-law to an author of popular renown, Leckie was also son of a Peer of England. At the end of their first private conversation, Mr. Campbell said, "You have attracted a most unusual girl. She is far from the usual run of today's society gem, I am sure you have discovered."

"Indeed, sir. That is what attracted me to her."

"Well, then, in any case, I am thrilled. My family is happy."

The Archibalds, relatives of the Campbells, offered to host a weekend engagement party at their country estate. "St. Valentine's Day would be perfect," said Lady Janey Archibald, aunt, teacher, guide, and confidant to her affianced and much beloved niece. That evening all were assembled, the party in full flower. Guests from the Archibald side of the family, the Campbells, and Captain Leckie's family, friends, fellow officers of the Captain's, and the local gentry were there. At ten, after hours of dance and refreshments, Phyllis spoke with her aunt.

"Aunt Janey, Captain Leckie and I must have a frank, private conversation. Where would you prefer we have it? And when?"

"My dear, your uncle's library. Dinner will be at eleven."

With a generous smile, and humor in her voice, Phyllis said, "Private, Aunt Janey. No ears at keyholes. No glass tumbler to the wall."

"Secret panels, perhaps? My dear, you impugn my character. But who is to say that a spirit will not overhear and plant the message in my ear?" She laughed, but a small laugh. "You have serious matters to talk over with Dr. Leckie, I am sure. I leave you to your discussion."

When Malcolm had closed the sliding oak doors behind him Phyllis said, "As you see, Auntie, as I call her, my aunt Lady Janey Archibald, would enjoy the connection with your brother in-law. She savors the aromas that waft from the British Psychical Society's chambers. An ardent occultist, Aunt Janey adores Sir Arthur Conan Doyle even though he is a Scotsman. Still, she says, an English writer after all. She had taught me about matters mystical, spiritualistic—all the disciples and mysterious practices and saw to it that I am well schooled in the arts. I hope that I do not have too much of the artist about me. I assure you that

The Engagement

I am not very good at any of it–poetry, dance, singing–but I enjoy them all a great deal. Nor too much of spirits and fairies."

"Never too much. I have seen your intelligence and good sense."

"I had the good sense to accept your proposal, did I not?"

"Except for that perhaps. There may be a lack of good sense in that. So nice of your aunt to arrange it–the dinner, the party," the newly affianced Leckie said. Then, softly, "Now that we are engaged. . . . .This usually signals a change in how society–capital S–views affianced couples–what those pledged to marry are permitted to do." He reached for her hand, pulled her close to him, and moved to kiss Phyllis' cheek.

"No further, for the moment, my dear. As progressive and moderne" –she emphasized the pronunciation–"as Aunt Janey is for the theatre and arts, when it comes to etiquette, her expectations are of the society of Queen Victoria's day. With the good queen in mind, might I have a cigarette before we go in?"

Slipping a thin cardboard container from his jacket pocket he said, "I brought a few packets of Isis cigarettes with me from Egypt. I had not a moment to transfer them to my cigarette case. I apologize." In their decorative cardboard box, the cover a feast of ancient Egyptian imagery, the cigarettes appealed to Phyllis even more than if they would have been in a silver case.

"A touch of Egypt. I am the queen of the Nile. But at least while we are at Aunt Janey's house, we will be under the good queen's regime of good conduct." She continued, "After she was presented at Court Aunt was told the old Queen considered her demeanor polite and her curtsey very pretty. Aunt adored the queen. I am afraid she will insist on chaperoning whenever we visit until we marry."

Malcolm lit both of their cigarettes. They smoked in silence for a few moments. Then he said, "Give her a moment to adjust to your leaving the family nest. Besides, she, and all the family, must like me, at least. Don't you think so? The rest will expect us to spend time together. We will humor your champion, then," said Malcolm. "Though I wish we did not have to wait so long to marry, my darling. I wish we could do something private. By a magistrate or pastor. Not to tarry long, a poet might say." They smoked their cigarettes, both quiet again, for a moment.

She: "It would be lovely and I favor it. But the word would out and there would be social hell to pay. You've been away too long to remember how these matters linger in society's opinion."

"I'm only wishing. I know. I was immersed in the social life of the Empire. Though I must admit, my dear, that I have doubts about myself," Leckie said.

"I am used to the bachelor officer's life. Good at whist. Devotee of backgammon. Good horseman. Rather stiff, unctuously ceremonial. Unexpressive, you might say. Perhaps I am amenable to change, but I have no great hope. If I am a squib. . . ." He paused in mid-sentence, drew deeply on his cigarette, slowly exhaling the smoke. "I hope you won't find me too much of a bore, a disappointment."

"Have no fear, my dearest. With my aunt I attended a performance of Mr. Shaw's 'Pygmalion', his newest play, a few evenings past. You will be my Pygmalion."

"Someone in Greek mythology? I don't recall the story."

A sculptor fell in love with a statue of a woman he carved, wished her turned into a real woman, and so she was. Shaw's based his play on the story. As Shaw tells it, a professor of phonetics bets his friend that he can present a Cockney flower girl as a refined society lady. And he succeeds. In our case, I will loosen your traces, as you horsemen would say, instruct you in the mores of the new generation. You will fit in. You will be all right." She laughed gaily. "But I believe you already are."

"Are what?"

"All right."

"I hope so, my dear Phyllis. I enjoy a comedy. Light opera, Tales of Hoffmann. That sort of music. In that regard I'm rather an old stick." Malcolm said, "An evening of Gilbert and Sullivan, perhaps."

Patting his shoulder, she said, "There is so much to discover, so much to enjoy together."

"I believe I have the capacity to love, because I know I love you. I enjoy your company. I hope time and encouragement will do."

"You shall see," she laughed. Phyllis picked up a crystal globe from her uncle's library desk and, peering within, took on the voice of a gypsy fortuneteller. "Ardor is within your grasp. Good sir, you will enjoy one another for the rest of your lives." With a sweeping gesture her arm ended with an embrace about Malcolm's neck, she said, "All this is new to me as well. I have been courted. But none of the men, nor what they had to offer, was the least appealing to me." Again she laughed.

Malcolm said, "It is as if you come from a world I did not know existed," he said. "Your interests, your vivacity, your smile, your glow. I had come to think dour smugness was universal. What you are is wonderful, all so appealing to me." Taking her hand and drawing her close, he said, "You fascinate. I am eager to learn." The smoke from each of their cigarettes mingled and twined in the air between them.

"There are passions to savor." Jokingly, she said, "I hope you, man of the world, are not too jaded."

"A hunger, they call it. And you, one of the New Women."

"I have fresh ideas, new beliefs. Mother and Father permit me a great deal of freedom. Aunt Janey has led me to people whose ideas I value highly. Even so, I have ideas of my own which clash with convention," she said, a tinge of excitement in her voice. "Whatever we will do, we do to please ourselves. Not as in my parents' day, a duty, a social obligation."

They held hands.

She: "Have you read the poet Yeats?"

He: "He is a tempest, a storm of feeling. 'I went out to the hazel wood' begins the one I favor."

"'The Song of Wandering Aengus,'" she said. And, from memory she recited the poem.

Concluding, she said, "He shakes the soul, awakes the imagination, makes us treasure longing and regret."

Leckie replied, "He is a young man with a brilliant future. A mystic, it is said."

"He takes his inspiration from many sources–the wind, water, the very air itself. I have heard the actress Florence Farr read his verse to the accompaniment of a psaltery, I believe it is called. Most affecting."

"Though, my dear, I am not much of a poetry lover either. In the end, I'm much more a Kipling reader than your Yeats."

"No matter. None at all. Read what you like. Listen to what you choose. Just love me."

"Much of me in the wandering Aengus? Am I old with wandering, my dear? These many years I have wandered. Can I stay in one place?

Even now the Battalion might call. Such a change in life. Maybe I will become an old withered stick, as Yeats would say, if I stay in one place."

"We shall travel, dear Malcolm. I will not tie you to a cottage and a village with a few meager lanes to explore. The world is before us."

They share a long kiss and a silent embrace. Malcolm said, "Silver apples. Golden apples. You are my glimmering girl with apple blossom in her hair."

She: "I am afraid we must cool the ardor the poets write of. Yes, we shall love one another and thrill to life's pleasures, I am sure. The older generation. Rarely a word of love or tenderness."

He: "Business and clubs and the conventional life."

As they readied to leave the library, their "serious talk" over, they kissed gently, their passions quelled, good sense intervening.

"Each of us has interests and obligations," the captain said. "If I am called to the Battalion. . . ."

She: "And I go to France, a nursing aide, when war begins, as it surely will, and soon."

He: "I would prefer you stay in England. Not safe. I do not think it wise of you to go."

She: "I must see war. It will be a part of our time. I will do some good. Finish your cigarette. We must go out. We don't want to make Aunt anxious. It makes her flinty. She regrets it afterward, but she can't help herself."

They extinguished their cigarettes in an agate ashtray on the library desk and rejoined the party.

Chapter Nine

Malcolm Leckie, Prisoner of War

Convent and School of the Sacred Heart
Mons, Belgium
August 24, 1914

> *Malcolm Leckie Burial, after Aug 28,*
> *1914, Register B 202, Plot 1, row B.*
> *Grave 1. Frameries Communal*
> *Cemetery. Age 34.*
>
> *8 December, 1914. DSO. First British*
> *Medical Officer to die in the war.*
>
> *London Gazette*

After Surgery

Captain Malcolm Leckie awoke to the smells of ammonia, bleach, and blood. His breath exuded the odor of ether.

Bandages wrapped the captain's head, face, back. Resplendent in his officer's uniform, Hans Dieter Mueller, Captain, Commandant sat in a straight-backed chair, crossed left leg bouncing lazily, a shining boot swinging toward and away from Leckie's hospital cot. "Great pain, I am sure. Morphine helps. We do not know how long you lay in the field before the litter-bearers brought you here."

His English thickly accented, he spoke slowly. "They found you face down, your left eye cut by a piece of detritus, slag you would call it. Unfortunately, horses also haul wagons there. If you are lucky, sepsis has not set in. You are prisoner in a war hospital and camp. I care for you under the rules of the International Red Cross, German Section, and accord you the privileges due an officer. Though I am sure there will be many, you are my first British officer. And you, sir? Your name?"

Drugged, groggy, the soldier mumbled, "Leckie, Captain."

"Medical Corps. Your insignia. I would put you to work in my surgery if you were able."

Leckie muttered, "If I was able I would be on the battlefield or an army field hospital."

"However, I will keep you from the lower ranks. You needed a doctor, Doctor."

Leckie saw the smirk on the captain's face, enjoying his own little joke. "Nasty wounds. Shrapnel. Back. Neck. Chest lacerated in the fall. You'll not be as handsome as you must have been, eye missing." Leckie heard the reputed cruelty of the Germans, a cultivated, sarcastic manner.

Leckie took in the room. Clean, crudely plastered, whitewashed walls. Paintings of saints blessed the walls. A carved crucifix, Jesus in his agony. Hand-made chairs and tables, the furnishings shoved into a corner. A chamber for humble nuns. Hospital cots in rows, just enough room between for a nurse or an orderly to shuffle in sideways.

He read the commandant's personality in his face. The far-away look pale-blue-eyed blond men often have. Lacking color, contrast, they miss the full palette of expression of a person fully present. The commandant had the look of a dreamer, an abstract thinker, no realist.

While the Commandant talked and Captain Leckie listened, aides delivered the wrecks of soldiers, lifted them from litters, laid them on cots. The room quickly filling. A music of groans, whimpers, shouts of the afflicted. For verses, curses. Soldiers stifled their crying. Some called for mothers, Jesus, God.

To an orderly Mueller said, "Make the captain comfortable. Nail up a rope. Hang sheets. Privacy for the Captain." Then to Leckie: "Sir, our accommodations are plain. The convent belonged to an order of poor nuns. They now comfort and care for the wounded, like angels, with their caps as wings. I thought they would be able to administer last rites to Catholics, but they tell me only priests can. I stay at a merchant's home across the road. We keep a simple mess–vegetables and a bit of meat. Sorry you will not be able to partake. Warm water for twenty-four hours. Then broth, if you are with us that long." Captain Leckie caught the sly implication. "My soldiers are fencing the courtyard to hold prisoners. The townspeople stay in their homes. They do not cooperate."

A matron bustled about giving orders, making up linen. Anguish marked her countenance. The eyes of the new nurses were glazed. Not one could have foreseen the devastation the day would bring.

"We won the day," Leckie managed to say.

"Terrible. You cannot imagine. The dead. . . . I am overrun with wounded. Many will die before they reach hospital and more will die before we reach them. Soldiers are collecting the doctors from the city to come and work. We occupy the city. Administration is in our hands."

"By right I should leave the enemy to suffer and die, his dead, food for vultures and maggots," Mueller began. "The rules of war, foolish. Wounded and dead treated the same, no matter which side."

"One of the tragic ironies of civilized war," Leckie replied. "Brutality and chivalry in one."

"'All akin in death.' Is that not so, my dear Captain. A simple fact of life." Mueller's wit flickered in the atmosphere of sarcasm.

Another Meeting
August 26, 1914

Two days later they spoke. Face drawn, haggard, having spent every waking hour in the turmoil of surgery, administration, and war, Mueller did not remember the medical officer's name. He glanced down, read from Leckie's medical chart. Drained of energy, barely able to stand, to think. "See, my friend? I am almost done in. Exhausted. After one day we are overrun. I tell you the work is killing me." He laughs. "Pardon me. I amuse myself."

The past night Captain Mueller hauled the doctors of Mons and the surrounding villages out of their beds and put to work in his surgery. He shared the German view on recent events, complaining to Leckie, "These Belgians. Donkeys. The Kaiser asked them politely to let our army pass through their beautiful country on our way to France, bothering no one. They refused, made us fight our way across. Many now dead. Towns destroyed. Fools."

"I do not know what you are talking about," said Leckie.

"We spoke of this earlier. It does not surprise me that you do not recall. You were, as you would say, befuddled. The trauma and the surgery."

"You Saw Them?"
"Yes. Clouds Turned to Golden Angels."

The German doctor said, "I cannot count the number of amputations

I have done. My arm sore from sawing. How many certificates of death I signed, how many. . . ." Mueller set a glass on a little table next to Leckie's bed and pulled the cork from a green bottle. Pouring liquid into the glass, he said, "I did not know nuns drink schnapps. My aide found several bottles. Excellent quality. Apple, pear, plum, and, best of all, cherry. Kirschwasse. Here. Smell. If you were in better health we would drink and exchange toasts. I take my rest at your side. Are you progressing? No, I see by the chart. I will drink for both of us." He raises his glass in mock-salute. "Swift victory for Germany." He slowly drank the schnapps, savoring it.

The weak voice of Leckie replied, "Swift defeat for Germany."

"I applaud your wishing, but what you wish is not possible. I admire loyalty to country. A virtue. I am told that the roar of our artillery already reaches the Parisians' ears." He sipped the Kirschwasse. "But let us not argue. There is something. Not quite military, not quite a personal nature. If I ask something that sounds eccentric, you will not hold it against me? Gentleman's honor?"

"Eccentric? What do you mean?"

Bending close to Leckie's ear, he asked, "During battle did you see anything out of the ordinary?"

"That is not personal."

"Depending upon your answer, the personal question follows."

"I saw the mangled, the perishing. If that is what you mean." Leckie recalled the events. He expected light, thin lines, soldiers hard to detect, hard to hit. Instead, the German Army streamed over the rise, marching down the slope, a wave of Germans, toward the Mons-Condé canal's edge. A frontal attack. Perfect for slaughter. A tactic the British least expected.

Mueller waited, hoping his prisoner would say more. Mueller leaned, turned his ear toward Leckie's mouth. Leckie spoke in a weak whisper. "Who am I to criticize your generals? But a frontal attack."

Leckie recalled the British soldiers let loose. The mad minute. He stopped, gathering his breath. He remembered masses of bodies littered the ground, in some places grew to a height where they served as a breastwork. He said, almost without sound, "Horrid deaths. I'd been in battle before. South Africa. Nothing like this."

Mueller replied, "Here I treat them. And the dead strewn across the battlefield, along the road to our doorstep, into these very rooms. But that is not what I mean. Anything you might call supernatural? A strange sky perhaps?"

"Sky?"

"Clouds, you know?"

"I am in a fog." Leckie closed his eye, groaned, the morphine wearing off. Then resumed: "Clouds. Yes."

Leaning forward, eyes wide with expectation, the commandant whispered, "You saw them, too?"

"I saw them?" asked Leckie.

"Yes. Clouds turned to a golden angel. Immense. Light too bright to look at. Then angels took part in the battle. Fought against our army?"

"So?"

"You might do me a kindness."

"We are enemies."

"I treat you with the courtesies due a gentleman. Imagine two—in your courts you call them affidavits, I believe—written independently by a German officers and a British officer attesting to the presence of angels."

Captain Leckie understood what Commandant Mueller had in mind. Leckie said, "Find someone who can take my dictation. I can not write. I cannot sign. I will need a British soldier to witness my words and mark. I read German well. Do you read English?"

"You hear me speaking, don't you. What do you think?"

Mueller called for someone from among the British prisoners to take down Captain Leckie's words. An orderly brought pen, paper. Mueller retired to his office to write his account of his seeing St. George and his angels on the battlefield at Mons. A soldier from the Northumbrians, a wound to the chest tightly bandaged, sat beside the Captain and wrote what the doctor said. Then he made a second copy, one to keep and one to give. Commandant Mueller did the same. Captain Leckie and Mueller exchanged documents, read what the other had written. Leckie spoke. "I suppose you saw some things a bit differently. You write, 'The angel's feet turned to blood that fell upon the ground. His head caught fire,'" said Malcolm Leckie. "I did not see blood and fire. I saw him in the sky and on the ground. The Germans died in multitudes behind the canal. Then I saw no more." The Northumbrian spoke up. "We saw them, too.

They saved our army. God blessed us."

Leckie said, "What you wrote is right enough. I'll sign. Witness?"

Mueller wrote a note explaining how the two had composed the statements. When they finished they spoke. "Maybe," began Leckie, "Someday someone will discover these documents and wonder. For now I expect the soldiers who saw them will tell of the angels' work that day."

"We saw something worthy of record, did we not?" Commandant Mueller said.

"For posterity's sake, if there is a posterity, we attest to what we saw." Mueller added, "I will get mine to my wife. Thus you shall have life eternal. In my safe."

"I will keep mine with me. A memento."

"My friend, you shall not outlive the war, even if it ends in a week."

The Captain unscrewed the cap from his fountain pen and handed it to Leckie. "I hope the pen does not leak. Leckie," the commandant said quietly, and lightly laughed. "Always a chance for humor in the smallest detail." Both signed the four copies. The German orderly and the Northumbrian signed as witness.

In Parting

"A sip of fine schnapps for you. The bottle is nearly empty. The rest is for you. Drink. Enjoy. The best. You go to a British hospital."

"Am I better? I feel worse."

"I am afraid that sepsis. . . ." He stopped, the rest of the idea clear in Leckie's mind. "Yes. Alive for the moment, my friend. For the moment you have your wits about you. That is good. Infection rages. Gangrene. The smell permeates the ward now, coming from so many, you among them. You will soon be gone. So a bit of schnapps cannot hurt."

"Is that why you are sending me?"

"No. A Lieutenant Von Arnim was wounded and captured by your English today. His father is now our Governor General of Louvain. You are being exchanged for him. I did not know you were so important."

"Nor did I."

"Here you are the only aristocrat. Your lineage? Are you also Sir Malcolm Leckie?"

"We do not talk of these matters."

"Do not let humility stand in the way of deserved family pride. I am interested. Please. You are of good family and well educated. You are entitled to the pride of pedigree."

"We use that word when referring to our breeding stock."

"Come, come. Gentlemen keep no secrets."

"My father carries the title."

"Are you the oldest?"

"Yes."

"So you will be. . . . Sorry." Mueller smiled at his own realization. "Do you have a younger brother?"

"Only child."

"But we are gentlemen who, under ordinary circumstances, would play at billiards and drink fine schnapps, smoke a good cigar, chat about the state of the world and our places in it. But you are my prisoner, patient, and guest, and I, your jailer, doctor, and host. It has been difficult for me to be a gracious host. I hate the English by training, by conviction. Hating the British is a national passion. Its roots run deep in our philosophy, our view of the world. You are a British gentleman, but a gentleman. Even so, I had to grit my teeth, as you say."

"Ach! We will be home by October. France will be easily beaten. It will be easily controlled, easily exploited. Our empire will cover the face of the earth. But you will not be here to see it, I am afraid. Where will your affidavits go? You will soon join those angels. Perhaps not the ones who fought against us, but you shall go to the angels."

"They must end in the care of my father. My sister and brother-in-law must see them. Sir Arthur Conan Doyle? You may have heard of him. Sherlock Holmes?"

"I am doubly honored, sir. I am a reader of Sherlock Holmes. Maybe that is why they chose you to trade."

"I must leave you now. You will be shipped as soon as the lorry is filled with petrol. I have slipped the affidavits into your tunic pocket. I hope Sir Arthur Conan Doyle makes use of them in a story. I hope to read it some day."

Chapter Ten

Greetings and Farewell

Jeanne D'Arc School for Girls
Frameries, Belgium
29 August, 1914

> *In the London Gazette of 9th December 1914 it was announced that there were to be 20 new Companions of the Distinguished Service Order. Of these, 3 were officers in the Royal Army Medical Corps who had served at the Front in the first few months of the war and had distinguished themselves by acts of bravery. One of them was Captain Malcolm Leckie (deceased) who had already been mentioned in French's dispatch of October 8th. His award was for "Gallant conduct and exceptional devotion to duty in attending to wounded at Frameries, where he was himself wounded".*

Malcolm Leckie, Wounded, Returned to British Care

The doctors and nurses had been on constant duty from the day of the battle of Mons through the fighting at Le Cateau. There had been fighting in Frameries itself, where the hospital was, Mons fifteen miles to the north, Le Cateau fifteen to the south. Those needing bandaging or minor surgery, those with broken limbs which could be readily set, were treated at stations along the way and sent to safe rest areas. The more serious cases were sent by train to hospital, delivered at any hour of the day or night. Some died on the way. When the trains arrived soldiers detailed for the work sorted the dead from the living and those who could be saved from those who could not. The most severely wounded were treated first. Even then, so many arrived that some the staff treated, died. At the same time the staff was ready to pack up the hospital at any moment. They drilled in this–pack, load, move, unload, unpack. How they would transport all the patients was another matter.

Phyllis Campbell, Nurses' Aide, Voluntary Aid Detachment, and the Hospital Enquiry Sheets

Nearly done in with fatigue after days and nights of exertion, Phyllis Campbell took information from the soldiers newly delivered for the Hospital Inquiry forms. Standard information. Name, rank, battalion, company, injury, its severity, where the soldier had been when wounded. She interviewed the soldiers in an unlit arched entryway to the school. Many were bandaged, limbs, trunk, head, face. Some could barely speak. Comrades who knew them gave her the information she needed. The groans, cries and sad noises of those in pain often made it hard for her to hear. She had to lean close, attending with her ear while she wrote down the information.

Nurse's aide Campbell came upon a soldier in such a condition. She noted the insignia on his uniform, Royal Army Medical Corp. Then asked the routine questions.

"Name, Captain?"

"Captain Malcolm Leckie," he muttered.

She dropped her pen. Her hands covered her mouth, withholding a cry. She thought, "Malcolm! Oh God! Nothing could be more awful!" but did not speak. "Malcolm," she said. "Phyllis," she said. "Your Phyllis."

His voice became clearer. "My darling Phyllis, what could be more fortuitous?"

"So it is, my dear."

"Wait, then, dear Phyllis! I have good news. All that you believe about a world beyond is true. I know it. I saw angels in the heavens. St. George fought for us. Many saw them. Shrapnel struck me. A voice said, 'I vouchsafe you this secret. What your loved one tells you about the life of the soul is true. You will die and live.' Oh, I bring you good news!"

"Malcolm, you are in delirium. You have lost much blood." She smelled the gangrene.

"Dear Phyllis. Reach in my tunic pocket. Two sheets of paper. Affidavits. Take them. Two accounts. One mine. One, a German officer's. "

The Angel of Mons: St. George, Intercessor and Salvation

"The flame flickers, soon to go out. But I must tell you. At Mons. The sky turned the brightness of the sun. Gigantic figure in the sky. St. George." He said, "I am delirious. You cannot be my Phyllis."

"Malcolm, I am your Phyllis."

After a pause, Leckie went on. "I might be dead already, and you, a memory. It grows dark."

Phyllis Campbell said, "Please go on with your account." The nurse's aide turned the page of her hospital inquiry sheet and wrote what Leckie said, phrases, words. "Facing us. Behind the German front. Pointed his lance at them." And he stopped, exhausted. "Louder than thunder."

She did not know what he meant. Her thoughts were a tumult. She thought how cruel. I have you in my arms, dying.

After a time of restless quiet, Leckie muttered. "St. George. Golden armor." Then, "You the believer, me the skeptic. Now I believe." His breath slow and shallow. He was again at the scene of the events he recounted. "Hope of victory. Thrilled the soldiers." His hand weakly pointed to his chest. "Keep it." Then "'Golden Arrows of God.'"

Captain Leckie's eyes fluttered open, then closed. He exhaled a tremulous breath. His heart stopped beating. The captain's body fell limp. After seeking a pulse, Phyllis called out, "Litter bearer, soldier gone. Captain. Medical officer." She gazed at the face she admired and loved, its repose, a memory to cherish. Phyllis took a handkerchief from his tunic pocket and covered her fiancé's face with it. Tears rose, which she wiped away.

Phyllis turned over the lapel. A little pin. A gold arrow. She unclasped its hook, put it in her apron pocket. She reached into his blouse pocket. Two folded pieces of paper. Put them in her apron.

A sergeant on a litter across the archway overheard the conversation. Through his own stupor, he sprang to life. "Miss, what the Captain said is true. I was closer to the fight than him. I saw the angels. I'll tell you

116

my story. Not now. If I live."

"As you say, duty calls. Sergeant, I heartily thank you."

When the *madame presidente* heard about Phyllis Campbell' fiancé dying in her arms, she gave her a sedative and sent her to bed. Phyllis slept, weary and worn. When she awoke she felt empty, like an empty amphora yearning to be filled.

The next day she searched for the old sergeant. Him, feverish, the wounds clean, stitched, bandaged.

"I'll tell you God's truth, what I saw. Put my name to it. I ain't been the King's soldier for all these years and now and I'm gonna put my name to a falsehood. I honor the King and my name. Church of England. I'll not go to my maker with a lie at the last moment of life."

"I'll write what you say." She wrote on the back of a fresh inquiry sheet. Feverish, he repeated himself. "Fifteen years' good service. I won't make a fool of myself making up a story."

He began. "South of bridge. Mariette. Bosche a mile away. Are you writing? Miss, I saw the same as he. One from a cloud."

"One what?" she asked.

"Knight in armor. Plain as plain could be. Soon another at the big angel's side. In the sky. My mates. Saw him, too. They were fierce, them Germans, They kept coming. We killed 'em by the thousands that day. "

"I wrote what you said. Now might you sign this?" she asked, handing him a fountain pen.

"Read what you wrote." She read. He signed his name, a scrawl, his hand shaky.

The little he said comforted Phyllis. Two accounts, signed. A few sentences from the sergeant. Two affidavits. She would spread the news. She would report to the world this miraculous intercession. She, a messenger of a miracle.

BOOK 3

ANGELS AT LE CATEAU AND THE VICKERS TEAMS

Chapter Eleven

The Quarry, St. George,
and the Angels of the Golden Mist of Salvation

Le Cateau, France
26 August, 1914

> *"We were saddled with pack and equipment weighing nearly eighty pounds and our khaki uniforms, flannel shirts, and thick woolen pants, fit for an Arctic climate, added to our discomfort in the sweltering heat,"* one Reservist recalled. *New boots, the heat, and the strain of continual marching along cobbled roads brought many soldiers to a state of collapse.*
>
> *Mons 1914: The BEF's Tactical Triumph*
> David Lomas

Without Pity or Remorse

(In the words of Private Paul Carmichael,
Vickers Team Ruffian)

For three days the sun had beaten down on us without pity or remorse. Each night sogging rain. The night before, a long drenching thunderstorm.

Three days since we beat the Germans at Mons. We marched through Malplaquet, paid our respects to the Duke of Marlborough. Bit of a history lesson along the road.

The Bosche struggled, too. Maybe worse off than we. The Germans expected to jump on trains and lorries and make their jolly way across Belgium to France. Their people sent them off with cheers and song and bands a-playing to a quick victory. They were accustomed to having girls

121

throw flowers, children toss chocolates, mothers and fathers pressing cigarettes and bottles of wine and beer on them. In Belgium they did not receive the greeting of friends and relations–King Albert of Belgium and Kaiser Billy being cousins. Found themselves as welcome as the plague. They thought the Belgian generals might put on an exercise, review the troops, and send them home. Symbol to uphold the country's honor. Then the Belgians would let the Germans walk across the country to fight against France.

But fight the Belgians did. Skillfully and well. They delayed the Germans, disrupted their timetable, messed up their plan. This gave the British and French time to get in place to fight.

The Bosche were worn out with fighting. The supply line, thin, attacked, broke in places. Their generals had not planned on using as much ammunition as they had, having as many soldiers killed, wounded, captured. So that the German general's soldiers can fight, they must eat. They took what they needed, gave the farmers and millers and merchants IOUs with Kaiser Wilhelm II's signature. Said the Kaiser would redeem his pledge as soon as he won the war. The British prisoners needed food, too, and guarding.

A Lovely Place. A Deadly March.

We killed the German infantry in the thousands at Mons. Since then the Bosche generals rethought their strategy. The open rolling plains and farm fields of the region were ideal for artillery. Artillery and cavalry to clear the way, the infantry to fight well protected.

We were several miles northwest of Le Cateau, the map told us. Except for a church spire, which looked like a cross sticking out of the ground, we saw nothing of the town. Without the spire we would have thought that all in front of us was flat expanse, like the roads and fields we marched through. But below was an ancient town, and a major train line, and the ancient Roman road. We were making our way across farm country, undulating hills, Lombardy poplars, neat hedgerows. Most of the crops in, some still ripening. Simple cottages of stone or brick set back from the road. Terra cotta and thatched roofs. A lovely place. A deadly march.

The Quarry

All that Remained was to Wave the White Flag

We were the only Vickers, the same old Ruffians. Me, the boss, Godley, and the two comedians. And young Atkins. The heavy artillery having gone off with the main body, C Company lacked protection and defense. "The general must dislike the 2nd Royal Irish's band's playing so much he assigned it to draw the Germans aside," said Catchpole. We came under the company band's wing. "A Vickers crew commanded by a bandleader," said Palmer, disgusted. I said, "Not as bad as it sounds. The band is first-rate soldiers, fit for battle. Soldiers first, musicians after. And Quartermaster Fitzpatrick knows the fighting business." We were rear guard for the main column, pestering and delaying the German advance long enough for II Corps to reach a place where it could make a fair fight.

We scuffled our way along. Stirred up a lot of dust. Make the Bosche think there are more of us than there were. Make them think the main body is where it is not. Lead them astray. Then make our way back to the battalion as best we could.

Like most battles, the battle called Le Cateau did not take place just there. We fought along the line from Cambrai fifteen miles east of Le Cateau and to the west a dozen miles. Find a depression, a puddle hole, a swale to drop behind. Find a clump of trees, a stone fence. We ran between fields, up and down hills. We marched down cobbled roads in new boots, stiff as wood. Murder on the feet and legs. Strain and exertion drained us. Every step was half act of will, half mechanically unconscious, the body marching itself. Exhaustion all around. My eyes, bleary and bloodshot. The world swam around me. Couldn't tell if I was asleep or awake.

No one seemed any better off. Not a joke or a quip from Catchpole or Palmer, who were always good for a witty remark.

Quartermaster General Sir William Robertson, of long service and deep military wisdom, had supply wagons come before us, drop caches of necessities at crossroads and in fields. So we had food and water, ammunition. But we traveled so fast we had to leave much behind. The Germans thought we dropped supplies so we could run away faster. They thought we had surrendered in spirit. And they ate what we didn't have time to grab.

The Quarry

This morning the men fighting on our right had a bad time of it. Along the march Uhlans killed many and wounded more. We strained to drive them back, kept at it all day. Attack, withdraw, attack again, retire, as we moved south.

A quarter of a mile away was a thin strand of wood on slightly raised ground. We stopped for Sergeant Fitzpatrick to confer with Godley and the rifles. Pointing ahead with one hand, his bandmaster's baton in the other on the corresponding spot on a map from the Franco-Prussian war of the area, Fitzpatrick said, "Narrow, shallow ravine just beyond those trees. In the spring there would probably be a river of melted snow. This time of year, a dry, rocky bed. We'll cross over, go up the other side, and fire from across the ravine. We'll take up a front of three hundred yards. Vickers, hold the left flank. Let the Germans come to us. Give them a taste, then,"–his baton inscribing another line behind the first–"Hold them again here." To all of us, "Give 'em a hearty helping. A good taste of British bullets, men. Then keep south to the main body. You'll be relieved there." Sidney Godley acknowledged the orders. Fitzpatrick went back to his men. We headed for the ravine.

We found that ahead was not the ravine the old map showed, but a wide, deep blue rock quarry, no longer operating. "Will you look at that! Old maps don't always tell the truth," I said.

A steep declivity. Below, waste rock, broken blocks of all sizes, shards, busted boulders littered the floor and slopes. To the east, at the quarry's opening was a roof supported by poles where stonemasons shaped and finished the rock. Next to it an equipment and lorry garage, a supply warehouse, a tool shed. There were three-sided storage sheds, a weighing platform, watchman's shack. At the entrance was an office made of the stone quarried here. Scattered about were rusted cranes, rusted bins, iron bars, strange shovels, sledgehammers, picks, the handles split and dry. A frayed rope kept trespassers out, the French here being law abiding, except for the boys.

To the west, a pit brimming with rotting leaves, algae, scum, and the smell of decay. Operating quarries pump ground water, natural springs, rain, and runoff out to get to rock below the surface. Diggings fill with water in abandoned quarries. The pit to our west wide and likely, deep. It went around a bend, so we could not see its full length.

Geography told us we could not go around. To pass the depths we would have to go back where we had come from into open fields. Or we would have to make our way through dense brush on dangerous slopes, keep below the ridge. Otherwise we would expose ourselves to German fire. The Huns were now close on us.

To the west the pit bounded us. Ahead, a treacherous decline. They would come in the entryway. No way out.

To the Bottom

A German aeroplane spotted us, turned back to report the good news. The Uhlans would gallop over, be upon us quickly, plug the entrance. Artillery and infantry close behind.

"We stand no chance here," mumbled Godley, more to himself than to us. "We'll have to go down, us and the band."

The quarrying had been done on the wall to the north, the side opposite the rim where we stood. Though this side was worked in places, too. Rain had carved a few trails which snaked through dirt and vegetation. These were the only way down. Fitzpatrick ordered us to the bottom where we could make a better—to our minds, futile—defense.

Before we took off down the wall, Sergeant Fitzpatrick made a short speech. "They think you are street musicians armed with pop guns. You will show them, and not how beautifully you play."

Clutching at branches and limbs, vines, exposed roots, outcrops of stone, the men slipped, found footholds, handholds, fingernail holds. They made their way down the one hundred feet to the bottom. Carried full packs and rifles. Hard, slow going. Every moment spent was a moment less they had to get set. The descent cost bruises, scrapes, a few strained ankles, torn uniforms. Some skinned their knees or shins, tore fingernails.

The band would fight, hiding and sniping. The soldiers hid among the boulders and rocks, in the scraggle of brush and saplings, behind trees.

The Problem of Manhandling the Gun to the Quarry Floor

We could not carry the gun and ammunition cases down from the quarry's rim. Bulky, awkward, heavy, the way too treacherous. Three yards back from the quarry's rim grew a tall tree. Pointing up, Godley said, "Private Atkins, that third limb up overhangs the wall. Climb out, loop rope in front of the crotch where it branches. Drop the rope end. Carmichael and Palmer will rush down to the bottom." He turned to Catchpole. "Tie the gun and the ammunition to the rope. Let it down."

Atkins: "I'm terrified of heights. You would better send someone else."

"You're the only one light enough," said Sidney. "Any of us would break the limb."

"How do you know it will hold me?"

"If it will hold any of us, it will hold you. We have to try."

Just to get him going took all we could do. Threats. Insults. Bits of cheerful comment.

Catchpole said, "Don't be a liver-lily mouse."

"Lily-livered, you mean," I said.

"I mean coward. Won't go out on a limb to save his mates."

William tied the rope for the gun around Tommy's waist so he would have both hands free.

Not to be left out, Ziggy said, "Runt of the litter. If you were a puppy dog you'd have been drowned. You're luck, to be with us."

The knot secure, Godley said, "Done, boy. Time to climb. When you come down we'll acclaim you a brave soldier."

After the tying and fuss, the rope's end hung down to the back of his knees. "You got a monkey's tail," said Gunner Palmer. To the rest of us he said, "Tommy told me he thought Darwin was right." William Catchpole flapped his arms, scratched his armpits, chattered and screeched. "Get up that tree. Go back where your ancestors come from."

The young private could not escape our jibing, all intended to get him up in the tree. This was how we encouraged him.

The lowest limb was too high for Tommy to reach. He had to climb onto my shoulders. I held his calves. He grabbed the limb, struggled to haul himself up.

When he reached the third limb he stood thirty feet above the quarry's edge, one hundred thirty from the bottom.

"I'm terrified of heights," he shouted down.

"Then don't look down," said Godley. "Just toss the rope where I told you to put it. Then you can come down."

Ziggy and Carmichael down the Wall

As soon as Atkins perched on the limb Ziggy and I scrambled down the wall. Catchpole and Godley stayed at the rim to guide the equipment down.

Godley tied on the gun and tripod base, pushed them out over the rim. The weight bent the limb dangerously, almost tumbling Atkins to the ground, and death by accident. They pulled the gun up. Godley unknotted the rope, took off the tripod, tied the gun back on. Tried again. The limb bent, but not as far.

By the time the gun reached the ground two from the company band had made their way down. Private Simon Peter Mastiller, bass drummer, and Kendall Haydon, company bugler. I called down to them, told them to untie the load, stack the goods as they came down. Two gunners were on the way down.

The ammunition boxes needed careful tying so they would not slip out. They took longer to lower than the gun's two parts.

Ziggy Palmer and I reached the bottom. Palmer looked about. "When Will Catchpole and I work a theatre for the first time, right off we looked for the back stage exit. In case of trouble. No exit here. No way out."

In the midst of boulders, thick brush, and trees we set the gun—Vickers Team One, Ruffians, front line, center. The plans had changed. No flank to hold. I sent the musicians to the pit to get water for the gun.

Valley of the Shadow of Death

The Hun cavalry had number and position, artillery and infantry not far behind. And we were trapped.

When all the ammunition and supplies had come down, looking below, William Catchpole said to Godley, "I don't know much Bible, but I know the valley of the shadow of death. Where is our St. George?" Then, "Listen. The jingle of tack." Catchpole said. "Once their artillery and infantry are in place, doom will be upon us."

"What do you think of war now?" asked Godley. "We still have to get Atkins down."

Sooner than Palmer and I had wished, we heard horses' hooves clattering on the stone footing of the quarry. A squadron of Uhlans paraded into the yard. Their pilots told them we were there. Horses stolen from farms and liveries pulled limbers. Some were our own, we had to abandon gear and supplies at the rim. The Huns formed a line along the entrance between the main building to the left and the scale, loading dock, and crane on the right. A hundred of them, lances and sabers ready. They were tired and dirty. Palmer and I saw determination on their faces.

As if they were on review, putting on a show for the trapped enemy, the Uhlans went through maneuvers. They did not seem to worry that there were British hiding in front of them. We watched, ready to fire.

One minute, parade, then the air thrilled to the shriek of whistles and bugles, the rumble of drums. Bosche officers barked orders. The cavalry charged. Fitzgerald gave the signal. We gunners and the infantry got right to business. The gun, primed, oiled, belts of bullets coiled, our Vickers unleashed her fury, chattered her chant of death. We shot the horses first. They reared, bucked, twirled, twisted, fell. Their sounds, hideous. Hooves thrashed, reins tangled up Uhlans, grabbed lances. The stirrups caught one's boot and held him when he needed to jump. An animal crushed a man. All around, mayhem and tumult. Then we shot at the soldiers.

For the cavalry, all faith in the horse, the lance, and saber. Many, thrown to the ground, took to their rifles. I said, "Look at that, will you! They shoot from the hip. They don't aim! Dumb luck if they hit anything. Thank God they are poor riflemen."

Shorthanded, we Ruffians thought death certain. But we would take many of the Kaiser's soldiers with us. I ran the first belt, Ziggy Palmer feeding the block. Haydon and Mastiller watched the gun's handiwork. It aroused their blood. Mastiller said, "Them to hell, us to heaven."

"Gabriel, blow your horn!" said Haydon.

Mastiller replied, "We are few, but fierce."

They went at it like sloganeers, sideshow barkers. They were used to the impromptu riposte.

I said, "Steady. You are soldiers of the King."

A defective bullet jammed the barrel. I stopped firing. Terror filled the musicians' eyes. "What now?" asked Haydon.

Asked Mastkiller, "Do we just sit here?"

The Quarry

"You have rifles. Shoot!"

I grabbed the bullet extractor, pulled out the bullet, and reset the belt. Then let short bursts go.

All the while German bullets flew at us from all directions.

At the start we had the advantage, the cavalry deprived of its way of fighting. Then the Bosche set their guns behind a heap of quarry waste a distance from the entrance. So we couldn't see them. The guns had to be far enough away from the target to do any good. The German artillery let loose a barrage. The quarry walls rained maiming, fatal shards and splinters. Rocks tumbled down. Slabs split away and crashed to the ground. The quarry shook from the concussion, which alone could kill.

"Trapped," said Haydon.

Mastkiller pinched his nose to squeeze the sound, a school teacher's voice. "Our Sylla and Charybdis."

Haydon retorted, "The devil and the deep blue sea."

"The devil with you," said Palmer "Pay attention."

"Fish in a barrel, my American friends say. All this nautical stuff," said Haydon. "It's fishy, ain't it, gunner?"

"Devilish funny," Mastiller said. "Fish in a barrel? Why would you shoot them? Blast holes in the barrel. Better take them with a net."

"You don't have any American friends. No friends to speak of," said Haydon. "Second, that's Americans for you."

The musicians had turned into giddy zanies.

I said. "Straighten up. You are soldiers. The Uhlans are forming to attack again. " I went on, "It's go down fighting or stand up and wave the white flag."

"Die for the King or kiss the Kaiser's arse," said Palmer. "Royal Fusiliers."

"Same for the Second Irish!" shouted Haydon.

Drummer Mastkiller chimed in. "A quick death doesn't seem awful terrible. Cursing and moaning on the battlefield, I wouldn't care for that."

I said, "Pray for deliverance." I let loose with Victoria to face the second charge.

Soon soldiers could not hear each other, nearly deaf from the discharges and concussion, a loud ringing in the ears only.

What Tommy Atkins Saw

(In his own words)

From my perch I saw the Bosche infantry marching across the fields toward the quarry. The battle would avenge the Germans' defeat at Mons.

I signaled to Private Godley. The gunner and Catchpole would have to let out the rope so I could get down. I tested the knots, tested them again, hesitated. "Don't let me hang where the Germans can see me," I said.

Catchpole said, "Don't worry. If they see you they'll think you're an angel come to help us."

Said Private Catchpole, "After Mons the Bosche think we are in league with demons."

I lowered myself from the limb. The two let me down a few feet when I whispered, "Hold. Pull me back up."

They stopped lowering me. Godley said, "Don't give up now. You can't spend the battle in the tree."

"Something queer in the sky."

"Aeroplanes?" asked Catchpole.

"Cloud. Gold. Lets light through."

Catchpole hissed, "Admire nature later." To Catchpole Godley said, "Lower away. He's a target."

Godley said, "Trick of light, Atkins?" We heard the pop of rifle fire. The Hun infantry was near.

"The cloud is falling toward the ground. Immense! See it? Pull me up! A bubble, a shell. Something moving about inside. Light shining through."

The German infantry now occupied the quarry rim. Behind trees, the sun at their backs, their grey uniforms mixed with the rocks. They were invisible to the soldiers in the quarry. They spotted only a few of us below, but knew many hid in the brush and rocks. From below I heard cries and curses, soldiers struck.

Then Godley and Catchpole saw what I saw.

I said, "No cloud. Pure light."

The light filled the sky and the quarry, so bright it pained the eye. Blinded by the light, the Bosche couldn't see.

"The Huns must take this as a sign. A blessing from Thor," I heard William say. "Since they have us at their mercy."

When we visited the factory where our guns were made we went to the foundry. We watched molten iron pour from a cupola. The foundry men appeared as shapes before the streaming iron. Inside the light ahead of me I saw such shapes.

Then a whirling funnel of light enveloped me.

Tommy Atkins' Second Encounter with the Divine

Suddenly the rope went slack. Godley and Palmer fell to the ground, the resistance gone. No frayed rope followed. The men knew it had not broken. "Atkins must have slipped out of the harness," Private Godley said. "We had no time to teach him about tying a safe harness." They heard no cry, no thud of a body hitting the ground. Looking up, Godley saw the dangling rope, empty, Atkins not to be seen.

Angel Lieutenant Maurice Dease appeared to Tommy Atkins, called him little brother, led him to the whirling cornucopia's mouth.

"What the hell!" Catchpole said, "Couldn't just disappear."

The whirlwind of blinding light spun, encompassed them, its opening high and wide enough for a man to enter. "What the hell!" Catchpole exclaimed again.

The two gunners heard the wind, as if it resounded in a cave. The air trembled, rumbled like rolling thunder.

Catchpole again: "What in hell," as if it was the only thought his mind could muster.

A sound arose, like a voice on a crystal radio, indistinct, but speech. The words repeated themselves again and again, becoming clearer each time "It's Dease's voice! I recognize his voice." Godley exclaimed. Finally a complete, clear sentence: "Enter, ye who would be saved."

When a schoolboy, Gunner Godley had read Dante's *Inferno*. He said to Catchpole, "'Abandon all hope ye who enter here.' Over the gate to Hell Dante wrote.

"Who the hell is Dante?"

"Never mind. Listen to what it says. The voice repeated, "Enter, ye who would be saved. My brothers, Golden Arrows of God, enter." The word "follow," echoed four times. "Step beyond the edge. Follow."

"That is madness! Do not do it. You will surely fall and die." William Catchpole cried. Private Godley stepped beyond the rim. The cone of golden light, brilliant as the sun, swept him up. He became invisible in the light's intensity, disappeared. Catchpole cursed again, "What the hell," and himself entered the place of salvation.

The three Vickers gunners floated across the quarry at the rim's level one hundred feet above the floor, deposited on the quarry's other side. Looking down, as they traveled, it was as if they were watching cinema pictures of the quarry photographed from an aeroplane. They saw the battle below, the deployment and Fritz's action. The bombs seemed to travel at the speed of a struck cricket ball.

The Ascent out of the Pit

(In the words of Paul Carmichael)

It seemed that the light of the sun had descended upon the quarry. All was a-shimmer, aglow with golden light. Nothing visible. We kept firing, but could not see our target. Still, we heard the shouts in German of pain and anger. Our bullets and those of the company band must have done their work. Then a spinning vortex, a maelstrom of white light, descended out of the golden glow. We heard the neighing of a horse immediately in front of our gun, feet away from the muzzle. Had a Uhlan broken through, falling upon us now? Enthralled, we looked and saw a pure white horse, more farm animal than steed, the armored St. George, his massive shield and iron lance in hand, astride. He spoke. "Messieurs de St. Georges, Golden Arrows of God, my soldiers, you served with diligence, courage, nobility." Though he spoke in a whisper, it was as if he expelled fire. "For this I will save you." His voice embodied the dragon he killed, his words the dragon's spirit.

Without a moment's hesitation I said, "All. Save all. The band, too. All or none. They prayed to their patron, St. Paul. Second Royal Irish'll play you a halleluiah anthem when this is done."

"Here or in heaven, salvation for all who fight for Belgium and France," Saint George answered. Wherever the men hid, already fighting, they rose, started in amazement and wonder. St. George raised his shield and lance over the roar of gunfire. An ethereal silence enveloped us–silence within silence. In the silence the soldiers heard the words, "Follow. Array! Array!" the saint's voice now the thunder of a thousand bass drums, and snare drums whose music was of shrapnel striking steel. His words reverberated from the ravine walls and caverns, for all to hear again and again. I wondered, could the Germans hear him? Did they understand English? A few, surely. Officers. Or did they hear him in German? Or was his message for us alone?

Lance held high, the saint stood in his stirrups. His horse rose up on his hind legs, neighing loudly, seeming to step on air, wheeled toward the south wall. We gathered up our pack and gear, dismantled the gun. Then a horn's clarion call to march. The south wall. No hand holds, tracks, trail, no path, no vegetation to grasp.

Suddenly, before us stood Lieutenant Dease, all golden light, his shape only visible. "Lieutenant!" I exclaimed. "Lieutenant Dease in the flesh."

"Not possible, not true," said Ziggy Palmer in disbelief. "He's there. But not flesh."

"He's as much man as you and I."

"Not flesh at all," said Palmer. "Not at all. Touch and see."

Dease saw us, his mates, heard what we said. We saluted. "My men," he said. "St. George blesses you. He leads us. Brothers of St. George. Golden Arrows. He saves you." Something beyond our training and instinct moving us, the men gathered smartly. Entranced, in the thrall of the power and spirit of our old lieutenant, his will subjugated our own. Our response was beyond obedience to a command.

St. George and the Lieutenant went ahead.

All of us, the BEF, caught in the quarry, marched toward the south wall, blind to the impossibility of climbing it. Suddenly we were ascending rock steps cut in the quarry wall. So it felt beneath our feet. We trod the path our eyes could not see. The way the hand finds the mouth–thus we made our passage.

Half way up the wall rope ladders descended from the top. Each rung called for less effort that the rung below, until we were floating upward. As if we had turned to dust, to cloud, to air, and yet were still ourselves.

In a moment's time others joined us in the light. Even the wounded were restored and swept up in the cylinder, the swirling cone, marching in air toward the wall.

It would have taken hours for us all to climb to the top of the wall, if it would have been possible at all. German snipers surely would have picked us off, every one, let alone what artillery could have done. Yet here we were, ascending, surrounded by light. vaporous forms guiding us.

Our hearts expanded with joy. Down the line I heard a bandsman sing,

"We are climbing Jacob's ladder,

We are climbing Jacob's ladder,"

His fellow musicians joined in.

We are climbing Jacob's ladder,

Soldiers of the cross."

As if we were again in the world of Biblical events. And on and up we went.

We came in on:

"Every rung goes higher and higher,

Every rung goes higher, higher,

Every rung goes higher, higher,

Soldiers of the cross."

Some with us had been killed in the battle. We could not distinguish between those who were alive and those who were not. We were not even certain ourselves.

As we approached the wall's top a voice called each by name, rank, and serial number–the voice of a headmaster, an examining magistrate. As if they read from a questionnaire, a hospital admittance form, an insurance application. Separating the living from the dead.

A fallen bandsmen asked, "Are we alive? Dead is painless. Is the memory of my wound's pain erased? The way we forget our births?"

St. George answered to the mind of each. "You are beyond the body. Alive in spirit. Your bodies rest here, consecrating this ground, this rock."

Some the voices called aside. Private Kendall Haydon, bugler. Private Simon Peter Mastkiller, drummer.

"How do you feel, soldier?"

"Feeling fit, sir. When do we march?"

"No more marching for you, soldier. Your marching days are over."

"My legs?"

"No. Your life."

I didn't know when the two bandsmen were shot. Preoccupied with dismantling the gun, I lost sight of them in the flurry of the flight. But I could tell they were dead, one lacking a head as he marched, the other, his blood falling in the air as we ascended. "Not to be seen? Gone?" I asked, reaching out my hand to shake bugler Haydon's hand, grasping nothing but air. I said, "Thank you, soldier. You helped save us. Will a salute do? You deserve that, at least. Maybe in heaven you'll be St. Peter's bugler."

No letter to give a loved one at home. No more zany Kendall Haydon. No more Peter Simon Mastiller.

Let Death Rest from Toil

No sooner had the voices died away than St. George and Lieutenant Dease reached the rim, stepped over and out of sight. None could see over. When we reached the top we stood in fields of stubble–the harvest hereabout being over–rolling as far as the eye could see, rising and falling, lines of trees separating field from field, vineyards, orchards, farm houses, barns, sheds. Through his binoculars Private Godley searched the fields in all directions. The Ruffians were not surprised that the two saints were gone. The helping angels had already faded into a mist out of which they had appeared, the mist itself dispersing into clear sky.

The Ruffians placed the gun to shoot down on the Bosche who lingered below, looking for the British, mystified that the soldiers disappeared.

St. George's voice called out from inside the minds of each Ruffian, though the sound seemed to be everywhere, "Let Death rest from toil. My minion angels will bury the many dead whose blood soaks the ground from Cambrai to Le Cateau. Multitudes of dead will follow." We heard the German bugles blow "cease fire." Spared the fight. Spared the disaster. Lives spared, for the moment.

Chapter Twelve

St. George and the Angels of the Dark Clouds

Le Cateau, France
26 August 1914

> *By mid-day General Smith-Dorrien's tasks had become one of the gravest difficulty. And this was but the opening phase of a movement which, I venture to think, will be accounted by the historian as one of the most astonishing pieces of work in military history. I refer not to the Retreat as a whole, but to the work of the Second Corps and its leader from 3 a.m. of the 24th to about midnight of the 26-27th. An eternity of years was encircled by those few hours.*

> *Liaison, 1914: A Narrative of the Great Retreat*

Brigadier-General E. L. Spears, Late, 11th Hussars

On this Vast Plain

(In the Words of Henry Sanders, Sergeant,
Gunner One, Vickers Two, The Victors)

On this vast plain, the terrain undulating farmland that we are trampling underfoot, the companies entrenched to make our stand.

The Victors climbed over a waist-high stone wall and hedge dividing one farm from the neighbor's, or one crop from another, turned about, now facing the direction we had just come, crouched behind, tore down enough stones so the Vickers' muzzle had free play right and left. Only the muzzle protruded, sniffing out its prey.

Before us the stubble of a grain field after harvest, behind, corn not yet ripe. Ahead the ground fell away to a flat expanse and rose gently again four hundred yards away. Beyond that, the ground rises and falls like gentle Channel swells. We knew the topography, having just marched over that ground to get where we were. We had come south from Mormal and now turned southeast. In hopes of catching the Huns in their impatience, ignorance, and arrogance, and mowing them down like a crop of maize, we set the gun. The sun was at its hottest at this time of day. Light shimmered over the ground, everything shifting images. The Bosche knew we were ahead of them. Our trail, our lines of march, were perfectly plain to see.

Making its way south, the army spread out over a large expanse, taking to the roads, and tracks, trails and fields, out of sight, making as much speed as possible. The two companies in rear-guard, we waited in pockets and clumps here and there, hot, tired, hungry, thirsty, out of jokes and jests, impatient. We wanted the Bosche infantry in range of our hungry mother, Vickers Two, who wanted to eat them, it being time for afternoon tea. We heard artillery drawing closer, sporadic bursts of rifle fire in the swales and valleys—before, to each side, behind—all about. We lacked artillery, it having gone on with the army to hold other points. And we thought ourselves strong enough to give the Germans a thump and a rout, turn them burned and bloody.

A flock of jackdaws feasting on ripening corn rose from the field, circled, flew off. "Funny what comes to mind at odd moments," Hardy said. "Those birds. A line from Froissart on the Battle of Crécy, not far from here. 'Also the same season there fell a great rain and a clipse'–he called it clipse—'with a terrible thunder, and before the rain there came flying over both battles a great number of crows for fear of the tempest coming.'"

"Birds all right, flying like hell out of here," exclaimed Jessop. "It's the booming of the guns, not no tempest chasing 'em."

"No rain. No eclipse," said Lang.

"Just a line in literature. That's all."

Two Tethered Bosche Balloons

Two tethered Bosche balloons in the shape of dirigibles rose not six hundred yards away, tied to ropes. They floated one hundred feet above the ground, and from the top of the hill at that. Spotters in woven rush baskets.

Said Walter Sage, "Closer than I thought they were."

"Close enough to make a worthy target," Howard Lang said.

We began with them. Exposed our position a bit, but a couple of short bursts popped their balloons. Both crashed.

"Good shooting and good sport," Lang added, "As our aristocrat hunter friends would say when the duck and the dove are in the bag."

Soon we heard the sputtering of an aeroplane engine. And soon it was in sight, circled a while, then flew off. The pilot spotted us and would report our positions when he landed.

The Enemy Arrives

It did not take long for the German guns to appear. "See the horses drawing the limbers to high points about?" I said. "With the distance they keep from us, we are good targets."

Gunner Jessop, said, "Height extends their range. Bad match, infantry against artillery."

"Bad conditions for a fight," chimed in even Nancarrew, the quiet one, adding nothing new.

"That's all right, boyo," I said.

Lang: "You watch. Their infantry will come out on forays when the chance arises."

Jessop: "Or when their bloody officers order them. Like at Mons. Bloody slaughter. I think we wiped out half the German army. I hope our generals have better sense."

"Who knows?" said Walter Sage. "We've lost a lot already."

Our talk was pointless, obvious. But we needed to relieve the tension, keep our minds busy while we awaited the attack.

Just then we saw German infantry in front of us, their formations and disposition taking shape.

Walter Sage went on, checking the belts, coiling them neatly, his face and body a study in concentration, not on the belts, but on what he was thinking, seeing in his mind's eye. "How many out there?" he asked, not looking up. "How many against us?" At Mons the Germans were numerous as bees from a hundred hives. This day their infantry were few, their artillery–batteries and batteries–taking the field. Not to say that there were no rifles. The infantry clustered about the artillery for protection.

I said, "However many there are, fight we must and fight we will."

Soldier Jessop piped up. "Didn't have much schooling. Was a mechanic all my life. But we learned Shakespeare, a line or two." He raised his arms, pointed in the direction we faced and recited:

'Once more unto the breach, dear friends, once more,

Or close the wall up with our English dead!

In peace there's nothing so becomes a man

As modest stillness and humility;

But when the blast of war blows in our ears,

Then imitate the action of the tiger:

Stiffen the sinews, summon up the blood.'

Hardy said, "Shakespeare. Henry V," a sneer and genuine disgust in his voice. "Every schoolboy learned the speech by heart. The real national anthem in time of war."

"Right you are, Hardy," I said. "But why such a tone? Mocking the Bard? What is wrong with the poetry?"

"Nothing with the poetry. Its the sentiment. The honor of dying in battle," said Hardy. "Shakespeare inspires us. Stir men up till they are eager to die. But here I am, like it or not, of my own free choice."

We were quiet after that. Why did he remind us? Our eyes on the way we had come—north–for the enemy.

Artillery fire became a barrage, more accurate as their reconnaissance spotted our positions. Comrades were getting it. The Bosche pulled light artillery in close enough so the gunners could see us directly. I grasped the triggers again, killed two of their batteries in five minutes. Then their infantry let loose and the battle proper was on. The Huns came closer. Rifle fire and the clatter of machine guns. We heard the shouts of our men, hit. Suddenly the Bosche were on our flanks. The old claw–pinch us between–the nut in the nutcracker. If we needed to, we could disappear into the cornfield behind us. The Bosche would not know where we were, but their bullets and bombs would soon find us.

I fired off another belt, short bursts, warming up the gun, shooting at pockets and clusters of Hun infantry sneaking toward us.

The Air was Still

Three or four butterflies flitted about. In the days of late summer bees circled flowers, looking for the right angle of attack. Yet suddenly clouds appeared just above the northern horizon, above the ridge and treetops whence cometh the enemy. Maybe five miles away, dark, torn, thin, but opaque, streaked, ragged clouds–as at the front of a coming storm– swirled, flattened by the wind driving them, wisps astray, fog-drift brushing the ground. We were trained to read the sky, the clouds, for weather. Cirrostratus they should have been, white, translucent. The wrong color this time of day, the wrong type of cloud.

Jessop's voice: "A wild sort of storm. Who knows what weather they get from across the Channel? Sea weather. "

"It's not coming from the west. From the east," said Lang.

Gabriel Jessop repeated. "The east. What happened when the weather was weird at Mons."

As the clouds drew closer, I thought I discerned shapes. I realized that, exhausted, overheated, hungry, thirsty, I was prone to hallucination. I set my sights back on the advancing enemy. "Keep to business," I said, as much to myself as to the men.

Nancarrew the quiet looked up, rubbed his eyes. "I am seeing things. Shapes in the sky? Sergeant, I'm going barmy."

I glanced up, saw shapes, too.

Keeping his eyes on the Germans, Jessop muttered, "A mirage. What can they be? Wishful thinking."

"I see them, too," I said. Then we all gazed.

The barrage and close fire went on. I stepped over the rock wall and out of the thicket of brush and trees to see what was happening. Up and down our line I saw worse than I had guessed. Two hundred fifty took the field, two companies and a few more. I saw about seventy-five left. The Germans crept and slouched closer. "Too late," I said. "Surrender or be killed. We can't do any good dead. We might be able to do something later, but for now. . . ." Sickened by the death I saw around me.

"You know best, Sergeant," said Sage. "Myself, I prefer living, too."

Gabriel Jessop: "Heaven is promised, but I've been lied to before. Like when they took me into the army. Thought I'd repair lorries for the Army, trot home at night for dinner with the wife and kiddies."

"But here you are. What of the clouds?" I asked. "They are more than four miles off and high in the sky. What does it mean?"

"Surrender? What does the manual say? When you are outnumbered and unsupported, fight like hell!" Jessop went on, sarcasm in his voice.

"You surprise me, Jessop. I expected different of you, cold as steel, sharp as a bayonet. But I don't mind living a little longer. Just getting the hang of it, you might say," Sage said.

"But I see horses in the sky!" said Nancarrew.

I didn't answer, not knowing what to say. Horses they were. The Germans were upon us, the horses far off.

"The Bosche will take us prisoner," I said. "We'll see things from the German point of view."

Hardy said, "I'll write tabloid exposé stories, you know." His left hand marked the place of each word as if in the title of an article or book. "'What the Craven Beast Wants,' 'What the Fat-Headed Bosche Soldier is Really Like.' Expose their thinking. Then the story of our heroic escape."

I did not want to see more perish. I tied a white handkerchief to my rifle, waved it in the air. I felt terrible, letting down King and Country. Against regulations. Against training. Against instinct. Revulsion at the thought.

It took a while for the Germans to see the flag, longer for the shooting to stop. In the meantime more of us were shot, a few more killed. Then we saw not just horses in the sky. In a loud whisper Lang exclaimed, "Cavalry!" The hair on the back of our necks rose. Dark as night, the horses advanced, trotting. As they drew closer, still at a trot–three miles, then two–we saw banners unfurled.

The Germans Came up to Us

The Germans came up to us, now not shooting, honoring our surrender. If the Germans could see what was coming they would skip the pleasantries and fire. I whispered to the men, "Jabber quietly among yourselves. Occupy yourselves with the gun. Be a bit rowdy. Keep the

Germans' attention on you. Don't point! Don't look up at the clouds."

The German officer saw my insignia. I stepped up to him. He spoke English, good English. "Sergeant, I was educated in your England. I know the British. I like the British. So civil. So reserved."

In looks and bearing he manifested what was most despicable in the Prussian Junker. Stiff in his tight grey uniform, his high black boots. Smugness written all over his face, nostrils flared, chin raised, steel blue eyes. The telltale scar across the cheek. Saber-cut, mark of initiation, sign of good breeding, important social connections, brotherhood, and the virtues the dueling fraternities proclaimed to show themselves part of old, brutal Germany. His accent that of an aristocratic German who had mastered English at a British university–Oxford or Cambridge. He said, "I do you a courtesy. I come as a gentleman and an officer to explain what we will do to you." In German, to his soldiers he said, "Too cowardly to give battle." Snide. He did not know that as well as he spoke English, I understood German. Taught myself. No one knew it. A private secret. Poor in conversation, but I could translate, a substantial vocabulary and grammar.

Herr Lieutenant went on, his voice dripping sarcasm, his face writhed in contempt and pleasure. "Therefore, I apologize for what I must do now. As you know, Paris awaits. We are moving too quickly to take you along. I would take your parole for your good behavior, but my General, not having the advantage of an appreciation of the British, has different ideas. He has no patience and has lost trust in Britain since you've betrayed Germany." He went on, "The general says," now affecting a general's deep voice and brusque tone, "'I thought English were our brothers. They went to war against us! Your King and our Kaiser, cousins!' 'Dastardly' is the word the general used. Yes, a dastardly deed. So he orders us to take no prisoners." He was having a fine time making his speech. Abruptly he changed his tone. "Get your policemen–for they are no soldiers–away from that gun! Order them to stack their rifles and toss their revolvers in a pile."

I knew his story was a lie. We saw many captured and taken away. Malevolent was all he was. I said nothing. "Order them!" In a mocking tone he spoke to me as an equal in rank, almost as if he was putting his arm around my shoulder, speaking comrade to comrade. "Terrified you are, thinking of your death. When Germans die, they think of the glory of the Emperor and the German Empire to come."

All the while, the cloud advanced slowly. At the pace they were coming, they would reach us too late to do us any good.

The German reverted to the tone of brutal killer. "You are not mute," he shouted into my ear.

"Nor deaf," I said.

At least one other Hun knew English, a stocky soldier, a man from the city, moustache etching a perpetual grin across his face. "Er sprecht!" he said. The rest laughed.

Thereafter, he translated what I said. Though, because his comrades needed to wait for him to translate, it was as if a comic delivered his line, the audience laughing half a minute later. The German soldiers took pleasure in the merriment, the humiliation their Lieutenant inflicted. Something in the German spirit.

"Not deaf?" he shouted. I saw the veins on his neck pulsing. The muscles that produced his grimace were taut. "Speak! But no!" He slapped his boot loudly with a riding crop.

The question struck me. Were the Germans taught these ways, or did cruelty and brutality come naturally? His terrorizing had no effect on me. The Germans thought they knew the British soldier. They made up stories about the British they told themselves. Perfidious Albion they call it. News they call it. Propaganda it was, and good for us. We could tell that the enemy knew nothing of our character, our ability. They had silly ideas. A bunch of policemen, bobbies, they thought us. A contemptible little army the Kaiser called it. His army he called the mighty Huns, who swept Europe long ago, and would do so now. They will not have to fight us, but arrest us, needing only to send their policemen after us. Such nonsense. We intended to teach them differently. For now, our situation was difficult.

I did not flinch, looked Herr Lieutenant Tries-to-Frighten-Me right in the eye, though courage was all I had. The clouds drew closer, but were still far off.

"Angels Saved us Before. Why not Now?"

Behind me the Victors muttered, mumbled so as not to be overheard. "Angels saved us before. Why not now? We are St. George's army," said

Howard Lang. "An arrow pinned inside my tunic pocket says so. What happened at Mons tells me so. We can fight for him only if we are alive," he said, patting his chest. "You and your school logic. We're as good as dead. The German is toying with the Sergeant," growled Jessop. "He will shoot us before an angel or storm can help. Even now, shrapnel and rifle fire. Say your prayers, I say. Make your peace."

Herr Lieutenant Sardonic

If he could have heard them, Herr Lieutenant Sardonic would have at least looked about. Instead, full of himself, enjoying himself, he plowed on. "Command your men to attention in the presence of a German officer, you bobby!" and made as if to slap my face with his gloves. "Have you no . . .?" He broke off, either at a loss for words at our stupidity, or unable to find the right words in English, or too exasperated to speak.

Herr German officer and his men enjoyed taunting us, so I gave him plenty of ammunition, you might say.

I interrupted him with a wave of dismissal. "The bully's swagger and bluster. Now you will offer us terms under insulting conditions."

The German officer laughed derisively. "I shall offer you no conditions, my friend. You are as good as dead, as the English saying has it."

"Go ahead, then," I said. "No sense wasting your pretty speeches on someone who will soon forget them. We are British soldiers in His Majesty's army. You are my enemy."

The translation, then the Hun crew laughed again.

"Nicely put, my friend. Very honorable. Good. That makes me feel less? What is the word?"

"Guilty?" the translator offered.

"Yes. I will have fewer regrets, knowing that you don't mind being shot. All for good King George. Well, then. Enough."

Mimicking his tone of voice, his attitude, I shouted back, adding a touch of the supercilious. "You, sir, are disingenuous and snide. Your smirk tells me so."

"Smirk? What is smirk? Army slang, perhaps? I admit, I am not up on that. "

"And coy." Making the gesture I said, "You speak as if you laughed behind a hand held over your mouth."

"As you can see, I do no such thing," he said, adopting that very gesture. "Or perhaps I am sharing a private joke with my comrades?"

Translation. Then laughter.

I gave him plenty to arouse his ire and contempt. "Sly mockery and belittlement," I said.

To keep matters lively I reminded him of what I knew he already rejected, quoting the Hague Convention on prisoners of war and the white flag of surrender.

Of this he made fun. "The very idea of treating the enemy as any better than vermin. Der Tag has come," he said.

"Der Tag?" I asked. "Today is Wednesday."

"You don't know what I'm talking about."

His loud voice and the resounding laughter had attracted an audience. His two dozen Bosche infantry had gathered about, each pointing his rifle at one of the Victors, enjoying the performance, my performance of a lifetime.

"Yes. Wednesday."

And again his men laughed, as if they had just heard the greatest joke in the world. And in a way, they had. I knew what "The Day" meant. We had read of Der Tag in the papers and magazines for years. The Day the Germans fight, defeat the hated, accursed, duplicitous British. Their big secret. Their code word. Their great hope and aspiration. Their prayer. Their toast at parties, receptions, wherever convivial, patriotic Germans gathered.

I kept him talking, enjoying himself, entertaining his men with drollery and wit– the cat teasing the mouse–kept him interested in the game. For my part it was stall, delay.

Finally, Lieutenant Fear-Imposing looked about, saw that we still held our guns. My distracting him had played itself out. He shouted, "I ordered you to disarm! You disobeyed!" He took his pistol out of its holster and shot about Nancarrew's feet to make him dance. Carrew stood still, looking him in the eye. Then the German shot him in the heart. The Bosche killer said, "You see? I do not have to shoot you in ceremony or good order. I can even shoot you myself if I choose." He laughed uproariously, stretching out the agony to enjoy it all the more.

"War. Look out there," he said, pointing with his pistol. "No ceremony. No order."

The gloom was all over Hardy's face, in his slumped shoulders. Too much fellow-feeling, compassion.

There was nothing we could do. We were grief-stricken. We held our faces rigid, not expressing the grief at the brutal death. Nancarrew the quiet was silent forever now.

We had expected to be taken prisoner. That was the rule. But the German lieutenant was going to shoot us. The Germans disdained the civil conduct of war. We heard about brutalities and atrocities they inflicted on the Belgians–burning, looting, raping, torture, murder.

A Front Row View

The German soldiers with the lieutenant spread out so each could see what was happening They edged to where a glance above the horizon and north would reveal what the sky contained. No sound. No sign. At that very moment, and half a mile away, the clouds, now clearly cavalry, changed from trot to canter, and canter to furious gallop. The ethereal horsemen circled, passed over the Germans to the southwest. Their horses' and their own bodies obscured the sun, casting darkness and light like that which falls through the leaves of wind-tossed trees. The shadows struck the Germans as grotesque monsters infecting the earth, now nearly upon them. Then they looked up, forgetting the British.

The summer air turned cold. A wind came up, whipped the corn behind, bending and creaking, the leaves scraping together, rustling, like sand paper on wood, and a disordered whooshing. Then a cannonade of rolling thunder.

"Who is cursed, us or the Germans?" Hardy asked.

"Who can say?" said Sage.

"If what we had already seen wasn't enough to topple the wits of the half-mad," Jessop shouted. The clouds swooped up and down like a flock of birds. Then, straining toward the German lines, the horses passed over our heads again, now a dozen feet above the ground. Looking up in terror and awe, we and the Germans saw their underbellies and tails, hooves churning the air. We heard the creaking of saddle, the jangle of reins, bridle, bit, of horse and rider's exertions in frantic gallop. We saw the leather soles of horsemen's boots in iron stirrups, iron spurs behind. We saw lances pointed forward, sabers flashing in the light. We breathed the smell of horses.

Some of the cavalry wore uniforms and carried the gear of one age, some of another. The warriors from above attacked with their lances, striking many Germans, killing many. Knights in armor of old and cavalry of a later time–of Wellington or Marlboro's time–came to ground between us and the Bosche infantry, on its way to wipe out the remnant of our two companies. I saw a few dressed in today's uniform, kit, and weapons. Stranger yet, I saw a man in a modern frock coat, a dandy. From our odd angle, we could not tell more.

Then thundering hooves pummeled the ground. We felt the ground tremble. We heard horses' neighing and nickering and shouts of orders and commands in a language I recognized as Chaucer's English.

The Sky of Three Suns

At the very moment, in mid-air and to the west, sundogs, seemingly spun out of the sun's light, stood to its left and right. I knew this minor curiosity from grade school meteorology lessons.

"Sky of three suns," said Thomas Lang. At first without form, the lights took vague shape, then became angels. In the middle was the actual sun. To the left and right, sun-dogs. Immediately we knew the one to the left in whose thrall we served. St. George on his horse. The one standing to the right, Lieutenant Dease, holding the horse's bridle. St. George looked down upon the Bosche soldiers with a fiery gaze. Dease, the interceding angel, now knelt, clasped his hands as in prayer for us.

On the ground between our line and advancing Germans, at the head of the host of angelic horsemen we made out St. George, clad in golden armor, astride his white charger. The horse reared up on his hind legs, circled, his master surveying the battlefield. Other knights surrounded him. Golden light emanating from him, set him apart. Saint George was in the sky and on the ground all at once. When he raised his lance in command below, he did so above. Like seeing an object's reflection in a mirror and the object at the same time.

147

The Angel of Mons

The Rocks Arise as Soldiers

In a moment of quiet, "Shush! What's that sound?" whispered Hardy.
"Gun fire and shouts," I said.
"No, not that. Put your ear close to the rocks," said Hardy.
"The stone wall?"
"Yes."
First we heard a tinkling, like limestone breaking apart in the fire of a lime-burner's kiln, or clinkers shaken in a furnace. Then the rocks trembled and shook, tumbled apart, rolling off in all directions, as if they had been thrown.

Out of each stone arose a mist, smoke, the smoke becoming tangible wraiths, soldiers from the past. This happening all along the stone wall. "I wish Andrew Lang could see this, realms of being confirmed," Howard Lang said. "The Psychical Society would be thrilled."

In our midst, out of the stones, before and behind, archers, swordsmen, men clad in felt tunics with metal studs arranged in neat vertical rows, and helmets like metal pots, mailed leather hauberks, iron greaves at the knees, rose up out of the stones and joined our ranks. They were armed with ancient implements of war–knives, broad-bladed daggers, swords, pole-axes, bills, a few pikes. Some had long bows, others crossbows. They wore not trousers, but hose. I read their character in an instant. Though they wore proper uniforms, some red and white, some green and white, they were brigands, cutthroats, criminals. Crude, unclean, yet trained, obedient.

Among them were soldiers from yet another time. Some wore tricorn hats, others grenadier caps. In their red coats and blue coats, frogs and braid, lace, bright britches they were dressed to parade-review perfection. Easily spotted. Soldiers with muskets and socket bayonets. Each had a ball-bag and priming flask hung from leather straps and bandoliers crossing his chest.

Two days before we had marched through Malplaquet, ten miles south by east, place of the famous battle. We paused at the stone monument in a farmer's field just off the road. Victory of Marlborough and the King's army. Carved in bas relief foot and cavalry dressed in the very uniforms and armed with the same weapons as those who joined us now. They threw themselves into the fight, ten of them for each of us, adding number and strength.

It was as if a picture book depicting "The Pageant of British Arms" had come to life. We looked on, astonished, but now accustomed to the uncanny, the unexpected, the impossible.

"Like Cadmus and the dragon's teeth. Sowed them, and armed men, warriors, jumped up from the earth," Howard Lang said. "*Spartes*, sown men."

"School boys. Always the books, the classics," Jessop said in disgust, breathing long on the "a" in classics, his eyes closed, chin up-tilted, in mock derision of the educated. "So these are the Spartans?" he asked. "Look British to me, though of old. Come to save us, then?"

"Must be. What else?"

St. George! In the Flesh!

Up and down our ragged line those still able to raise their voices shouted like men in a madhouse, "St. George! In the flesh! St. George! Come to do for England!"

"God save us!"

"Sweet saint, I'll worship at your feet forever." Some nearly wept. Heavenly reinforcements. And the soldiers about cried in relief, "Heaven's knight, save us." An instinctive moaning and involuntary sobbing, breath drawn deeply and quickly expelled.

Seemingly in reply to our cries the phantom warriors roared the ancient salutation, a summoning shout, though in speech of Chaucer's day:

"Sente George! The longe bowe and the stronge bowe."

The voices of all, as in chant or call, resounded above the shrieks and blasts of the artillery, machine guns, and rifles. "Comen we to saufe merrie Englonde!"

"Joynen as a bretherhede!"

"The bowe and the swerd, the launce and the pike!"

In words and speech closer to what we spoke, we heard the same pledge of aid. Their bloodcurdling yells died away. The officers of the King's Own Something called out commands. The drummers beat the signals to the troops. The soldiers faced straight ahead. As if we weren't there. As if they were real while we were not.

The celestial soldiers and cavalry covered the field, devouring the Germans before them. Blasts of horns and trumpets assailed the ear, fifes and drums tore the air, beat louder and louder until it seemed we were in the midst of interminable thunder.

The Bosche Lieutenant Bluster glimpsed the horror galloping toward him—an angel warrior. I wonder what he thought in those brief seconds. No time for remorse over how he had treated us. The warrior came at the lieutenant across the front. Lance passed neatly between the leather belt and tunic, the angel lifted the German off the ground. He clutched the lance's shaft. If he let go, the horse's monstrous hooves would crush him. The knight swung his lance to the left and lowered it toward the ground. The German's boots scraped the ground, pulling him flat on his back. Caught in his belt, the lance twisted and pierced his stomach, and came out just as quickly. It had done its work, the horse and rider galloping on. Lieutenant Superior sprawled, still alive, the depths of surprise mingled with terror and pain in his eyes. I would have liked to know his mind. He did not eat his own cruel words. He spat them out, blood. And he died, unshriven.

The cavalry caught up with the Germans, stabbing with lances, slashing with sabers. We saw the glint of swords' flashing steel, the sunlight on knights' armor.

In the fury and fiasco, the mingling of cavalry with cavalry, the German horses broke from the line, bolted in all directions, their eyes wide with terror, foam streaming from mouths and nostrils, blood dripping where the bits cut their mouths when the cavalry tried to control them. Some horses falling, others wounded. Some reared and plunged, wheeled in circles where they stood. Advance ceased. Many riders toppled to the ground, some trampled, bones broken, bleeding from wounds. Hun cavalry cried out, trying to steady the horses.

The archers plucked arrows from their quivers, nocked their arrows, drew the bows. We heard the twang of bowstrings, the whirr and whistle of arrows in prodigious numbers. Saw clouds of death singing through the sky. Strange to see sticks of wood throw Germans to the ground, gyrating in mad dances and convulsions, like acrobats and tumblers gone berserk. Arrows, feathers and all, sticking out at all angles.

"Hedgehog-like, they look, prickled with a dozen arrows." Sage laughed, savoring his own wit.

The clatter of ratcheting rack and pinion cranking the whipcord tight, the buzz, the vibration the string set up when the bolt was shot. We heard the click and release of the bolts flying invisibly, so small and swift, to bury deep in flesh. Heard the dry crackle of musket fire. Even as inaccurate as the weapon was at a distance, the rain of musket balls struck down many a Bosche. Puffs of smoke, then clouds obscured the ground, the musket added to the row.

Following behind, foot soldiers finished the work. Swordsmen hacked away, severing limbs, decapitating heads from torsos. Pike-men ran many through, the guts being soft, a large target, easy to withdraw the pike. The maimed, dying, and dead choked the battlefield for the length of two cricket fields, three hundred yards long and double the width. They became an impediment, cluttering the way.

The Germans ran. None stayed to tend the wounded. Though their cries were piteous, they did not arouse our sympathy. They would have eagerly killed us.

Years ago our editorialists and essayists had introduced us to the Germans' true religion: kultur. The idea of German superiority and the necessity, therefore, of making the world its empire. But Herr Smug was going to kill us after we had surrendered. In so doing he honored himself according to German values. The angelic host judged his values and intentions. God and his minions are ruthless with men who behaved despicably. So much for kultur. So much for the Germans, the Chosen People.

"Shoot an Angel of God?"

(In the words of Howard Lang, The Victors)

Mechanic Jessop talked to himself, but without knowing it he was speaking out loud. "Is this how it is then? The angels doing our fighting for us? This is something new. Even Joshua fought at Jericho, didn't he?"

We were keyed up for the fight. Nerves taut. Eager and ready all at once. We had never laid our weapons down. We had Vixen. I could read her thoughts. "Shoot, my boys! Kill, my men!" Ahead and behind and in our midst the fight raged.

I said, "If it wasn't for our protectors mixed with the enemy, I would fire. I dare not shoot. Can't tell if they are made of matter."

Jessop: "I dunno. Ask them."

"They act like they don't see us."

A warrior angel, longbow in hand, took an arrow from his quiver, pricked my forehead with the tip, drew blood. My whole body vibrated. I heard blood pulse in my heart. I felt my flesh melt away so I was only graveyard bones. A resounding voice filled the air, though only I heard. "When the way of righteousness is imperiled, the unseen world helps the righteous." The voice came again, "God is no mere onlooker. He casts his lot with the righteous."

My senses opened to another world, showed me this world differently. When something of great importance happens—a sweetheart's first kiss, a child's birth–it is as if time halts. So it was now. Even though the horses were at a gallop and the phantom soldiers in our midst charged forward on the run, time was taking its own time. I savored every moment, wishing it could.

With the words of the voice, I knew that our bullets would pass through the angels, make no pain, leave no trace. They were immortal, and, though at the moment, material, immune. Strange as it was, I believed my thought. "I will fire my pistol," I told Hardy. "I'll do them no harm."

"How do you know? There's no way of knowing. Don't. I wouldn't."

I said, "I'll do it."

"If you are wrong?"

"This is war!" said Walter Sage.

"Shoot, then," Hardy said. "We are on the edge of annihilation anyway. There are hundreds of us dead already, maybe thousands. Give it a try. A small mistake like that. Not the Vickers. Just your pistol."

"Shoot an angel of God?" said Jessop, aghast.

I shot at an angel swordsman, hoping to strike only the outer flesh of his thigh, miss bone and artery. The bullet passed through him, through his shield, and killed a German who had enjoyed his lieutenant's performance minutes before. The ancient warrior marched on, untouched.

"Lang was right," said Jessop. "Fire away."

The Onslaught Halted

The German onslaught halted. The Bosche spun about, running back the way they had come. No longer the eager foe, but frightened, terrified men. The pandemonium of horses wheeled and bolted, heard their riders' cries.

"It ain't earthly, it's divine," said Walter Sage. "I've been blessed. Not like church on Sunday morning. No, this is real. God's presence among us. The saintliest vicar in England ain't come as close to God as we."

It took two minutes to break down the gun. Its weight, the ammunition, the belts, the water canister hampered us, but we did not fall far behind. We joined the chase, rushed forward to catch the enemy.

"Look at the Bosche run!" Sergeant Sanders shrieked. Enthusiasm lit up his face, animating his limbs. Gleefully, he said, "I hope St. George doesn't disapprove of our fighting after we surrender. Ungentlemanly to break a pledge. Not cricket." We all laughed.

"No chance of that. He's leading the fight," Sage said.

The Hun artillery could not adjust to our movement quickly enough. We were too close for their bombs to do any good. Their spotters signaled the firing to cease.

Before we could set up in a new place the Germans were already out of range. They did not counterattack. When the angelic host is after you, you better keep going.

As Swiftly as They had Come

As swiftly as they had come, the angels flew off. It was as if the angels mounted an invisible hill in the sky, separated into two rivers, the bowmen and pikes men and knights heading southeast, those of the Eighteenth Century going to the northeast, became clouds again, flapping like immense, unfurled banners, then a flock of birds, then disappeared beyond view.

"We are saved!" Jessop said.

"For the moment. The battle's not over. The war neither," said Walter

Sage. "Plenty of time. I shall remember this as long as I live."

"You may not have long," retorted Jessop.

I said. "But we are not dead yet. We are still alive."

The angels saved the Victors, and many others. But many died. Our little golden arrows protected us, except Nancarrew, gone. We grieved for his death. We wondered. For what purpose were we being saved? Bear witness and report after the war is over? Because we are men of virtue? We could not bury Nancarrew. The hope was a burial team would give him Christian rites. "These golden arrows are not absolute protection," said Walter Sage. "They do not stand between us and death. Men kill. Bullets kill. Death does not kill. Thank God, Nancarrew did not suffer. He stood bravely. Honor him in prayer when we can."

The squad began its march across the field strewn with bodies, arrows stuck in the ground. "What will their burial teams report to the general?" asked Jessop. "That the British fought with bows and arrows?"

Sergeant Sanders said, "I would like to be a fly on the wall. See the general's anger at such foolishness. Why, those blokes will be in stockade before he finds out they told the truth. What will he write in his battle report tonight?"

Said Sage, "Best skipped over if he wants to keep his command."

"He'll write his men fought like demons," I said. "Who knows how they will prosper elsewhere today? The battle line is long. What about the Ruffians? I hope they are safe."

"What will our general say?" asked Jessop.

I remarked, "The generals are smart. Easy to describe what happened in the language of an ordinary battle report."

"Who would believe us? War weary, exhausted, frightened, they would say. No sense in trying," the sergeant muttered almost to himself, as he surveyed the scene of slaughter before and about us.

Souvenirs

I said, "I'll collect some arrows and bolts."

"Souvenirs? Each should take some," said Walter Sage. "Memento of the day heaven saved us again."

Jessop replied, "Can't carry arrows. Won't fit in our kit. But a bolt or two should be easy to hide. Might make good hand weapons if the need

The Angel of Mons

comes."

Sanders said, "We will put a few in the ammo box."

I said, "Souvenirs are not what I had in mind. Evidence. British Psychical Society. Those gentlemen will want to study them."

"Gentlemen, nothing. Crackpots," someone uttered.

"Crackpots, nothing." I said. "They are scientists and thinkers. Not to be fooled. Besides, we saw. We witnessed. Experienced. Have the bolts in hand."

"How to get them to England?" asked Hardy.

"Surely when we go home the Army will expect souvenirs, as Sage said. Crossbow bolts. Souvenirs."

Jessop objected. "They are buried in the dirt or some Bosche bloke's back side."

"I'll dig it out of one of these unfortunates, as you may call them. What's a bayonet for?" I replied.

We collected a dozen crossbow bolts stuck them in a German soldier's kit we took off his back, buried it in the ammunition cart.

BOOK 4

THE ANGEL OF MONS,
CONAN DOYLE,
W.B. YEATS,
AND WINSTON CHURCHILL

Chapter Thirteen

Sir Arthur Conan Doyle and
Captain Leckie's
Letter from beyond the Grave

Windlesham Manor, Surry
August 26 1914

(Attested to by Sir Arthur Conan Doyle)

Uncertainty Lay Heavy upon the Heart

England was in a low mood. All were appalled by the barbarity of Germany's attack on the poor people of Belgium and France. The German army was sweeping toward Paris and victory it claimed to hold close at hand.

Saturday evening. A pestilential vapor, a gloom inhabited the dining room at Windlesham. The size of a ballroom, for which we sometimes used it, the room covered the width of the house. To dispel the gloom, Lady Doyle and I entertained Sir Oliver and Lady Lodge. He, eminent physicist and President of the British Psychical Society–to which I belong, founding member. Mr. Sherlock Holmes was our guest as well. We ate at a bay window extending fully a yard out from the main body of the house–surrounded by fragrant flowerbeds–perfect for the small gathering. Dinner, a light meal befitting the season and the weather, vegetables and salads from the garden, fowl. The talk ranged from the cost of beef and eggs in the country, bee keeping, brewing ale and beer in Belgium, and Holmes' recent monograph on German espionage in England. Even so, the conversation circled back to the sad affairs of that moment.

In everyone's mind was the war with the German behemoth.

All knew that in the opening moments of the war many British soldiers would be killed. In English homes fear and uncertainty lay heavily upon the heart. There were tales, accounts from past wars, of soldiers appearing as apparitions or in dreams to their kin, telling of their passing, this before the Army sent telegrams to the home to deliver the unwelcome news. Several of us anticipated phenomena that might enlighten us as to the question of life after death. We discussed the Psychical Society's interest in the matter. My late friend Myers compiled five thousand accounts of such events not only from soldiers' relatives, but of people from every station and every age of life. I reached for the book which happened to be near at hand. "Oh, Arthur," my wife, Jane, said, "You are not going to read and preach."

"Only a few words, my dear." I had marked the passage with slip of paper. "Frederick wrote, 'We gradually discovered,'" I began, "'That the accounts of apparitions at the moment of death–testifying to a super-sensory communication between the dying man and the friend who sees him but while that death was yet unknown to the percipient, and thus apparently due not to mere brooding memory but to a continued action of that departed spirit.'" I said such apparitions came from the victims of murder, accident, and disease, drowning, and even suicides. I handed Myers' tome, Human Personality and its Survival of Bodily Death, to Holmes. "Believe his explanation or disprove it," I said.

"Yes, we hear tales of such phenomena," said Sherlock Holmes. "Lady Doyle, may I open a window and sit near it? I wish to smoke a pipe."

"Please feel welcome. I shall call the butler."

"There will be no need. Please allow me." He opened the window, filled his pipe, lit it.

"Tales? Perhaps." Smoke curled about Holmes' face. Jean remarked, "At this moment, Mr. Holmes, you look like a medium wrapped in what they call plasma, presumably the signs of the presence of a departed soul." A blithe spirit, my Jean. Holmes waved his hand about to dispel the cloud, as if to dispel the notion of mediumship, and to acknowledge a clever observation, Jean demonstrating that she shared a shred of skepticism in matters of the spirit surviving bodily death.

Sherlock returned to the argument. "Mr. Myers' accounts are not proof. It is not the number of stories, but their veracity. The theory breaks the laws of our Mr. Newton's physics." Turning to Professor Lodge, he asked, "Is that not so? Every proposition needs to be tested. That is what physicists do. And so it is with these most unusual pheno-mena, is that correct?"

"Even more so, Holmes. Hypotheses need testing, experiments."

Holmes muttered softly, "You hunt out deception and fraud? That is not the same as testing hypotheses."

"There are many such cases, of course," said Sir Oliver. " We seek to find out and expose those who deceive."

Then, his pipe stem pointed toward me, Holmes observed, "Conan Doyle, in your stories you invent ingenious devices. You concoct fantastic possibilities. Your tales' laws and logic are consistent within themselves only, creating interesting fictions."

I replied, "My stories have nothing to do with the matter."

"Much like your stories, Doyle. Spiritism. Spiritualism. Whatever you choose to call it. Hocus pocus. The occult. Full of holes in logic. Events that do not hold up to facts of science and physics. Madame Blavatsky and her ilk. Feeble thinking. Blatant foolishness. I am afraid these characterize your psychical fuss." Turning to Sir Oliver he said, "Sir, you must pardon me for saying so, but I am surprised that so eminent a physicist would preside over such an organization, let alone associate himself with it."

Professor Lodge held forth. "Physics of Mr. Newton's day, and much of our own, accurately explains and predicts phenomena at the level of the everyday, even to the motion of the planets. But Mr. Newton had not the tools or theory to explore the extremely minute nor the immensely huge stars. Indeed, in his day these magnitudes and phenomena was unknown. Contemporary discoveries, unknown even as recently as our youth, reveal laws we are just beginning to explore. No doubt the names of Planckt and Rutherford are familiar to you. But their ideas are beyond the understanding of all except theoretical physicists."

Shelock Holmes said, "All that you say so far is true. I await hearing your thinking on the connection between the new physics and the accounts we find in Mr. Myer's book."

"I shall attempt it. Study in the worlds of atomic forces and galaxies and stars reveal phenomena new to physics. Our Psychical Society looks to see what new hypotheses worthy of exploration the new laws invite. Chemists, physicists, biologists—we are serious scientists. Not the wishful pursuing hopes of Heaven and reunion with loved ones. We leave that to occultists and mystics."

"Thank you, Sir Oliver. A most cogent explanation. I, too, wonder what the new sciences will reveal."

Lady Jean, a student of such events as well, said, "However, Mr. Holmes, with so many likely to die, if such phenomena should arise from the horrors of war we must study them, benefit from them, not merely weep and lament."

Lily Loder-Symmons and Automatic Writing

"Sir Arthur, will you invite our guests to the drawing room? Let us take coffee there. We shall be more comfortable."

We seated ourselves in what Lady Doyle called the conversation nook.

"I notice something new on your desk, Miss Loder-Symmons. At least new since the last time I visited. If I may ask?" said Sherlock Holmes. "That apparatus? What is its purpose?"

Since they were young ladies, Lily Loder-Symmons and my wife, were the closest of friends. Both great beauties. Highly intelligent. Lily was, practically speaking, our permanent houseguest. Even at a young age Lily suffered from chronic bronchial disorders, which I treated. Grown frail, delicate, she was confined to bed much of the time. Lily spoke, "Mr. Holmes, several months ago a learned doctor–oh, I am sorry, I've forgotten his name–delivered a lecture about automatic writing at a Psychical Society meeting. I decided to learn it." She went on. "The theory is, if we open ourselves to the spirit realm, we can become a transmitter of messages in writing. Enter a trance and let the spirit speak is the idea."

Said Lady Jean, "Lily tried her hand at it when she was well enough to get about. Arthur set up a suspended sling that lets her hand and arm move freely. I gave her a fountain pen. It does not require dipping in an ink well."

Miss Loder-Symmons added, "The contraption makes it easy for me to write whatever my hand is inclined to record. Sir Arthur provides me with paper. I can scribble away to my heart's content." Added Lily, "I thought automatic writing might contribute to our knowledge of psychic phenomena, the world beyond. I pass my time profitably. I must admit, I am not very good at it. In fact, quite inept, to tell the truth."

I said, "Of course, I am interested in such phenomena. To study, not to practice. Lily was our experiment, a test, this drawing room, her desk our laboratory."

Just then, the maid brought in a tray with coffee pot, cups, and saucers. I removed the stopper from a decanter of fine Scotch, poured for the men. "In a snifter, gentlemen. To be savored, bouquet and flavor. Unmixed." Raising our glasses I toasted, "To His Majesty and his health."

"Here, here," all replied.

Professor Lodge and I indulged in cigars from Cuba. I jokingly offered them to the ladies. "You are a bad man and a poor example," chided Lily.

Stifling a laugh, a mere smile breaking out, Lady Lodge added, "Even in jest this is in terrible taste, Sir Arthur. You, Miss Loder-Symmons' physician, treating her for a lung disorder. For shame."

"Sir Arthur, behave yourself," scolded Jean, in mock annoyance. "Ignore him, Lady Jean. Most of his jests are in poor taste. His barbarian Scottish roots. You would think he was raised a peasant. His mother and father would be horrified. We must excuse him his harmless pleasure." Sherlock relit his pipe.

Suddenly Lily fidgeted about. Her face took on a strange cast, a look of perplexity, as if pushing something away, rejecting it. I asked, "Did I offend with my rude humor? I must apologize, dear Miss Loder-Symmons."

Wanly, her voice weak, she said, "If you will excuse me, all. I feel strongly the agitation that accompanies a message's arrival. This more strongly than before."

Lily's writing desk was at the wall opposite the nook. She faced into the room and had a splendid view through the windows across the room as far as the distant stands of trees. Lily stood, unsteady on her feet. "May I help you, Lily?" I rose to join her. Haltingly, leaning heavily on my arm, she made her way to her desk. She took pen in hand, placed her arm in the apparatus.

To me the detective whispered, "An entertainment for my benefit? You old Scottish jokester." And to the group, but still more to himself: "I believe they are taking us in. The coincidence of our conversation and this event is too striking."

None replied.

Short of mortification, and on the heels of our present conversation, I did not look forward to Lily demonstrating her meager talent as an automatic writer. "This is most unusual," I said by way of excuse, apology, knowing the quality of Lily's transcriptions and what we were likely to see. Her writings contained many errors—the wrong name, or place, or time. Mistaken accounts of events. Much of it seemingly pure whimsy, like bad versions of Edward Lear's nonsense verse, or pure gibberish. Much of it made no sense at all. I wanted Miss Loder-Symmonds to have something to engage her interest, so I had her keep on with the practice. I read all she wrote over the past weeks. I regretted that the arch-skeptic should see folly reveal itself. And with the Lodges in attendance.

But, ever the amiable host, I said, "By all means. Lily is new to this. She does it principally for entertainment. She is not serious about it."

"What do you mean, Sir Arthur?" Lily fumed. "I take this with the greatest seriousness. You wound me, sir. Upon my honor, you owe me an apology. If I were a man and this any century other than the present one, I would slap you with my glove. Then it would be pistols at twenty paces or swords. To say such a thing, let alone think it!" She being near trance, it was almost as if a personality other than Lily's spoke. While I had offended, her outburst was most uncharacteristic.

"I do apologize," I hastened to say. It was an hour of apologies, me the offending party.

Returning to my chair, my back to Lily, I heard a violent rattle, a clatter of the contraption shaking. At the same time a sharp, deep growl arose from Lily's throat, followed by irregular gasps, as if someone was forcing her to breathe, a lifeguard resuscitating someone pulled from the sea, nearly drowned. I turned and looked at Lily. She shivered. Perspiration broke out on her upper lip and forehead. She was under terrible strain. She trembled convulsively. I worried that she was suffering a seizure, a fit of some sort. Then, as if shocked, Lily's body stiffened, "Something extraordinary is happening. The word 'transpiring' comes to mind," she said, laughing loudly, unladylike. She went on. "An unfamiliar part of my mind speaks now. Not the ordinary Lily." Then she gasped, her lungs inflated as if a sudden rush of air had filled them. Then she blew the air out, her sternum dropping deeply into her chest, followed by another deep inhalation. "My breath seems to be breathing me," she said, laughed again. "Transpiring. Breathing across, if I recall my little Latin, root and prefix." Her eyes rolled up, only the whites showed. Her hand began to move, then descended on the paper and wrote.

All observed. "I hope nothing is wrong," said Holmes. "You are her physician. But from your offer of a cigar to someone with lung problems, I should say a bad one."

"But it appears to do with Lily's automatic writing," said Sir Oliver. Turning to me, he continued, "If anything noteworthy is to happen, your home would be a likely place." He turned to Holmes. "Don't you think so?" he asked.

Sherlock Holmes did his best to mask his exasperation. Yet he was puzzled. His thoughts at work, reason and cogitation in his febrile brain manifested themselves in his wrinkled brow and left leg crossed over right slowly bouncing, as if, of all things, he was confounded, dumbfounded.

Up until now Holmes believed all instances of what is called psychic phenomenon to be fraudulent. Even now he could not tell if this was fakery. We rest, on the other hand, watched in eager interest.

Then, almost as soon as they began, the tremblings ceased and the sounds–unintelligible vocalizations–died away. Lily entered into trance more deeply than she ever had before. The whites of her half-closed eyes stared vacantly. The four of us stayed where we were so as not to interfere with what was happening. Twilight darkened the room. Lady Oliver clasped her hands tightly on her lap. My wife, who had taken up her knitting, a scarf for the butler's baby daughter, set it down, watched.

I motioned for my guests and Jean to quietly cross the drawing room. The Lodges and my wife seated themselves on a sofa alongside Lily's desk, though too low to see the top of her desk. I stood beside them, also too far to read what she wrote. Was it legible? What message might it convey?

Quiet as a cat, Holmes approached close enough to look over Lily's shoulder, watch her pen write, seemingly of its own accord, across the page. He was not close enough, however, to read what she transcribed. In her earlier attempts Lily wrote in haltingly, spasmodic jerks, the writing difficult to decipher. This time Lily's hand glided smoothly, purpose-fully. She would pause momentary and seemed to listen intently. Then her fingers took up their task again. In the past the sessions lasted for a minute or so, and the communication would end. I took out my pocket watch and noted the time she began writing, and when she stopped. She wrote fully three minutes, stopping as suddenly as she had begun.

Lily slowly returned to herself. We remained quiet, did not move. Holmes approached her desk. "May I, Miss Loder-Symmons?"

"Indeed, sir."

He took up the pages and read. His brow wrinkled in perplexity. "Humph," he said. "Conan Doyle, come look." Holmes went on, "Whose handwriting is this? Do you recognize it?"

Captain Leckie's Handwriting

I thought, what sort of question is that? As if I would recognize a spirit's handwriting. Holmes added, "Please come, Lady Doyle. You, too."

"I fear you have bad news, terrible news. Tell me, Sir Arthur," Jean said.

Her brother, Malcolm Leckie, and I were the closest of friends, though twenty years apart in age. We delighted in each other's company and conversation. When he visited at Windelsham in good weather, during the day we played lawn tennis, billiards all evening. We hunted together, fished, even boxed each other, and fenced. A medical officer in the Royal Army Medical Corps, he was attached to the Egyptian Army for the past four years, serving in the Sudan, up the Blue Nile and in Upper Egypt. We corresponded regularly, but saw each other rarely. A few months ago he returned to England, now Captain Leckie. Our reunion was heartfelt, a pleasure for us all.

Germany declared war on France. On 4 August King George declared war on Germany. Eleven days later Malcolm sailed for France with the First Royal Fusiliers, among the first of the British Expeditionary Force to reach Belgium.

Before my eyes, the message. The slant of the letter, the bold stroke. A pen in the hands of a military, medical man. The horrid punctuation for which he was infamous. I hastily read the first words to myself–"I am dead in body. Nevermore shall we meet in the flesh"–my heart came near to bursting, tears rose, blurring my vision. "One moment, please." I wiped the tears, wiped my fogged reading glasses.

I skimmed the document. I said to myself, then aloud, "Malcolm tells us that he is dead in body, but he lives on. His writing this message confirms that his soul lives on."

Jean gasped when I spoke his name. Indiscreet on my part, but what was I to say?

She cried, softly sobbing. "Malcolm! My dear brother," she moaned. "My dear, dear brother!" My wife loved him with the deepest love a sister can have for the splendid brother he was.

"Sir Arthur, will you kindly read to us Miss Loder-Symmons' transcription?" asked Holmes. I took the paper in hand and said, "I will read it, dear Lily."

The note told of St. George and a horde of angels standing between the British and the German army, saving the BEF from slaughter. It told of Malcolm being struck in the neck by shrapnel while tending the wounded near the battlefield at the Belgian city of Mons on August 23. In Surry we knew little of Belgium, nothing of Mons or a battle. We knew that there was bound to be fighting, where or when we knew not.

There had been no news up about the fighting. Military censorship.

The message said the Germans captured him. When he was dying of his wounds, he was exchanged for an important German soldier–a Von Arnim, Lily wrote. Who he was we had no idea. Malcolm was treated in ambulance hospital, dying in an angel's arms, another angel lifting him up, carrying him to his new life. He died this very night, just hours ago, in military hospital somewhere across the French border, Frameries. His transmission told of many deaths, divine intercession, himself dead but still in battle. How could that be? Still in the battle? Confusion in the letter it seemed.

Malcolm's message ended with the words, "Even as Lily writes, I am in this room with you, my dear ones. I can report the words spoken, who is there. Since Lily was in the room these could be taken as her observations. I am Captain Malcolm Leckie, now in spirit. I greet you from the other world."

Lily had scrawled the word fiancé across the page, at the end of the communication. I did not know what to make of this.

All were silent. The message had struck us dumb.

A Test

After a pause of several moments Holmes said, "As to his death, that will await notification from the Army. I hope that Malcolm lives. I know Miss Loder-Symmons is honest and a loving friend to Malcolm. What happened? Was this a quirk of the mind? We must test, determine if the message is authentic. You agree, Professor Lodge?"

"Indeed," the eminent physicist replied. "Arthur, you must formulate a test question."

Conversant with the practices of psychical research, nonetheless, my dear wife was distressed by our attempt to communicate with her brother. Especially if we confirmed that he was dead–her greatest fear. To Jean I said, "Dear, we must determine if the message is from Malcolm." Then I said, "Allow me a moment to reflect, Sir Oliver."

Then, turning to Lily, I said, "I will write and dictate a question. Malcolm's spirit, if it is he, will have two channels for receiving the message. After you read the question, we shall see if an answer comes, and if it does, if it is correct. Neither prompt nor resist any words or writing that wish to come through." I wrote my question and its answer, sealed it in an envelope, and gave it to Holmes to hold. Then I said, "Malcolm, what is the significance of the guinea coin attached to my watch fob?"

We waited. By my watch, fully two minutes passed. Then, with the same rapidity with which she wrote before, Lily wrote, "Friendship, kinship, remembrance." Lily stopped, as if frozen, then wrote the words, "First fee a patient paid for my medical services. I gave you. Token of professional connection." The writing stopped again. We thought the message was finished. Then it took up again. "Attached guinea, keep friendship in mind."

"Mr. Holmes," she said, "Please read." He read the reply.

I said, "That is precisely correct. It can only be a communication from Malcolm."

Sherlock Holmes asked, "Is it not possible that Lady Jean or Miss Loder-Symmons overheard the conversation. At some time in the past Malcolm mentioned this?"

"No," I said. "Ladies, did you ever hear me or Malcolm talk about this gift? Speak honestly. A great deal depends upon it."

"No, my dear," said Jean. "I never wondered. I never paid any attention to the coin."

"Nor I," said Lily. "However, your question and Malcolm's answer quite frightens me. I doubted that the soul lives on after death. Doubted, as any sensible, intelligent person would, in the face of uncertainty."

Adding his sentiments, Holmes said, "Though not thought of as a man of great sympathy, largely thanks to your husband's portrayal of me, I feel deeply for you, Lady Doyle. You, too, Doyle. I know Dr. Leckie is much loved and esteemed. You speak so highly of him. I yet hope to meet him one day."

Even so, Holmes persisted in his skepticism. He raised again the possibility that Miss Loder-Symmon had heard an account of the coin. "Perhaps without your recalling ever having spoken about the guinea and no one recalling having heard mention of it, such a conversation took place. We are poor at recalling every conversation, especially when at the time the information seemed trivial, insignificant."

Lily Loder-Symmons spoke to Jean, her voice small, weak, quavering. "I am so sorry. The words came so swiftly. I did not know what words my hand had written. I see ugly words. I am terribly sorry." She said, "I knew no more what is on these pages than you did before you read it." She buried her face in her hands and sobbed.

Lady Lodge moved a chair over and asked, "May I sit with you, Miss Loder-Symmons? These past moments have tried you greatly." She opened her shawl and wrapped Lily's shoulders in it, calming and comforting her. "You shiver, my dear."

Jean wept softly. I went to her, held her hand.

Lady Lodge spoke up. "I should like us to be able to sign an affidavit in good faith, a document for history, for posterity."

Holmes absorbed the import of what she said. He said, "Sir Arthur, you know I am deeply skeptical in these matters. Before I sign such a declaration, I need to be closer to certainty. Our signatures are a bond, a pledge that what we attest to is true." Holmes asked, "Sir Arthur, would you be so kind as to ask a second confirming question? This is a matter of great moment, as you say. A second question, please, sir. If I am satisfied with the question, and the query elicits the correct answer, I will sign the document you propose, Lady Lodge."

Sir Oliver said, "Your reasoning is sound, Mr. Holmes, just as it always seems to be in Sir Arthur's stories about you, sir."

"Thank you, sir. However, in the case of the tales of Sherlock Holmes, all the reasoning comes from the mind of our friend Doyle himself. As well as his mischaracterization of me, and his fictional, foolish Dr. Watson, who cannot seem to put two and two together. By that I mean his Watson cannot draw perfectly obvious conclusions from evidence. He turned to Conan Doyle and asked, "Have I given you sufficeient time to formulate a question?"

As if she had not listened to the conversation, Lady Lodge interjected, "A tragic, horrid dilemma. In one way we wish the message to be authentic, in another, wish it not to be. My dear, you are surrounded at this moment by those who understand and love you. We shall see this through."

The Lodge's youngest son, Raymond, along with one hundred thousand young men, was readying himself to enter his Majesty's service. I saw the worry on his parent's countenances. Surely, they thought of the risk their beloved son would face, especially now, when they considered Captain Leckie's death.

Just before Malcolm left to rejoin his battalion, we played a last game of billiards. Ordinarily I won. However, in that game Malcolm played well, beating me by a substantial score. I had not played since. The counters for that game still hung on wires over the table. I wrote, "Who won the final billiards game we played? What was the score?" I wrote at the bottom. Leckie won 500 to 477. I slipped the sheet of paper into the envelope, and stamped the melted red sealing wax with my signet. I returned to the drawing room, handed the envelope to Dr. Lodge.

The Answer

"I wrote two questions and answers," I said. By now Lily had composed herself. She sat at her desk again to receive the message. She closed her eyes, placed her arm in the sling, hand poised above the paper, pen ready. After a few moments the mechanism shook, though not violently as before. Soon she wrote "500 to 477. I won."

Dr. Lodge opened the envelope and read my note. I took them to the billiard room to see the beads marking the counters.

Holmes said, "This is the best we can do for the moment. Since you psychical fellows believe in a vast number of so-called phenomena, it is yet possible that there is yet another explanation. The evidence is fascinating, compelling, but not yet conclusive." Pausing as much to think light as to his pipe again, Sherlock Holmes continued. "Until we know that he who we would mourn is in need of our grief, it is not yet time to adopt the mourner's face and garb. Beyond that, we must discover that if he died before Miss Loder-Symmons received this transmission. After all, it is possible that he is alive now, and will not be so in the near future."

Professor Lodge said, "In any case, Holmes, you concede that this information was not transmitted by speech or writing."

"Yes, Sir Oliver."

Lodge said, "Please, Sir Arthur, write up a memorandum of these events for us all to sign. Are all agreeable? Any with insurmountable reservations?"

"Pardon me, Sir Oliver. Please allow me to draft the report," said Sherlock Holmes.

"I would expect the person with objections to be you, Holmes," I said.

"All the more important that I write the document." Holmes turned to me and asked, "Have you a typewriter?" To the right of the baronial staircase and beneath it was my secretary's office. I set Holmes up there. When I left him he closed the door. We heard the slow clicking of typewriter keys, the machine being new to Holmes, a pause, and typing underway again.

Recovering herself, ever the woman of good sense and decorum, ever the hostess concerned for her guests, Jean asked, "Could I offer anyone more coffee or tea, a drink while Mr. Holmes writes?" We passed our cups to her for filling. Lodge and I smoked our cigars. All were silent. In ten minutes Holmes emerged from the office, a single page memorandum and three carbon duplicates in hand. "Please read. I have been brief, yet thorough. If revision is necessary, I will type the document again."

We read. The document was forthright, plain, accurate. It avoided the language of psychic phenomenon, but did not misrepresent what had taken place. Holmes had typed in each of our names and a line beneath upon which to apply our signatures.

I said, "Miss Loder-Symmons, your pen, please." Then to all: "You must press rather hard. We want all the copies to show your signature. But not so hard that the ink runs."

Lady Lodge and the maid helped Lily to her room.

Then I saw the Lodges out, bid them good night. Holmes was shaking my hand in parting. I said, "Sherlock, a moment, please." We stepped back into the vestibule. I said, "I will not be satisfied until I know the facts about Malcolm. As you said, we do not know for certain. May we lay plans?"

"Of course, my dear Doyle."

"Come back in. Lady Jean will join us."

They sat again in the room where Lily had transcribed the message. It began, "I thought I would request a meeting with Winston Churchill. He's an active sort and able to get things done."

Lady Jean already had a plan. "You will do no such thing, my dear. Malcolm is my brother. You will only aggravate Winston. He wants to get his hands on you, I am sure, for your letter to the *Times*. I know you, my dear. You will engage him in debate. He will send you away before you even present your request. Here is what I will do. I shall arrange a meeting through Lady Churchill. We serve on charities to care for wounded soldiers. Even now, her sister works in a field hospital. Lady Churchill will be willing to help me find out about my brother. In that way your meeting with Winston will be a formality, giving him occasion to accede to your humble request for help. I shall write your script and you shall not deviate from it. There is too much at stake for me to risk your blundering."

"Excellent plan, Lady Doyle. Extraordinary evening, Sir Arthur."

The men shook hands and Holmes departed.

In the Library

(Memorandum to myself, private)

After Lily and Jean had gone to bed, I studied the two pages Lily wrote. I opened my personal diary, not my commonplace book, and wrote. "A new stage of my life has begun. I am convinced that the transmission we received from Malcolm Leckie is genuine. He is dead in body and living in spirit. I have seen one of the four 1215 'exemplifications,' as they are called, of Magna Carta and a Guttenberg Bible at the British Museum. Marvelous, monumentally important. This document stands apart, declaring a truth even more important than the declaration that even a king is subject to law, and Mr. Guttenberg's Bible. The import of the letter is greater than these. If I find that Malcolm is dead, and he died the way he describes I will be compelled to believe that the spirit lives on after death. We will have evidence beyond dispute that what religion teaches and many believe–bodily life is a phase and not life's totality–is true. And I will believe that Malcolm communicated with us. However, we shall have to wait."

I paused, mused, then wrote on. "There is no doubt that something compelled Miss Loder-Symmons' hand to write those words in that penmanship. The replies to my questions are evidence. Are there other means by which such communications could take place? Are the events the communication recounts supported by facts?"

"These communications erased my doubts that the soul survives death. Myers was convincing, but now I have first-hand evidence. I will discover at the cost of the loss of a dear brother in-law if our path does not end at bodily death. Is it worth the cost? Many will die in this war, with nothing gained or learned. Deep irony. As in fairy tales where a wish is granted, but the consequences of its fulfillment unforeseen, unwelcome." I set down my pen, blotted the page, and closed the book.

How long will we wait to find out?

Already I know that many whose sons, brothers, husbands, fathers, nephews, neighbors, friends are no more, would soon share our grief when the news of casualties comes.

Chapter Fourteen

W. B. Yeats, Arthur Machen's "The Bowmen", and the Battle of Le Cateau

Woburn Buildings
Lodgings of William Butler Yeats
London, England
26 August, 1914

If a man could pass through Paradise in a dream, and have a flower presented to him as a pledge that his soul had really been there, and if he found that flower in his hand when he awoke—Ay!—and what then?'

Anima Poetae from the Unpublished Note-Books
Samuel Taylor Coleridge

A Heavenly Army Arose to Save Them

(Yeats's Vision)

Yeats arrived at his flat, tired, consumed with the war just under way, agitated from a morning of political debate and wrangling. He had listened much, spoken little. Should Ireland stand with England or withhold its support? Who was in the right, who wrong? What of France? What of Germany? The spiritual dimension of the war was uppermost in his mind. This war, he fathomed, was between good and evil, God and the devil. Long and terrible it would be.

Hoping to calm his mind, he lay on his couch, closed his eyes, breathed rhythmically, recited an invocation to a meditation. The practice was simple, without trappings or ceremony. He asked for guidance, help, wisdom. Hierophant, or head, of the Hermetic Order of the Golden Dawn, he drew on the highest practices he had at his command, raised his spiritual vibration to its highest level.

His daemon had taught him prayers, postures. Years before at a séance a voice, the spirit of Leo Africanus–al-Hasan ibn Mohammed al-Wezaz, al-Fasi–called out, "Mr. Yeats, I have been with you since your birth." Thereafter, through séances, card readings, and automatic writing Yeats and Africanus carried on an esoteric dialogue. Africanus was his teacher, his guide, his Genius.

Soon, Yeats was taking on many forms–animate, inanimate–and many sizes–the sun, an amoeba, King Solomon, a dying dog. Often he was in several realms at once–inside a tree, within a horse, in the ocean's depths, at the earth's molten core. He could be anywhere at any time–moments in history, anyone, a simple peasant, an ancient mystic.

Soon–Yeats knew not how much time had passed–he was astride a horse, a Pegasus, high in the air, two hundred feet above the ground. The poet rode in the midst of cantering cavalry, dress and weapons a welter of past times–knights in medieval armor–riding horses caparisoned–cavalry wearing tricorn hats, long red coats, swords drawn, standards aflutter in the wind–ahead, behind, left and right, a horde. No soldier, Yeats was the only one not in military uniform. He carried no weapon.

The mystic heard his horse's breathing, felt its ribs expand and contract, felt its heart as it raced. He heard the clanking of ancient armor, jangling harness, swords in scabbards, saddles' creak. The odor of horse sweat was thick in the poet's nostrils. Suspended in sky, with the sway of the horses' running only, no clatter of hooves. Yeats held the reins lightly, the leather rough and warm in his hands, his feet planted in the stirrups. All about him was cavalry row upon row, pikes, lances, studded clubs ready. Before and behind, to the left and right, perfect formation. Sunlight glinted from steel weapons, helmets, armor. The faces of the soldiers about him were sternly empty, as if they were gazing into the void. Neither word nor whisper.

The ground grew closer. Below Yeats were farm fields of northern France. One hundred feet below and ahead, he saw the British Expeditionary Force, modern rifles, modern artillery. Facing them, the Germans, thinly spread, advancing. The soldier to his right, insignia of the caduceus on his lapel, turned to Yeats, spoke to him telepathically. "Mr. Yeats, sir, I greet you. I am Captain Malcolm Leckie, RMAC. Excepting you, every horse and rider here is in spirit only. In my case, shrapnel at Mons. Prisoner of war. Returned to hospital. This very morning passed on. Expecting you. Eager for your presence. Sir Arthur Conan Doyle–my brother in-law."

In utter surprise, Yeats replied, "Sir Arthur? Indeed!" Yeats knew of Conan Doyle's deep interest in psychical phenomena and questions of the soul's life.

Looking upon the panorama unfolding before them, Yeats said, "Captain, I have been here before."

"I know it, sir. I do not read poetry. Though my fiancée recited "The Wandering Angus' to me at our engagement party. I am again a wanderer in this realm new to me.

I learned from mystics in Egypt, India. You've been here in imagination."

"In *The Wind among the Reeds* is 'The Valley of the Black Pig.' What I see below I saw in the vision that gave rise to the poem." And he recited, as their horses and the company wheeled through the sky:

The dews drop slowly and dreams gather; unknown spears

Suddenly hurtle before my dream-awakened eyes,

And then the clash of fallen horsemen and the cries

Of unknown perishing armies beat about my ears.

We who still labour by the cromlech on the shore,

Being weary of the world's empires, bow down to you,

Master of the still stars and of the flaming door."

"This, indeed, is your valley of the black pig," Leckie said. "Below is something more, greater than the poem." Then he observed, "Few cross to the world of Spirit alive in the flesh. Enoch. Now you. Fewer return to bodily life. Jesus. Now you. This once, you are a messenger between worlds, our Hermes. Yes, you were given this poem. Now you see its events before you. Indeed, sir, you are privileged, and bear the burden of responsibility."

Out of his blouse pocket Captain Leckie took a prescription pad and pen, scribbled as they rode. "Deliver this note," he said. Yeats stuck the paper deep in his trousers pocket.

"To Conan Doyle?" the poet asked.

"To Conan Doyle. Yes, Mr. Yeats. Together you and he will piece together the puzzle's meaning. Each of you holds half. You, the mystic, he the seeker for the truth of realms beyond the ordinary. Together, you shall prosper in your quests."

For no reason Yeats could explain, the cobbler's son, who lived behind the shop at Woburn Buildings, Tommy Atkins, came to mind, and the words "eternal travail." Yeats knew what the words meant, but no idea to what they applied. Yeats last saw the lad in his crisp, new uniform, kiss his mum, shake his father's hand goodbye. The poet gave the young soldier a friendly salute. The boy returned it earnestly. Then arose the thought: The boy might be in this battle, young and fresh though he is. Then an image, real as life: Young Private Tommy Atkins, indeed, rising through the air in a whirlwind of golden light, he among many, saved from death by a miracle as momentous as Yeats's own. The mystic's heart filled. He sobbed with unexpected relief for the boy and his family, a soldier he knew only by sight and an occasional nod of greeting. A vision within a vision. A visitation from a distant event, Yeats was certain. Then the image faded, Yeats again riding, the horse's mane whipping in the wind, its neck thrust forward in fervid chase.

Then the horses plunged toward the ground, now straining at the reins, eager for battle. They ran to earth. The frantic hooves of hundreds of horses added to the symphony of war. The sound battered Yeats's ears, the feuding light of bombs exciting the eye. Dirt flew up from the ground spattering his clothes and face, his hands. The angel soldiers fast approached a field thickly strewn with rocks and boulders and German soldiers. Yeats was terrified. The horses would likely stumble over stones in the rush forward. Suddenly the stones and rocks rose up out of the ground into the air, becoming infantry of past ages.

"Deucalion! Out of Greek mythology. Stone turned to flesh, rock to warriors," Yeats exclaimed. Bows in hand and arrows filled the quivers, soldiers of the long bow. Others were armed with crossbows, yet others wielded swords unsheathed. Steel helmets and thick cloth armor mingled with infantry armed with flintlock muskets and bayonets, wearing red coats and mitre caps. The foot soldiers loosed a fusillade of bolts and arrows as thick as torrential rain on the German soldiers. The twang of the bowstrings' release, arrows whistling piercing the air, the click of the crossbows' release, the sizzle of the bolt tearing on its way to the target split the ear. The cavalry flew at a gallop, infantry and cavalry occupying the battlefield. From the infantry angels' mouths flew the howling of hunting wolves. The angel horsemen took up a cry, tearing the air with a mingled cacophony, the rumbling of thunder with lightning's ear-splitting crash. Instantly arose German shouts and cries of terror, pangs of the wounded and dying.

The faces of the soldiers of the British Expeditionary Force shone with relief, the anxiety and terror of the moment replaced by relief. They saw salvation in the clouds of angel warriors descending to their aid.

As suddenly as the event commenced, it faded to darkness and silence. Gone was Leckie, gone the horses, the soldiers, the battlefield. For many hours Yeats's mind traveled between the vision and present reality—on his couch in his flat in Woburn Buildings. Then he recalled the unearthly battle, envisioned its outcome, uncertain to him, its violence vivid.

Yeats's experience was pure, transcendent, indelible. Reality beyond reality. The mystic apprehended several dimensions simultaneously, inhabited several states of being all at once. Time and eternity met, the profane intersected with the divine. The phenomenon lasted between an instant and an age. No way to measure time. The tick of time not followed by the tock. No time at all. The outer world disappeared.

From the shock of revelation Yeats's body shivered, trembled. His hands twitched. Even now randomly muscles spasmed. Sudden involuntary deep gasps, as if the breath breathed him, followed. Yeats's brow was drawn in deep concentration. The voice of his daemon, Leo Africanus spoke.

"This will shake the pillars of the metaphysical world. Reward for the initiation you underwent. You will be blessed with poetry deeper than what you wrote before, abundant. You shall earn high place in this world, and the Other."

Yeats was in rapture. "Such bliss. I am shot through with the fire of joy."

Africanus replied, "Yet another reward. Though, I must warn you. Tumult lies ahead. Alister Crowley, perpetrator. Arthur Machen, the dupe. Banish the one. Admonish the other."

For hours Yeats's mind traveled between vision and present reality–him on his couch, him in the saddle coursing over the field of battle.

He finally awoke at twilight, at first dizzy, mildly nauseated. Yeats smelled the dyes and polishes and leather from cobbler Atkins' shop below. He heard the tap tap of the cobbler's hammer, the whirr of the machine that trims the heel and sole to a fine finish. The jingling bell when customers came in and left. He reflected. For a time he lived in two worlds. He slept, he dreamed the vision again, he woke, and slept, dreamed, woke again. A day and a night passed. All the while he had not stirred from his flat. He could not recollect the sequence of events.

Yeats In Mackerson's Pub

28 August

Yeats seated himself in a booth in old Mr. Mackerson's pub, Mackerson himself, the publican's garters holding his shirtsleeves tight around his thick, folded arms, taking his order. Mr. Mackerson asked, "Pint to greet the day, Mr. Yeats? Though, from the looks of ye, its a cup of coffee you need."

"Coffee, please. Piece of steak and kidney pie. I am famished."

"Been at the poetry, have you? Keeping you busy?" Pouring a mug of coffee from a carafe, Mr. Mackerson said, "Your good luck. Hot from the oven." He called the order to the cook.

Yeats asked, "What do I owe, Mr. Mackerson? I'll pay now so as not to trouble you later."

"No trouble, Mr. Yeats, but pay now if you like."

From his trouser pocket, the poet drew out a handful of bills. Among them was the scribbled note. Its meaning overwhelmed Yeats. As Saul, struck by revelation on the road, became Paul, so William Butler Yeats, Hierophant of the Hermetic Order of the Golden Dawn, Keeper of the Vault, in Mackerson's pub, drew forth a confirmation. After decades of cultivation–diligent study of a multitude of mystical texts, training, devoted practice, discipleship, initiations, tests, explorations, rites, rituals, ceremonies, invocations, and meditation–came the harvest, proof of journey, proof of his quest's success. The living battle. A doctor's prescription page, name and rank, a few words scrawled.

Yeats muttered to himself, "How long did the apotheosis last?"

Overhearing, but not understanding, Mackerson asked, "What's that, Mr. Yeats?"

"Sorry. I spoke without realizing." A headline on the day's copy of the Evening Standard a customer left behind caught his eye. He read the story, turned to the page where it was continued to read the end. On that page was the title "The Bowmen" and the name, Arthur Machen. "Take the paper if you like," said Mackerson. He read while he ate, surprised and amazed.

Yeats finished his slice of pie, gulped his coffee, and hurried off. "Good day, Mr. Mackerson."

"So soon, Mr. Yeats? I had hoped to have a word with you. Your opinion about this war."

"My view, sir? Yeats mused, "The nations of Europe are at each other's throats. You can smell blood in the air. Politicians, propagandists whip up the crowd's fervor and Europe is hysterical. The world is a carnival, a circus, a rowdy fair. Soon, Mr. Mackerson, we will see."

"A short war, do you believe?"

"When have they ever been short? In ancient days only. But not now, I don't think."

"Hoping you are wrong, sir."

"So am I. Thank your wife for the pie. Good as always. The pie, I mean. Your wife as well, of course."

He reached into his pocket, felt the paper, reassured himself that opening and reading the note was not itself a hallucination, residue of his recent vision. If not for this scrap, he would think it a wild fantasy, keep the matter to himself. The poet wondered if the Times would report a battle in northern France, and give the date. Perhaps the battle, but not the horde of cavalry on the wings of the air, angels, warriors returned from the dead, he was certain.

The event opened the realm, if not of paradise, than at least the certainty of a beyond. Not yet sure what it meant, nor what it portended.

Yeats, The Hermetic Order of the Golden Dawn, and the Angels of the Dark Cloud

That night Yeats convened the Sphere in his flat, the three principal members and himself, the inner circle of the Hermetic Order of the Golden Dawn. In a magisterially uncomfortable chair sat MacGregor Mather, who brought the Western Mystery Tradition and angelic magic to life. Sober of judgment, his opinion was sought by initiates and adepts alike.

From the kitchen cove came the clatter of kettle and teapot, the tinkling of teacups, saucers, and spoons and the oven door's squeaking as Maud Gonne set out refreshments. Favored with great beauty, deep intelligence, political acumen, and insight, her opinions were also valued. Tall, elegant in posture and movement, dress, well-spoken with a penetrating, melodic voice, she had captured Yeats's heart. He had inducted Maud Gonne into the order, partly in the hope of romantic success, partly because she was eager to develop her considerable psychic powers. They awaited the arrival of the Praemonstratrix, Florence Farr.

Pacing the floor, Aleister Crowley, arch-magician, practitioner of the dark arts, a member, but not of the Sphere, barely contained himself. "I gave up an enjoyable evening. I've waited for Florence long enough. Begin without her." The mystical, esoteric, and occult societies shunned Crowley, perpetrator of many scenes, the center of scandals, object of complaints. Aleister Crowley, massive in frame and face, dark hair matching his dark, hypnotic eyes, his modulated voice, and flamboyant gestures made him a compelling figure. He spoke with authority and bombast, drawing adherents and sycophants, as well as detractors and enemies, to his occult notions. A chameleon, he insinuated himself into occult societies, then did all he could to control them.

Having recommended the young author, Arthur Machen, to the Order of the Golden Dawn, of which he was a member, he attended this night at Yeats's insistence.

From the kitchen Maud Gonne spoke up, "Your convenience and comfort do not come foremost in everyone's thoughts. Your bullying gains you no friends."

"Why call on me, then?"

Carrying the tray, Maud entered the parlor. "My friend, you shall soon learn why we are here. We will begin when Florence arrives."

Years before, under a full moon, Yeats and George Bernard Shaw saw Florence Farr as Priestess Amaryllis in "A Sicilian Idyll". Both loved her starling beauty. Shaw wrote Louka in "Arms and the Man" for her. For Florence, Yeats created the character of Aleel, the minstrel, in "The Countess Cathleen." Aleel peers into the Spirit world, just as Florence did as Praemonstratrix in the Order. Expert in alchemy, Egyptian magic, and the I Ching, Miss Farr's greatest strengths were in skrying in the Spirit Vision and divining with the crystal. Yeats took her to be his poetic muse. Her voice alone he judged worthy of reciting his poetry.

As a church bell tolled midnight a knock came at the door below. Yeats went down to greet Florence. "I'm tired, Willie. The performance tonight went well. Your play opens soon. Too soon. My character still eludes me. But you said we are to talk about Arthur Machen. He is advancing in study and practice. I expect good things of him."

"Of course, we shall see."

"Is he here?"

"He is not here." They reached the top of the stairs. "Tea? Maud baked scones."

Aleister Crowley grumbled, "It's about time, Soror Farr. I gave up a lovely night's entertainment to be here."

"Frater Aleister," she said petulantly. "Your greeting is not welcoming. I work at night. I am an actress."

Having poured tea for everyone, Maud sat beside Yeats on the couch.

"Now that we are all here we can begin." After reciting the Order's pledge, Yeats said, "To business. Aleister, you sponsored Arthur Machen. You are his mentor."

The acerbic Crowley snarled, "Barely know the man. Met him at a meeting of some sort. He asked me to introduce you, so I did. That is the extent of it. Hack publicist. Penny-a-word newspaper writer. People wrap their refuse in his words every day."

"From what you describe, you know him quite well." Yeats said.

"Reputation only."

"Slippery, you are Frater Crowley. For that reason I researched the minutes and find this," said Yeats, holding a handwritten page attesting to Crowley's mentorship of Machen. "Should I read?"

"Don't bother with your scribbles. Your point?"

Taking the copy of the *Evening Standard* from a side table drawer, William said, "Arthur Machen's 'The Bowmen'. What do you know about it?"

"A story? What should I know about his story? I do not read newspaper fiction."

Mather said, "Not a newspaper any of us read. What have you to complain of, William?"

"Headline caught my eye. Not even about Machen's story. Sometimes something seeming to mean nothing leads to something of importance. Such was the case here. My point: 'The Bowmen' represents a danger to the Order. Contrary to what you claim, Frater Crowley, you know a good deal about acolyte Machen's story. If we do not find out from you tonight, we will find out from acolyte Machen. For now we hold him incommunicado. He comes in the morning."

Yeats continued. "No need for hiding, evasion, deception. I know how Arthur gained his vision, my dear Brother Crowley. And so do you. Do you wish to speak and confess? Or be mortified when others hear me tell what you have done?"

"I have not been accused, so I admit nothing. You'll not trap me."

"William, what is your complaint?" asked Maud Gonne. "What happened?"

Africanus Comes to His Aid

Yeats sipped his tea, took a bite of scone, another sip of tea. All of a sudden his body quivered, then shook, his frame stiffened, rigid. Maud held him from falling from the couch. Shocked, the members of the Sphere looked on. His lips drew back, clenched teeth revealed. His breath came in deep, irregular gasps. A gurgling, a guttural growl came from deep in his throat. Tortured, ghastly, inhuman sounds. Garbled syllables tumbled over each other. His jaw gaped open, snapped shut, teeth clacking. He snarled like a wolf. A voice not Yeats's, accent heavily tinged with Arabic, boomed, hesitant, then shooting forth a word or phrase at a time, stammering, stuttering. Yeats's vocal cords slowly released, tongue cleaved from the roof, his breath worked at the Spirit's will.

"I am Leo Africanus, Lion of Africa, One of the Circle, Daemon to the Keeper of the Vault, his Genius, his ever-reflective soul. I occupy his mind, his voice and body to reveal the truth." In several words the voice stressed the wrong syllable. "I come to accuse, judge, and punish the. . . ." Anticipating what the Genius would say next, Yeats uttered the word "betrayer." A pause in the transmission, and shivering, quaking, gasps, groans. Leo Africanus spoke again. "Poet, do not interrupt. You are the goblet from which the wine of my words pours forth. Among you is an evildoer, an enemy. I will not speak the accursed name of the beast of three sixes."

All saw the numerals, vague at first, but more and more distinct, on Crowley's forehead.

The group was astonished. None had been in the presence of such phenomena. Each of the inner circle silently invoked Spirit, sealed themselves in white light to protect them from the evil manifest in the room.

"The arch-fiend, for such he is," Africanus bellowed, "Has much to do with Arthur Machen's story."

Concerned for Yeats's wellbeing, Mather asked, "Where is William?" Africanus said, "We are together as one." Yeats's body relaxed. He spoke in a voice greatly strained, but nearer his own. "I am William. I am two at once. I see through my eyes and his, hear with his ears and mine. He speaks with my voice."

Then Yeats's torso became rigid again, lunged forward, arms extended. He drew them back, his wrist raised as on puppeteer's strings. Inches from his face, his thumbs and index fingers touched, a triangle. Though this space he gazed, his eyes vacant, unseeing. Then the index finger of his right hand trembling, shot forth again, pointed at Crowley's massive chest. "Heart of ice, soul of filth! Maligner, destroyer by falsehood, rumor, lies. Frater Crowley plots to establish his own school of thought, Arthur his unsuspecting dupe, his tool. Machen incapable of achieving the vision he saw on his own." Now the daemon's voice, a harsh croak, addressed Crowley. "You intercepted the vision vouchsafed the Keeper of the Vault Yeats. Hypnotized Machen. You sent the vision to the gullible acolyte's mind. You told him this was an election, an anointing. He would lead the new school. You did not tell him you are the puppeteer, he the puppet." And to the group: "Thus he planned."

When aroused, Crowley would be possessed by a frenzy or feign posses-sion. He rose to this state now. "I do not care what names and titles you give yourself. You daren't speak this way to me." Maud and Florence watched in amazement and fear as Aleister Crowley's neck thickened, veins in his temples throbbed and pulsed. His grimace took on a killing, devilish look. Recoiling at the words from William's lips, he nearly toppled from his chair.

"Contain yourself, Brother Crowley. Peace, sir. Peace. William may have over-spoken, but you must forgive him in the spirit of brotherly charity," said Florence. She stilled his rage.

Yeats took a handkerchief from his breast pocket, wiped saliva from his lips. Perspiring, exhausted, he said, "I speak, but it is not me who speaks."

In fear of what Aleister might do, Maud said, "William, please stop. You go too far."

Africanus, spoke, "Silence, soror! Attend to my words! Listen and learn! Aleister Crowley believes he occupies the heights, he Chaos, father of Jupiter and Zeus. He is wrong. The Circle guards mankind and works through me. I come to chastise and cast out this devil's child, this doer of evil." The voice said truly what Crowley had done.

Aleister's heavy face flamed, the blood thickening it. His eyes bulged from their sockets. A man hungry to bring disaster, cataclysm, apocalypse, he saw that he was doomed, his treachery his downfall. Crowley's body shrunk back into its seat, then sprung forward, as if propelled from behind. He leapt to his full height, breathed deeply, his breath sonorous with rage, his body expanding, his bulk menacing, his face florid with indignation.

He rushed at Yeats, exhaled with a bellow, "You blasphemous accuser! Discredit me? Hark! Hark! The arch-liar accuseth me! Story, story! Humbug, I say! So I leave." Through clenched teeth, and as if reciting a set speech, in a mocking tone Crowley said, "I came to be of service. I am attacked and vilified. Threats and affronts. I remove myself from this god-forsaken club! Dilettantes and poseurs! A vile accusation upon my name and honor!" Anger sealed his face.

Then, sending a tea tray, teacups, saucers, lamp, and books to the floor with a violent shove, Crowley wheeled from the room and stomped down the stairs, slamming the door. The frame shook, the window glass rattled.

Mather spoke. "He was on the verge of physical violence. Spiritual violence as well." None was strong enough to withstand a bodily attack. Spiritually, together they could stand against him. "But for the moment we are safe," said Mather.

"Even now he is plotting revenge. A curse. Set some evil against me," said Yeats.

Mather said, "The antipathy is beyond reconciliation. What we heard from William's lips is true. Do you concur?"

All gave their assent. "We conclude our judgment upon Crowley. He is expelled from the Order, all power of initiations, rights, and privileges revoked. We shall hear Machen before we decide about him."

"It is very late. We are exhausted from what just happened. Even so, I must tell you what has took place this past Wednesday and after. I shall make my account brief." Yeats described the events. He concluded, "And as I rode through the sky the soldier beside me called my name. Captain Leckie had died that morning of shrapnel wounds he received in battle at Mons in Belgium. He wrote a note and pressed it into my hand. I stuffed it into my trouser pocket. Brother in-law of Sir Arthur Conan Doyle."

"An amazing, not to say sad, fortuitous connection," observed Mather.

Yeats finished his account, saying, "I revived sufficiently by this morning to take a stroll. Air and exercise. I stopped at a pub for lunch. "When I went to pay I took out. . . ." Yeats reached into his pocket, drew out the piece of paper. "With the bills was this." He handed it to Maud. "Read, please."

Unfolding the paper she read, "'Guinea. Watch fob.' Then two sets of three numbers each. And the word 'fiancée.' William, what does they mean?"

"I do not know. But I shall find out."

The paper passed from hand to hand, held like a holy relic. The four saw the Royal Army Medical Corps insignia, the name Captain Malcolm Leckie, the scrawled words and numbers. The room was profoundly quiet, all immersed in wonder and thought. The Order's very purpose was to find passage to another world. It was what they diligently sought. The teachings they studied and practiced all were intended to bridge the gap between the worlds of matter and spirit, time and eternity, the divine and the worldly. Each knew that of all men, William Butler Yeats most warranted this passage. Each heart was sad at the death of this Captain Leckie, but joyful of his message.

"I have more to tell." Yeats took up a page from a leather folder. Went to my encyclopedia. Two words rose to mind. Crécy. Malplaquet. The Battle of Crécy, fought on August 26. The same date as the battle to which I was transported. Thus, the soldiers in the battle dress of that time."

"Willie, this is miraculous," exclaimed Florence.

"There is yet more." He read his notes, then said, "The Duke of Marlborough fought the French at Malplaquet. Seventeen nine. Near the battle I rode in. Beyond this, the Deacons of Mons, the Knights of St. George, and the Golden Arrows of God–soldier-citizens schooled in Christian esoteric practices–fought alongside the Duke. Many were killed. Legend claims that their spirits lurk in the ground, arise in time of calamity and war. Thus, I say, the soldiers wearing the garb and fighting with the weapons of Marlborough's day."

Mather spoke. "Same date as Crécy. Near Malplaquet. Remarkable."

All retreated into their thoughts of the momentous occurrence. What this implied for the Order, the world. The veil between the worlds had been pierced, if only for this moment. Time and space transcended. Yeats had passed through. A message transmitted. Physical evidence. Culmination and proof of the Order's practices and hopes.

Arthur Machen's "The Bowmen"

(His Account and Admission)

29 August, 1914

Maud Gonne asked, "William, what has this to do with Arthur Machen's story?"

He described "The Bowmen", reading passages and describing the events. Yeats concluded, "The events I experienced were the events in 'The Bowmen.' Machen added a few details to heighten dramatic affect. Removed some specifics, I suppose to avoid detection by the censors. Otherwise, it is as I said, an account of what I experienced."

Allowing some moments for his friends to reflect further, Yeats brought them to present needs. "Tomorrow morning the three of you must fetch Machen," said Yeats. "I sequestered him with the Todhunters. John took him there earlier this evening on the pretext of giving him a teaching. I needed to make it impossible for Crowley to reach him, tell him lies about what had happened, Crowley's interpretation of events, you could say. You must escort him here. Let acolyte Machen think he is in good standing. Do not worry him. Say nothing about what you now know. Africanus directed me to correct the man, not punish him. He is the innocent victim, Crowley, the guilty perpetrator. It is remarkable that Machen received the vision. His skills are worth cultivating. Crowley, of course, is highly skilled. But he works only for his own benefit and the devil's, not mankind's."

"Therein lies the difference," said Maud.

It being so late, Yeats gave up his bed to the women, he sleeping on his couch. MacGregor Mather made his way home, it not being far away.

Next morning the members of the Sphere arrived at Yeats's flat, Arthur Machen along with them. "How do you do, acolyte Machen?" asked Yeats, extending his hand for the sign. Since their meeting several months ago Machen had abandoned the look of a Russian Orthodox monk–long curly black beard, long wavy hair parted in the middle. Now, clean-shaven, hair cut to style, he dressed and carried himself like a proper man of business. Affable, welcome everywhere in London, he was a Fleet Street man, star journalist, properly established. His eager, energetic step took him to events of the day for the Evening News, where his writing was esteemed.

"Greetings, Hierophant Yeats. I have something to celebrate."

"Do you, indeed? What is that?"

"Yesterday the newspaper ran a story of mine, 'The Bowmen.' The public's response is already enthusiastic. A timely tale, the war being on. The publisher is printing five thousand copies in pamphlet, paying me quite handsomely. Need to write an introductory note by tomorrow noon."

"Celebration must wait," said the leader. "I sent you to Frater Todhunter not only for a lesson, but to put you out of the way. I will explain later. You are here at my command. Yet it is your story that brings us together. I read 'The Bowmen' and shared excerpts with the Sphere last night."

Then Machen noted consternation on the faces of the others, and worried at what might come. MacGregor Mather spoke. "But first we must enter holy conclave." Turning to Yeats, he said, "Keeper of the Vault, pray and recite our pledge."

In studied cadence, Yeats repeated the words then said, "The pledge concludes, 'I will not abuse the great power entrusted to me.' Yet, in 'The Bowmen' you describe our practice for opening the gates of vision. Reciting the sacred formula, your narrator invokes Isis, Pythagoras, and Hermes Trystistimus, and prays for inspiration. With the induction you revealed an Order's secret. You violated the pledge."

Machen was frightened. "You are right. I did what the story says. Then I entered a near-trance and wrote what I saw."

"You do not know that the rites opened your mind to Aleister Crowley's influence. From that moment on you were his instrument. He was with you when this took place. I know it."

"He was."

"Indeed, I will tell you how the story came to you. Crowley took you deep into trance while you still believed you were fully conscious. He planted what you saw in your consciousness. Crowley demonstrated his extraordinary powers, not yours."

Machen's head drooped in fear. Terrified, he asked, "Do you speak in metaphors? How could such a thing happen? Frater Crowley told me. . . ."

Maud Gonne interrupted.

"No more Frater Crowley." Maud Gonne went on. "He is banished from the Order. Admitting Crowley was our failing, was it not?"

"Blame my pride. He persuaded me he would serve the good of humankind. I was duped when I should have known. But, go on Machen."

"Crowley told me that altering the invocation corrupted it, so it would not work," said Machen. "The order of the names is changed."

"The serpent's wiles are plausible and pleasing," observed Magus Major Mather. "Crowley lied to you and knew he lied. Even when altered, our rites and ceremonies are powerful, dangerous in the hands of the uninitiated and uninstructed."

"Arthur Machen, what I tell you now is of greatest importance. The same events that you saw in your vision, Hierophant Yeats took part in." Said Maud, "An event unique in the history of spiritual seeking occurred. William rode with the angelic cavalry you saw. Did you notice a rider wearing a frock coat?" Said Maud.

"I did, and wondered at it."

"It was the Hierophant himself. What happened to our leader is far beyond what the multitude of dedicated seekers have achieved throughout the ages, Enoch excepted, Jesus excepted. The Other World took him, spirit and flesh, and returned him, spirit and flesh. A great revelation of the World Beyond, and you expose it. Could anything be worse?" Machen shivered in fear. "The universe hinges on such events, and you . . ."

"I truly did not know," said Machen. "I am heartsick."

"And so you should be."

"What can I do to make amends? Is there anything?"

"Of that, later, sir," said MacGregor Mather.

Yeats said, "The Order serves spiritual forces which work for the good of mankind. Crowley works against them. Your slip of the pen jeopardizes our careful work."

Machen, who came expecting congratulation, saw that so heinous was his error that he faced chastisement and penance, if not expulsion from the Order.

Yeats said, "Your story revealed secrets only the initiated should know. Your oath bound you to report what you saw and how you came to see it to us, not, God forefend, the *Evening Standard*."

Florence Farr spoke. "Your story announced the news, like the evangels of old, but to the wrong eyes and ears. Through you, Crowley undermines the Great Work. We do not yet know the consequences. Will it affect the war? Its length? The outcome? The lives of many?"

She then directed Machen. "The pamphlet you spoke of will spread the news widely. It will make its way into the psychical, mystical, and occult societies. You will be, praised, quoted, sought out as the authority. You must refuse. We cannot allow your association with us to be known. Therefore, we must cast you out, at least for a time."

"Who knows what use Crowley will put it to? He will hound you with threats and demands. You must resist him," said Florence. "We will ask the spirits to protect you."

Crestfallen, Machen said, "Separation will be painful, but I understand why it must be."

"Your publisher needs an introduction for his pamphlet. In it you must make it clear that your story is a fiction."

Mather said, "Those who work for evil and darkness will afflict those who pursue the path of good and light. Crowley's heart is black with evil. Even now evil fills the German nation. You meant no harm. So you have learned. We send you forth with good hope and blessings."

Cut off from the benefits and joys of the Hermetic Order of the Golden Dawn, Machen was broken in spirit, angry at Crowley for his ill-use, afraid of what the dark soul would try to do to him.

Machen dismissed, the conclave closed with prayer and solemn words.

Florence Farr asked, "What is there to do?"

Yeats replied, "As Conan Doyle's Dr. Watson would say, 'Ask Sherlock Holmes.' I will follow Dr. Leckie's instructions, and ask Holmes' author, Sir Arthur. My request for an appointment will, no doubt, surprise him."

Yeats knew that communion with the Other Side was a crucial event in the life of the Order and his own life, too. But to what use to put it? He did not know. When the others had left, Yeats meditated.

In the midst of his meditation the voice of Leo Africanus spoke. "Student, your energies are depleted. Meet with Conan Doyle. Then quiet and rest. Others I have aided–great masters, alchemists, philosophers, shamans, yogis, buddhas. Your beloved Christian Rosenkrantz. I will help you. Keep to the Light and you shall be poet in the second rank after to the writer of The Cloud of Unknowing, the divine St. Theresa, the mystics Isaac Luria, Lao Tsu, and Rumi. You are at the beginning of the Great Work."

Yeats planned. I will ask Conan Doyle for a meeting, bring the bad news of his brother in-law's death. Unofficial news, coming from a suspect source, the evidence a piece of paper, a few scrawled letters and cryptic numbers. Tell him what I saw, what I did, what I know. Delicate, difficult business, to be sure. Though each of us knows of the other's writing, reputation, and interests, we have never met.

Yeats scribbled a note and posted it.

> Must see you. Important news to give you. How soon can we meet? Please reply directly.

> At your service, I am,
> William Butler Yeats

A reply came quickly.

Chapter Fifteen

Yeats Meets Conan Doyle

Windlesham Manor, Sussex
30 August, 1914

Yeats Worried

Yeats worried about how Sir Arthur Conan Doyle would take his report. Bring someone to lend credence to what he would say? But they shared no mutual acquaintance. A member of the Order? Their testimony could add nothing to what Yeats himself would say. Finally, he decided to go himself, brave the rebuke or anger that might await him. But he was certain he needed to give over the paper, deliver the message, as Captain Leckie had instructed.

While a journey to Surry was not out of the question, it called for time and expense, when Yeats, preparing his new play for performance, had little of either to spare. But the matter being of great importance, Yeats undertook the trip.

Arriving in midday, Yeats was greeted by Sir Arthur Conan Doyle's secretary and escorted to the drawing room. Immediately, Sir Arthur enter-ed. The two men shook hands and exchanged greetings.

"It is such a fine day, Mr. Yeats. Let us walk outdoors while we talk. Is that agreeable to you?"

"The fresh air of the country is always welcome," answered Yeats.

Doyle called for refreshments to be delivered to the gazebo where they would later sit. They walked a cobbled path. The air was filled with the humming of bees and the smell of flowers in full bloom. Doyle stopped, knelt to pick a blossom, and put it in his coat's lapel.

"Sir Arthur, I put myself humbly at your service. I hope that what I say does not offend in any way."

"I am, of course, greatly curious about your reason for calling on me. Your note's brevity and expression of urgency make it clear that the matter is serious. "

"It is. I have news from a source you may find beyond credulity."

"I do not know your meaning, sir. But I am sure you will soon divulge it."

"I believe I must speak around the point before getting to it. Please indulge me, then."

"Go on, sir."

"Is it fair to assume that you know something of my work in the esoteric?"

"No details, sir, but I know that your interest is deep. Hermetic Order of the Golden Dawn, is it?"

"Yes, sir."

"I know of such orders and practices. I pursue what some consider a more scientific path. My work in the British Psychical Society. Your purpose has to do with that rather than literature?"

"Yes."

"I am of an open mind. These days we might expect phenomena of an unusual nature."

Still hesitant, Yeats continued qualifying his position. "You know that much of what comes to our notice in these matters is fraud, foolish sophistry, and mere wishful thinking. In this instance, I have only my own word and a piece of paper as evidence. Pardon my hesitation, but I wish to be circumspect and respectful."

They reached the gazebo and sat down at opposite sides of a small table.

A Page Torn from a Doctor's Prescription Pad

Yeats laid his leather pouch on it, extracted the note, and handed it to Doyle. "After you read, I will be glad to tell you how this came to me."

As brief as it was, Doyle read, gazed in thought at the note, looked over the landscape, read again. Tears rolled down his cheeks, though he did not cry.

"I am so sorry, Sir Arthur, to bear such sad news."

"Thank you, Yeats. Sorrow and joy." He smiled, "Ironic. A prescription, yes. Even more, a prognosis. Perhaps for us all. I am silenced in the presence of what this means." Pointing to the note, he said, "As precious as any document in history."

"I am relieved," said Yeats. "What an event to share with you. We are bound by this."

Over the table that separated them the men clasped hands in friendship.

In sober reflection Conan Doyle said, "All these poor Tommy Atkinses, these almost anonymous men, one name serving all. I remember many, treated many on the veldt. Saw many dead."

The name Tommy Atkins again. A small irony there, too. The name of a boy he barely knew and the generic name for all privates. Yet, in the fluttering was a question, a premonition, too. Had their chance encounters transferred a power from the magus to the young man? The oddest sensation, a shiver, a "yes", passed through Yeats's body, and left him with a wondering.

"As I did, Malcolm could have served many in the war, saving many from death, seeing many beyond help. I say, this service is so much greater than that."

Tea arrived, and a plate of sandwiches. Doyle had the servant send Lady Jean and Lily to join them. "I will tell you what took place here a few nights ago. When they arrive, you must tell us how you came to have this." Doyle then explained the meaning of the cryptic words and numbers. "Before you leave, I will show you the message Captain Leckie sent through Miss Loder-Symmons. It contains more details than your note does. They will interest you, I am sure. I shall show yours to the ladies, if you don't mind. I am sure it will amaze them, after it shocks them. To know that you were with Captain Leckie after his bodily death. Amazing. Absolutely amazing." Doyle exclaimed, "Oh, I am filled with wonder! What a cost. The death of my dear friend and my wife's brother." As they talked, Sir Arthur was already formulating plans for lectures and essays, articles and books. His most cherished hope realized. The spirit survives bodily death. Though the other night's experience proved it to his satisfaction, this was confirmation. Proof from two sources, two modes of transmission. Yeats never heard of in the annals of spiritual history. At the same time he knew that the news must be closely kept, its value significant beyond that of individuals and families of faith, but to the government, as well. If St. George and angels had helped in this instance, what could they do in the future? Their power was beyond what humans knew and understood. Were they a secret weapon? Joshua at Jerico. Other angelic interventions.

The women arrived. Sir Arthur introduced Yeats. He told his wife and Miss Loder-Symmons of the note, handed it to them. Lady Jean read and wept. "Malcolm," she cried. "Messenger. Beloved brother. Now I know I shall see you again when I pass on. What hope! What joy! And, Arthur, what sadness."

Lily Loder-Symmons shivered, speechless, lost in thought. Jean took her hand lovingly. Yeats looked on, deeply moved, remaining silent. He knew that the note Miss Loder-Symmon had transcribed and his in Captain Leckie's hand foretold a future for each of them, and for humanity, different from what they would have predicted before. Joy abounding. A new age, a new era had begun. A door, unnoticed and unknown, had opened. Revelation.

For the next half hour the Doyles and Miss Loder-Symmons described what had occurred the night of the transmission. And Yeats recounted his experience of that same afternoon, to their amazement. He also told them about Arthur Machen's story, saying that the idea of angelic intervention would spread widely. "Miracles abound," said Lady Doyle. "And my brother was the instrument, you and Miss Loder-Symmons, the messengers, we the witnesses." She clasped her hands to her heart. "To be blessed with such election! Our lives are forever changed. I do not know what reward you will receive, Mr. Yeats, but mine is already in hand. The knowledge of the truth. Life after death. What could be more sublime?"

None wanted to leave this sacred talk and return to common conversation. Thus, a few words of parting. Though Yeats arrived by train and taxi, Doyle drove him to the station and saw him off. "I must think what use to make of this information," said Doyle. "It is revelation of the highest sort. No doubt it will make its way into the world. Perhaps others are having similar communications, other intimations. We shall listen to hear."

"For my part, I have shared it only with the Sphere, the inner circle of the order," said Yeats. "There will be repercussions from Arthur Machen's story, but we will let them reverberate as they will, have their own life."

The men clasped hands, looked reverently into each other's eyes, Yeats turning to the station, Doyle, to his car.

Chapter Sixteen

The Angel of Mons, Winston Churchill, and his Aunt, Lady Janey Campbell

3 September, 1914

Lady Campbell's Note

Before breaking the wax seal with his letter opener, Winston Churchill saw the crest of Aunt Janey, Lady Archibald Campbell. He thought she must be reminding him of his subscription to a dance society or literary club or a charity. Though this being a time to gather funds for refugee societies, orphanages, hospitals and *ambulanciers auxiliares* in Europe, it must be a request for money. War had commenced. He would send her a cheque.

Instead, he read:

Dear Winston,

Come to tea. A few moments only. Not about the arts. You know my niece, uncle's sister's daughter, Miss Phyllis Campbell. In Belgium and France with a Voluntary Aid Detachment. She informs me of something you must know. I do not want us to be overheard.

The First Lord was reluctant to go. He was in the midst of heavy, fatiguing work, assigning the ships their stations, men, armaments, supplies to ship across the Channel. Securing ports and landing zones, depots with ammunition and supplies, fuel. Keeping the German navy at bay required keen planning. The last time he had visited Weldon House was for the engagement party for Aunt Janey's niece and Sir Arthur Conan Doyle's brother in-law.

But "I do not want us to be overheard." Secrecy about information from her niece? He knew that Miss Campbell's training taught her to inform her superior of anything noteworthy. Nevertheless, Aunt must be mollified. Otherwise she would pester and wheedle in the artful way of an aristocrat, a lady of social prominence. In the long run it would take up more time to not go now and have to go in the end, than it would to go now, willingly and joyfully.

He penned a note and sent it to her by courier:

Dear Aunt Janey,

I agree. We must meet and talk. You have invited me to tea? This afternoon, then. A few minutes, as you say, should take care of our business.

Winston

Tea

Churchill arrived promptly at 3:00 at Weldon House, the Campbell London home, and left a quarter of an hour later. The butler admitted him, escorted the First Lord to the drawing room where Lady Campbell, comfortably seated, greeted him, offering her hand.

"You are looking very well, Aunt Janey."

A great beauty in her day, painted twice by the great Whistler– "Arrangement in Black," "The Lady in Yellow." She was the subject of a photogravure by F. Jenkins of Paris in his *Book of Beauty*, 1857. George Frederic Watts painted her. Other noted painters vied to capture her image, her spirit. Once their muse, she animated their brushes and pens at the time of her ascendency, and, dare Churchill think, her apotheosis. A Child of Graces, personification of beauty and charm, a daughter of Zeus, she still was lovely, dressing in the height of fashion. She lived the life of an aristocratic social matron, a woman of fashion and taste, intellectual, filled with curiosity and verve. Aunt suffered one eccentricity: the occult. She wrote often about faeries and the unseen world, mysterious phenomenon, encouraging others' interests in these and related subjects.

"Thank you, Winston. Come, sit down, my dear boy." Beside her on a lamp table between them was a tea service, a decanter, a brandy snifter, an envelope, and a letter opener. "I shall have tea. Though it is tea time, would you prefer a cognac, Winston?"

"How thoughtful of you, Aunt."

"Rather old, and good, your Uncle James tells me. I know my calling you away from your work is inexcusable, First Lord, but I must talk with you. Grant me two minutes. One sentence." Lady Archibald poured her tea. "Pour for yourself, Winston. You know how much you want."

"Thank you," he said, and removing the stopper, tipped the decanter over the crystal and poured. "I knew that your calling me away meant that what you had to tell me must be of great importance," he said, careful to display no displeasure at her inconveniencing him.

"And so it is. Archibald's niece–our niece–Phyllis, intelligent and trustworthy, has been my protégé for years. She has a remarkable story to tell about the battle at Mons. She managed to smuggle out a note."

"Come now, Aunt Janey. Nothing the girl could write would require smuggling. I am sure you overstate the case."

Insulted, she said, "Indeed, I do not, as you say, overstate. Phyllis treated a young soldier sent from Belgium for surgery to military hospital in London." She paused to sip her tea. "She pleaded with him to hide the letter so it could not be found, and, through a nurse serving at the hospital, a friend of Phyllis's from her training class, get it to me. I say, so much like snooping and spying."

Pointing to the envelope, she said, "Last evening the bell rang. When Wilcox answered, the nurse handed him this envelope saying it was for me. The butler asked her in. She said there was no need, and left. Three documents." Lady Janey picked up the envelope, lifted the flap, and removed the stationery. "A note to the nurse. Instructions."

"The other?"

"The letter she believed would not have passed the censors."

"That is doubtful, my dear aunt," he said dismissing the notion. "What could a nurse have to report that would not pass? What does she report, then?"

Handing him the paper, she said, "Phyllis's letter to me. Read it."

Dear Aunt,

I have sad news to give you. My beloved fiancé, Captain Malcolm Leckie, died, and in my arms. He called it a blessing, I, a blessing and a curse.

As grief-stricken as I am by Malcolm's death, I shall nonetheless have a remarkable account to write for the

The Angel of Mons

Occult Review. Malcolm saw the Angel St. George and a host of other angels over the battlefield at Mons, Belgium on this 23 August. With this the German attack faltered. The BEF withdrew from the attack intact. In the article I will not name him, but the account, I assure you, is true. What he said is corroborated by others in hospital and confirms our deeply held hope and conviction that there is an angelic realm.

I enclose a document verifying this account.

You know I am a slow, methodical writer, so it shall take a few days for me to compose. It is something I do for Malcolm. His account was a great gift to me. I will be grateful for it the rest of my life. In the few moments each day I have in quiet the writing will distract me from my grief.

I am sure Mr. Shirley will be eager to publish it.

In grief and sorrow, I am your beloved, grateful niece,
    Phyllis

    p.s. My hatred of the Germans has grown monstrous. I do not see how I could treat a German soldier, were he brought to hospital, even though we are to treat all as God's creatures and creations.

Churchill finished reading, sipped the last few drops of cognac, breathed in the fumes from the sifter. As if talking to himself, he went through many perplexities the few sentences raised. Stunned, at first he knew not what to make of the letter. What it implied for the Conan Doyles, Phyllis, his aunt he could readily see. But the government? He set that matter aside for the moment, though he knew that this was Lady Campbell's principal concern. "Terribly sorry to hear of your niece's–sorry–poor Phyllis's plight. The poor child," he said. "And Malcolm Leckie's death. Sadly, the Conan Doyles must hear of this through official channels. Do not announce it to them, Aunt Janey."

"I am not so foolish as to do such a thing. What do you take me for? But what of the letter, Winston? By your response I can tell that you have not heard similar reports. I wondered if you had."

"No such account has come to my attention." His face barely masked his bewilderment. "The occult, the esoteric, the mystical–I know they interest you. Phyllis, too. So it is more likely that you would hear of this than I. As is the case."

"There is a third document." She removed a piece of paper from the envelope. With lowered voice she said, "An affidavit. Signed by Captain Leckie and a German Captain."

Startled, Churchill blurted out, "What? What did you say? I must not have heard you. An affidavit attesting to what?"

"The envelope was addressed to me, so I read the document inside. Hence, we are meeting here in strict privacy."

Passing it to Churchill, she said, "Winston, I had you read the letter first so you could, shall we say, give vent to your incredulity. This, I believe, brings the matter to a conclusion."

"What! Let me see it." He quickly unfolded the paper and read. "An account bearing Captain Leckie's signature?"

"It shall take you all of a moment to read. Then you can decide what interest the government would have in the matter. Read, my boy."

Churchill read, showing no emotion. "An interest the government would have? Surely, Aunt Jane. What in this matter could interest His Majesty's Government?"

"You are a wise man, of this I have no doubt. Or you would not be where you are now. I mean your place in His Majesty's Government, not my drawing room."

"You can understand the gravity of what the letter and the affidavit declare." Churchill said, "You may not realize it, but this would be rollicking good fun if the MP's and Lords debated the matter in Parliament. I could see it now, a mockery made of the proposition."

Lady Campbell said, "Yet, I am afraid that we will hear of much suffering and woe ere long. Parliament will have much rhetoric, bombast, and high patriotic hot air to expel over this part of the war."

"You are correct. Men die and politicians make careers. I saw it in South Africa and we shall have it here in greater measure," said the First Lord of the Admiralty. "But this angels nonsense, and an article for, my God, *Occult Review*."

Churchill laid the letter on the table.

"Winston, what she wrote concerns me greatly. What can you do for your aunt? Rather, what will you allow your aunt do for her King and country?"

"You are already being of great help, funding the *ambulanciers auxiliaires* where Phyllis nurses the wounded and dying."

"Merely a philanthropic gesture on the family's part."

"Do you wish to be brought into affairs of state?"

"I have never called on you in your official capacity. I do so now."

"You have no standing in the Government. Do you fear for her safety, her sanity? Do you want her recalled from the war?"

"Don't be foolish. She is as sound of mind as you or me. I helped raise the girl. Strong as oak. Courageous. Send someone to interview her. To speak with her. Very likely she will lead you to other soldiers who saw the angels. Bring the matter of the angels help to the Government's attention. Surely you can do that."

"I do not believe we can count on angels to help. I will take the information in Phyllis's note under advisement, dear aunt."

She lay the letter down. "Do not put me off. This is important."

Irritated, he asked, "To whom? The Government has no interest in the occult. Your astrologers and spiritualists, the esoteric brethren, Theosophical Society crackbrains believe they receive information from sources beyond our ken."

"You saw the letter and the affidavit. You mock, Winston, and I am serious."

"As I am. These two pieces of paper. Not yet enough. Aunt, pardon me, but we are at war. I have a war to fight. We equip our soldiers with weapons, train them to fight. They are professional soldiers. Officers lead them. Our generals and admirals plan, scheme, pursue stratagems. If angels help, I am thankful, thankful for anything that will help defeat the Germans. Let your angels go about their business, so long as it is to our benefit."

He poured himself an ounce of the good cognac, sniffed, sipped, took a moment to compose himself, then went on. "Our cavalry, intelligence, and scouts reliably inform us. We have balloons that see the enemy, where he is, in how many numbers and how disposed. Aeroplanes fly over the roads and fields, reporting on movements and concentrations. I have yet to see such information from otherworldly beings. Does Phyllis know the enemy's plans? I went on maneuvers with the Kaiser not three years ago. I can deduce what he has in mind, the German plans. We watch them unfold, change. The War Council sees how things go and adjusts plans, actions, accordingly, taking advantage of opportunities that arise, avoiding traps, thwarting disaster. The Government needs no occult knowledge."

"Do not disappoint me, my boy. I do not ask much. Take this to the War Council."

"I must think about the proper course. I presume that for the moment only you and I know of the note."

"Do you think I did not share it with my husband?"

"Oh, yes. Uncle James as well."

Picking the letter up again, she said, "The note gives fair warning. Phyllis will expand upon what she wrote. It will appear in the next issue of the *Occult Review*. I did not want the publication to come as a surprise to you or His Majesty's Government." She sipped her tea. "People know we are related. I do not want this to have repercussions, to affect your place in His Majesty's Government, or affect the government itself. Questions in Parliament and such. You have your critics, I know. Even enemies, though why, I cannot imagine," she said.

"I wish I could console Phyllis. But I am sure she will remain in France." Her eyes began to tear. "I had quickly come to admire her fiancé. We were sad when they had to postpone their wedding, both of them being called away before the date they had set for their nuptials. Now it appears that it was for the best. Better to lose a fiancé than a husband. Widowhood, especially before the couple grows used to one another, grows in their love for one another, is a most horrid state. In a young woman it leaves a permanent wound. Always the question, what would have been? The dead man is ever after like a third party when the girl remarries."

On the Way back to His Office

In Churchill's breast pocket was the packet. He promised, he swore, that he would secure the documents in his private safe, return to his Aunt. She had argued that they belonged in the possession of Malcolm's father, a man prominent in business. While his driver sped him back to his office Churchill read the documents again. He lit a cigar, reflected. Phyllis, lovely girl, fine breeding, noble family, and keen mind, sensitive. In his mind's eye Phyllis cradled the captain in her arms as he breathed his last. In a foreign land, the midst of war, surrounded by the brutal enemy, a hospital overflowing with wounded soldiers, the maimed, the dying, assaulted by moans and cries, smelling waste and blood, bleach, ammonia, vomit. No wonder a story of angels, Churchill thought. Miss Campbell's angel had flown away. In the midst of misery, pain, and death, blossomed her own misery and grief. Did her fiancé say he had seen angels? Had other soldiers seen them, too? Sir Winston concluded that a family of markedly anti-German sentiments–Phyllis educated in France, indoctrinated in the pseudo-science of occultism (nonsense from start to finish) made such a tale almost inevitable. Exhaustion, grief, the terror of what she saw, heard, touched, ministered to, the very surroundings might well have pro-voked a dream of sufficient intensity that she could have mistaken the contents for real.

He thought more coolly, now that he had left Weldon House. Publication in an obscure not-too-reputable source, its readers of the crank variety, intellectuals of a strange sort. Such people likely to talk volubly about crackpot, hare-brain ideas. These people eager for signs, for confirmation of a world beyond the world. After all, this was war and anything could happen. Word of mouth. Soon the story would gain the status of fact. Even if there were no angels, and what was the likelihood that there were? The story was, a gift from God, he thought with more than a shade of sarcasm. Even a rumor at the proper moment, soon taken as fact, could do as much as report of a victory, more than a dozen editorials or letters to the *Times*. The government need take no stand on the matter, not utter one word of opinion about it. Neither confirmed nor denied. Simply unspoken. Let the popular mind promote it. The *vox populi*, the voice of the people. It will be wonderful to watch, observe its manner of working, see what it produces. It matters not that the story is fantasy.

Chapter Seventeen

First Lord of the Admiralty Winston Churchill Meets with Conan Doyle and Sherlock Holmes

Office of the First Lord of the Admiralty
6 September, 1914

> *The War Office and Secretary of State for War, Lord Kitchener constructed the story of the Expeditionary Force's 'miracle' escape from the disaster at Mons. The aim was to encourage the widespread recruitment he knew was necessary if Britain was to win the war.*
>
> *The Angel of Mons*
> David Clarke

Churchill has Much to Tell Conan Doyle and Holmes

The office staff had left for the day and all the officers were in conferences or at early dinner. Quiet. Unlikely that people would notice two civilians entering the building and making their way to Churchill's office.

First Lord of the Admiralty Winston Churchill rose from his chair, reached across his paper-covered desk, and shook hands with Sir Arthur Conan Doyle and Sherlock Holmes. "Welcome, gentlemen. Please take seats. Sir Arthur, Mr. Holmes, thank you for making yourselves available on such short notice."

"Not at all. I thank you, sir," said Conan Doyle. Holmes nodded his acknowledgement.

"Holmes, I am pleased to meet you. As many readers must, I wonder how close what Sir Arthur writes about you is to the truth. Perhaps in our visit this evening, I will be able to discover for myself."

"Sir, I shall save you the bother. Disregard everything you have learned of me from Conan Doyle's stories. He uses my name and my address. All else he concocts in his imagination. He satisfies his publisher and his public. Third rate writing at that, in my estimation. I prefer scientific writings, history, world literature, our venerable classic British poets and writers."

Churchill laughed heartily, struck by Holmes' forthright manner and wry wit. Turning to Conan Doyle, he said, "The subject of your most famous stories is not an admirer. For shame, sir. If you cannot satisfy him. For shame."

"Please do not mistake me, sir. I criticize him only as a writer. At heart he is a sterling patriot, a staunch Englishman, a shrewd businessman, and trustworthy in what he will say he saw."

"Trustworthy in what he will say he saw" set off Churchill's mind, a hound on the fox's scent. The First Lord's train of thought was barely interrupted when Conan Doyle said, "Holmes, I am sorry to say, sees me as a money-making dolt. In turn, I see my friend as a man who intrigues all who know him because of my stories. Whatever he claims, my Holmes is true to character, as you can tell by being with him even these few moments."

Without reply, Churchill moved to his subject. "Gentlemen, my wife spoke with me. Our wives' work on the ambulance hospital societies. I understand you are preparing a refuge at Windlesham for the hard-pressed Belgians. Very good, Sir Arthur."

"Lady Jean's idea, with which I most heartily agree. The least we could do, she said. Happy in any way to contribute. Myself included, of course."

"I'm sure of it, Sir Arthur," said Churchill.

"I pray for the ladies, indeed," Conan Doyle said. "The three of us have seen war. It will be a shock to them, the awful, bloody mess of it."

"You wanted to meet. Your wife told Lady Churchill you would not reveal the purpose until we were together. Even more intriguing, you bringing Mr. Holmes." Turning to Holmes, he said, "Of course, I am pleased to meet you, sir."

Replied Holmes, "I am here to stand witness to what Conan Doyle will tell you."

Holmes' remark puzzled Churchill. Trustworthy in what he saw? Stand witness? Churchill could not imagine what Conan Doyle could say that would call for witness and corroboration. The First Lord wisely suspected that Sir Arthur wanted to plead for a commission in the service, possibly even a field position. Churchill knew that Conan Doyle expected a family tie to be recognized–his Aunt Campbell's niece engaged to the recently departed Malcolm Leckie, whose death Churchill was about to announce. A meeting with the man of intrigue, Sherlock Holmes, in exchange for a commission? Perhaps that was all there was to it from the amiable Conan Doyle's point of view.

Doyle spoke up. "The purpose of our visit. . . ."

Churchill interrupted. "Patience, Sir Arthur I have not yet begun. Yes, all this made me curious, but not sufficiently to put you on my already-burdened calendar. As it happened, facts came to my attention that I want to tell you myself. Hence, our meeting. Two matters, gentlemen. Then I will hear what you came to say."

Assignments

Churchill rose from his seat, turned, and lifted the lid of the humidor on the cabinet behind his desk. His back to them, asked, "Cigar, gentlemen? I fear this will be the last evening for many a day when I will sit and converse with literary men. Henceforth, all military and government."

"Delighted with a cigar."

"If you do not mind, sir," said Sherlock Holmes, "I prefer a pipe." He filled it, tamped the tobacco to the proper firmness, struck a light, and smoked.

Churchill cut the tips of two cigars, passing one to Doyle. The novelist held his match so the flame did not touch the tobacco, but lit it by the rising heat only.

"Now, to the first matter of our meeting, gentlemen. As both of you know, being students of current affairs. . . ."

"Pardon me, Sir," interjected Sherlock Holmes, who called for clarity and precision in all that was done and said. "I am by no means a student of current affairs, if you mean the affairs of the Government."

"No, no, Holmes. I mean the state of affairs in Europe. It may be as you say, sir, that you are not well versed in the affairs of His Majesty's government. But you will take part in these affairs." Churchill lit his cigar, took several puffs, the smoke expelled from his nostrils, along with a scowl, the sign of a fierce spirit. "I have it on good authority that your skills will benefit England's cause. Your service, in any case, is commanded."

He looked down at his memorandum book, as if to find what he wished to say. His countenance assumed the cast of a Roman senator's bust carved in marble. The tone of his conversation changed, as if an irritation had risen to the point of an eruption. High dudgeon. Indignation.

"As much as we care for Germany, we care more for our pledge to Belgium. Germany suffers from *Die Grosse Zeit*. They see before them the panorama of conquest, victory over all of Europe, a European Empire. You have the perspicacity to see that this war will be of a severity never before seen on Earth." Churchill's oratorical powers were in full flower. "The number of soldiers. The stocks of armaments and ammunition. It will be a war of long duration. There will be no victory in the two months the German plan calls for. Two months will not even see full mobilization of the armies. We have men by the tens of thousands ready to enlist." The First Lord took in a puff of his cigar, reflected, spoke. "Knowing the size and training of the German armies and navy, their resources, their people, and the Kaiser's will, I foresee a long war."

Churchill fell silent for a moment, drew deeply of his cigar, slowly exhaling the smoke, watching it uncurl in the air. "The upshot. Gentlemen, you are at His Majesty's service. I need your eyes and ears, your keen impressions."

Turning to the Scotsman, he spoke to mollify his anticipated disappointment. "In you, sir, the reporter, roving journalist, correspondent, the man to keep up the home front's spirits. You will write regular dispatches for the Daily Chronicle and Times, articles for Reuters. Dispatches from wherever you are, and popular books for the British people giving a good and true account of their countryman's deeds. You will use all of this as the basis for a history of the war you will write. As I did in the Boer War."

Holmes picked up the thread. "And much good it did, Sir Winston. Much good, indeed."

"Thank you, sir." The First Admiral concluded his remarks on the matter, saying, "You will go with military designation as Deputy-Lieutenant of Surrey." Conan Doyle had received this appointment in 1902, an honorific title, with neither obligation nor privilege.

The writer thought a lowly appointment. Lacking authority. No command. A free roving reporter is right. Unconnected to anything of importance, as he saw it. Necessarily inconspicuous. Not even granted a chance to make a case for a field command. "You will be unofficially the voice of His Majesty's government and the voice of the people. I intend you to write extensively about the war. Depending on how long it lasts, perhaps several volumes." An attempt at flattery: "Who would you recommend? Kipling. Davis, Gibbs. I'll enlist a few others."

Seeing that Winston Churchill had made up his mind, the writer said, "Of course, sir, and greatly honored. Pleased to serve His Majesty." Then Churchill said Doyle would be attached, not to the Admiralty, as Doyle assumed, but to the Foreign Office. He heard the words, "To whom you will report directly, and from whom you will receive instruction." Holmes read further disappointment in Doyle's downcast gaze. Churchill rolled his cigar in the tray removing its inch of ash, cleared his throat to draw Sir Arthur's attention, then broke the silence. "I had hoped to cross the Channel myself. Raise a bit of the old bluster. But my position prevents it at the moment. I envy you. This time, gentlemen, we won't be fighting. But you, Sir Arthur, will be close–listening, observing, writing. South Africa was our day, was it not? In any case, I am taking you on as a pound a year man."

In a pique, the writer said, "I am honored, sir that you think I can afford it. I am no rich manufacturer or great Lord."

"The British people purchase your books, the source of your fortune and fame. You have a duty to your readers."

"I thought I had fulfilled that duty writing for their enjoyment and edification. Was that not enough?"

"In any case, I send you in a capacity you will enjoy."

"But, Sir , you . . . ." began Doyle.

Sherlock Holmes saw the squabble arising in Doyle's mind. He hoped the indignant Scotsman would repress its expression. Holmes knew the First Admiral had a salvo he could fire in reply. The insufficiency of defense at Scapa Flow that Doyle had written about in a letter printed in the Times. Better if that not be brought into the conversation.

Churchill interrupted. "I concede to your plea."

"I pled nothing, sir. I merely. . . ."

"I instate you, sir, as a private at private's pay. An end to it, then."

"Oh, no sir."

"What do you mean?"

"A pound a year suits, sir."

"Now you've ceased your clownery, sir. Of course you would rather be on the list of the pound a year's than the private's list."

A Private Matter

To prepare for telling the sad news he had to deliver, Churchill said, "Let us have a taste of cognac. This being a. . . ." He paused. The gravity and sadness of the message he was to deliver prevented Churchill from saying "special occasion." From a drawer in the cabinet behind his desk he took out a crystal decanter, three brandy snifters, poured his Hine VSOP brandy, and handed one to each man. "Cheers, gentlemen. King and Country," the three men raising their glasses, each taking a sip.

Churchill set down his snifter, took his handkerchief from his pocket, pressed a corner to his lips. "Doyle, I must move to a private matter, between the two of us."

Rising from his chair, Holmes said, "Excuse me, gentlemen. I shall, with your permission, wait in the hallway. . . ."

"Nonsense, Holmes. I prefer that you stay. Nothing to worry about, I am sure. Is that correct, Sir Winston?"

"I would not say so, Doyle."

"Well, then." Churchill's unexpected reply surprised the two men. Holmes hoped that this was not Scapa Flow coming forth for discussion. Doyle, sharing the same thought, steeled himself, but wanted Holmes's presence to soften the blow, to the extent it could. "Stay in any case, Holmes."

The First Lord said, "As you say, sir. To the matter, then. Sir Arthur, you remember my aunt, Lady Janey Campbell?"

Clearly not Scapa Flow.

"We celebrated the engagement of your brother in-law and her lovely niece, Phyllis, at her house a few months past. Aunt insisted I call upon her two evenings ago. She recounted certain events which Phyllis had passed on to her."

"She has heard from Phyllis, then? I would not have expected communication so quickly. Splendid."

"Not so again, sir. Miss Campbell sent a note to her aunt through a young soldier she had treated in Belgium and invalided to London." Churchill opened the memorandum book that lay on his desk. "Let me see, now." He turned a few pages then read. "On second September–four days ago–he arrived." Churchill paused, sipped his cognac, set it on a coaster, and went on. "Two days later Lady Campbell received an envelope from a nurse who Phyllis knew."

The cigar's ember fading, Churchill took a few puffs to revive it. "I saw Aunt that evening, as I said. I would have called for you earlier, but only now could I clear a moment after the work day to meet."

Churchill removed a folded page from a flap in the book's cover and passed it to Doyle. Sir Arthur unfolded the paper, torn from a stationery notebook. He heard Churchill say, "I am deeply sorry." The First Lord went on. "I have read its contents." The writing was a scrawl, revealing deep emotion and haste. Some of the ink bore the mark of tears, the ink forming blotches and puddles and the shape of streams. Doyle read the gloomy account. From the note he learned that Malcolm had indeed died, the poor girl cradling his head. Phyllis wrote "26 August" at the top of the note. The date Doyle's beloved brother in-law's spirit had spoken from beyond the veil of death.

"I am sorry, Doyle," Churchill repeated.

Doyle turned to Holmes. "How unpleasant for the girl," he said. "Captain Leckie died in her arms. Malcolm, the dear boy." The good doctor passed the note to Holmes. Doyle said to him, "This explains the word 'fiancé'."

"What do you mean, 'explains fiancé?'" said Churchill.

Conan Doyle said, "We knew. This is what I came to you about." Sherlock Holmes spoke. "The letter confirms what we sought to discover."

"Now I know my brother in-law's fate," said the writer. With that, Sir Arthur buried his face in his hands, lifting it a few moments later, now marked by agony.

While the esteemed detective read the note, Churchill asked, angrily, "What do you mean? Has my aunt been in communication with you? I warned her not to tell you. Told her I would have you in. One reason you are here. A family courtesy. It will be yet a week before the official reports of deaths and casualties are confirmed, visits made to families."

Doyle replied, "No. Your aunt did not talk with me, sent no note. We discovered by other means," said the writer, "Holmes and I had, let us say, a premonition."

"Premonition?"

Reluctantly at first, Sir Arthur and Sherlock Holmes recounted the events of the evening's events of the 26th. Holmes said that the communication from Malcolm mentioned his being shot during a battle at

Mons.

"Reports are coming in," Churchill said. "What the Army accomplished at Mons was of great importance. The success contributed substantially to the chance that the army could, as the saying has it, 'live to fight another day,' as the army must."

"Gentlemen," Churchill continued, "If the BEF had not held and delayed General von Kluck's advance, this war would be all too brief."

Churchill refreshed their cognac. "But let us drink a toast to your departed brother in-law and one of Britain's gallant soldiers."

Once again they raised their glasses, and meditated on what lay before them.

"Miss Campbell sent another document, an affidavit." He handed the paper to Doyle, who read in amazement, then passed it to Holmes, who read also. After a moment's pause, Churchill asked, "What do you know about St. George? The angel?" Stranger grew the accounts. Pausing to think, the First Lord sipped his cognac, two puffs of his cigar, sipped again. He counted. Doyle told of William Butler Yeats's experience. Of Arthur Machen's story. Four sources now. Five counting the strange affidavit.

When all was said, Churchill replied, "Mind, His Majesty's Government has no interest in angels. We've a war to fight. If angels help, that will be fine. But we cannot count on their aid. I foresee that the story will spread on its own wings. People will fervently wish it to be true. From what you tell me, it well may be true. Religion and our churches teach that the Lord is on the side of the righteous–in this case, the British."

"As you read, Phyllis plans to write an article for a magazine. I tried to persuade my aunt to have her niece keep it for her personal reading, her memories. My attempt was futile. Lady Campbell considers herself an authority in matters occult, sometimes writes for an obscure magazine, the *Occult Review*. Foolishness and wild speculation. She will see to it that this revelation is made known to the world." The First Lord went on. "How could I not believe? And this Yeats fellow? I am not a literary man, but his name is familiar to me. One of the bright lights of poetry. And Machen? I've not heard of him. The story of St. George and his angels should be making its way on the wings of rumor–recall the famous passage in the Aeneid."

As they spoke, Churchill thought. From the account of one angel there will be reports of hordes. From one appearance, the stories will be of many.

Of such words and such speaking do religions grow, myths take shape, national identities emerge, heroes and saviors arise.

"Doyle, please send my heartfelt condolences to Lady Jean. My wife will send a message to Miss Campbell. She may wish to come home. If she does, I will see to it that her passage is eased. Miss Campbell is in my care for the moment. Her father in-law-to-be, Lord Leckie, is her guardian. I will consult with him before I write. My aunt, also."

Churchill stood, came around his desk. He clasped Doyle's right hand in both of his. "I am most sorry, Sir Arthur. I had looked forward to a familial connection with the popular writer and beloved storyteller. But most of all I am sorry for the young couple–Malcolm and Phyllis. The poor girl must be grief-stricken. And surrounded by casualties and death. Many more fine men will die before this folly is over. Grief will spread its pall over our nation, our Empire."

The two looked deeply into each other's eyes, measuring each other's souls at this moment of crisis and sadness. Doyle spoke. "I shall send your aunt my thanks for her efforts. Jean will write a note. Please give our regards to Lady Churchill. The ladies' good work will be greatly needed, as you say, in the days to come."

"You know how you must conduct yourself. Do nothing to jeopardize your assignment. Go, Sir Arthur. Go and fulfill your duty to your King." Churchill rose from his seat and made his way to the door. "You came with two purposes. You now have your commission, though it is not what you would have chosen. And you have informed His Majesty's government and the War Council of unexpected aid. I did not treat your report with scorn. Indeed, you confirmed what I had already been told. No one here to show you out. Please allow me, my friend. Mr. Holmes, stay a moment." Churchill took Doyle by the elbow, turned him toward the door, walked him to it. They shook hands once more.

Doyle closed the door behind himself. What Churchill and Holmes discussed Holmes never said, but Doyle had a reasonable idea: espionage. Reporting to the First Lord of the Admiralty himself, most likely.

Holmes and Churchill Alone

Behind the closed door the conversation between Holmes and Churchill continued.

"You speak German, I presume?" said Sir Winston.

Holmes answered in German, "Half a dozen dialects. And other languages as well. Others I read, but do not yet speak."

"I thought as much. And not just languages. Polymath, they call it, do they not? Encyclopedic knowledge."

"Yes, Sir Winston."

"Holmes, I have some private business I wish you to undertake. Though, not private in the usual sense. The Germans captured my wife's sister, Nellie, and her fellow hospital companions at a hospital near Mons. They are being kept at Maubeuge, just on the border between France and Belgium. I want you to affect her release. Smuggle her out of the camp if you can, or, if you must, negotiate her release. Exchange of prisoners, perhaps. I am sure we hold some of their officers, aristocrats all. It would do the country's morale no good if the people knew the sister of the First Lord of the Admiralty's wife was a prisoner of war. Choose the method and the means. My office will assist you in developing aliases and the dossier and documents to support the identities."

"I must think and plan."

"Of course, sir. Come tomorrow evening about the same time. Beyond this, I wish you to stay in Europe. Get as close to the Kaiser as you can. Report directly to me. My assistant will brief you before you leave, but prepare to leave soon. Thank you, sir. By the way, what do you make of St. George and his angels? You are a man of reason and good sense."

"Thank you, sir, for the compliment. While much of what Doyle writes about me is fiction, he is right in seeing me as reasonable. I have gone with him to séances and other such events. While he easily believes what he sees to be true, I detect much fraud, and point it out to him. This matter is different. I was present the night the message from Captain Leckie came through. The test questions were correctly answered. While I do not know Yeats, I examined the note he gave to Doyle. Though apparently written while the men were on galloping horses, the handwriting is Leckie's. The prescription pad, authentic. Therefore. . . ."

"I see. Thank you, sir. You put my mind at ease."

Word of the Angels will Spread

Winston Churchill knew that the story of St. George and the angels would spread. Its truth or falsity did not matter. If the story sounds plausible, or even implausible, people would believe, strengthen their conviction that they were in God's favor, strengthen their resolve to fight on. Beyond that, the First Lord knew that the Government is not above shaping the news for military advantage. He drew in the smoke of the cigar, sipped his cognac. In time of war the press distorts the news and word of mouth distributes it, making it story and drama, myth and gospel.

He went back to reading papers piled on his desk, scribbling notes on some, signing others, all the while thinking of the strange, sad encounter with the two gentlemen, Sir Arthur Conan Doyle, and the remarkable Sherlock Holmes, both of whom he would hear from in the coming days. An odd encounter, and one whose repercussions would persist throughout the war.

Ready to Depart

The two assembled their kits, Holmes' consisting mainly of costumes and makeup, Doyle's of notebooks, pens, pencils. Doyle embarked on September 12 from Southampton, arriving without fanfare or notice at Le Havre. Holmes left two days earlier, landing at an undisclosed port, destination unknown. That was the last the two saw of each other until after the war, in a vastly changed world. Both men were changed by it and by the years. Of what happened between their parting and their reunion neither of them spoke, though Sherlock Holmes kept up with Conan Doyle's many writings. Not only of the war, which were voluminous and salutary to the British spirit, but essays, articles, books about life beyond the grave.

Book 5

The Last British Soldier Killed

Chapter Eighteen

Tommy Atkins,
Angel of Memory, Grief, and Tears

Nimy Bridge, Mons Canal
Mons, Belgium
November 11, 1918

> *On Monday, November 11th, before the "cease fire" sounded, the mighty successors of "the contemptible little army" were in Mons, a spot that was consecrated ground to them. By the most remarkable coincidence in history, the war on the British side ended where it began.*
>
> *In the last week of August 1914, five British divisions retreated from Mons. In the first week of November 1918, five British armies marched back to Mons. It was the most tremendous recoil in history.*
>
> *The new British soldiers wished to stand victorious in the Flemish colliery city (Mons) where their old Regular little Expeditionary Force of 86,000 men had opened the war against overwhelming odds.*
>
> *"The War Illustrated" 23rd November, 1918 "Star of Mons in the Ascendant"*
>
> Edward Wright

(In the words of Tommy Atkins)

Before All the Falderal

Yes. I am Thomas Atkins, Private Thomas Atkins, later, Sergeant. Some think it a pseudonym. Others sing about Tommy Atkins, all the privates, our dedication, duty, and sacrifice. Yet others say I am the soldier the generals had in mind when they picked the name for the sample Army Registration Card. I am none of those. I am plain Tommy Atkins, son of Ezra Atkins, cobbler, and Margaret Atkins (nee Gilbertson), home at Woburn Buildings, my father's place of business. We lived back of Father's shop. Always the smell of leather, polishes, dyes, rubber, machine oil. Before I enrolled in the army, above us lived a Yeats fellow, a man of great renown, I was told. Never read a word of his, though. We've passed one another on rare occasions, a nod, a touch of the cap brim, a muffled greeting. My father cobbled several pair of his boots.

I came of age to enlist six months before the war began, time enough to train then ship out before all the falderal. Before angels fought beside us. They saved the B.E.F. from annihilation, saved the few of us in the early days of fighting. That was years ago. My two uncles, military men, my mother's brothers, convinced me there was a fair chance for a young man who stepped into line before the war began. For they knew that war was soon to come. I would stand for promotion better than those who came along after the storm broke. I thought I was headed for an office post like my uncles', not knowing how low I stood on the ladder of skill and aptitude.

I stepped forward, took the oath, received the King's shilling, greeting, thanks, and letter of appointment. Sign your name and you are Tommy Atkins to the Army thereafter, one of the thousands of pieces the generals move about so the King can have his way. Then six months of training and travail.

The moment training started, I could tell that I had made a dreadful mistake, so far from my element. Gone were the conveniences of life I was accustomed to. I knew nothing of the world. Little more than a schoolboy in the company of hard men, I was the butt of pranks, tricks, jokes, japes, and capers. Why, they had it in for me in ten minutes. Last in mess line, ignored, assigned the lowest, menial jobs.

But the Army said I was made of something. I could not bring ignominy upon my family's name. I had the good sense to knuckle down. It wasn't easy, didn't appeal to my taste, didn't suit my nature. I made it through. I'd never be promoted on the strength of my qualifications. At the time I was too dim to realize it. What had my uncles been thinking? Me in charge over men of that sort? Once they saw the failure I was, and not wanting the family's names disgraced, my uncles must have pulled strings so that I would be lost to view.

Little by little the men eased up. Finally, they helped me along and said I was a good lad, but near an idiot and how did I ever get in the Army?

The Vickers occupied the backwater of the British Army. I was stuck on a Vickers team, what that little piece of hell turned out to be. None of high rank paid the weapon any attention. Maybe good for defense, and little good for that. Its clack and clatter and roar foretold a life of noise. Bullets fly so fast, they were invisible. Except for the destruction, the casings flung about were the only sign that they had been fired.

Everyone on the Vickers team saw as soon as I came on that I was a creature made for mockery, a butt of jokes. Slight of build, short.

Talk I overheard about myself:

"He reminds me of a hare the gardener finds in his vegetables, brains with his hoe."

"Brains of a pumpkin. A natural talent for the role of a vegetable in school dramatics."

"Cheerful, he lacks the sense to know the world. Naïve."

"His face with all the features of a darning egg—pug nose, thin lips, chin lacking, expressionless, pale eyes."

"Hair? Flops about when it is dry. Plastered, sticks like wallpaper to his head."

"Ears something to behold—handles on a jug. Rheumy blue eyes, reddish hair that glistens when it gets the pomade."

"Moping look."

"Not old enough to grow a moustache."

From what I overheard, my personality matched my face. I wouldn't know. I was not one to look within. And thus, I learned the world's opinion of me, or at least my chums'.

Like all Sixes, I began as a gear humper, scout, range taker. Everyone could fire the gun. Even me. I carried two boxes of ammunition, a rifle, and my kit. At first too much for a shrimp like me. My shoulders and back were always sore. I wasn't built for this kind of work.

In the Nuns' Woods

North of Menin Road
Four Miles from Ypres
11 November, 1914

The Germans attacked from three directions: north-east, east, and south-east. Nine days and nights we spent in the woods and nearby. Sometimes it was quiet, but often our side or theirs tried some maneuver. There were points that one side was keen to hold, the other equally keen to gain. The movement of our two guns was all within the range of the wood and surrounding farms and villages.

Quiet as a Sunday Morn

20 November, 1914

It had happened at Mons, at Le Cateau, everywhere, wherever we would turn and fight. In some places a platoon, a company, a battalion would march along and it was quiet as Sunday morning. At the same time the next village over, or a nearby neighborhood, or around the corner, or down the road, rifles and machine guns cough and sputter, a shell explode, a barrage would fall. Suddenly it was as if the gates of hell had burst open wherever the fighting was going on.

Soldiers say when your time is up, it's in for you. So it was for us.

I was hauling the canvas bucket from a brook. The Victors and Ruffians' crossfire killed Germans when they tried to cut through the line we held. A scythe cutting hay comes to mind. I didn't have time to shout, "Run!" A bolt of brilliant light, a blast, a rain of hot steel. A second followed, a third. Cries of anguish. Curses. Alive one minute, dead or dying the next. Me, a tear in my tunic, a nick on my left shoulder. I dropped the water bucket, ran about, checked each man for signs of life. All gone.

No need for medics. Burial team was all.

Life still in him, but fading, was Carmichael. I held his head up, rested it on my lap, so he could have some ease. We looked over the scene, stunned. The men were dead. At first, there were waves of light rising in summer heat. Then a golden mist, then a shimmering, like the tips of ripples on a ruffled pond. Each man became an orb of light, like Dease months ago. They hovered over us in the air. As if they spoke through a phonograph, voices remote and thin, they sang "For He's a Jolly Good Fellow". I heard one say, "Farewell, brother." "Carry on, Atkins." "Dease awaits us," Another said, "He is above. Calls with open arms." I swooned, but was awake. "Do us honor, Atkins," the sound now crackling like a worn recording, "Golden Arrow of God." Then, from my eyes pinpricks of golden light, shot forth golden arrows. The arrows became eagles flying straight into the distance, the future, bullets from my eyes, from the Vickers machine gun. My own flesh melted away. I was skeleton, yet standing, as if I did not need flesh or sinews or muscles. I saw the doom to come. Then I heard a mortal voice. Carmichael. His voice fading with each syllable, he said, "I see their souls rising. I join them." His dying words. Another brother gone. Like a swarm of golden bees spiraling off, his soul joined the others.

My brothers. My strength. Uncles mistook me. Parents, dull to any notion of me. What does a cobbler and his wife know of the world? Leather and last, nails, sinewy thread, wax, and polish. The Ruffians raised me, made me. Victors, too.

I would not abandon the gun, had to stick with it. Too heavy to carry myself. Too precious to leave. I enlisted soldiers coming by. Not to shoot, but carry the gun along. Keep it from the Germans, prevent being killed by my own Vickers. For surely they would turn it on us as I hurried off. Collected all the ammunition we could carry. In shock and grief I left, hoping the burial crew would take Christian care of my friends.

Not the Last of the Ruffians and the Victors

Whenever I fought at a moment of need, one of the Ruffians or Victors would appear. Gabriel Jessop or Carrew Nancarew might help me repair the gun, hand me a part. Catchpole and Palmer might march along to the trenches, full kit, singing a London stage ditty, its verses replaced with ribald lyrics to lighten my heart, make me blush. "How's old Vicki holding up? Had to piss in the canister to keep her cool when there is no water about?" Catchpole might ask.

"You uncouth old fool. Besides, I am Gunner One now. Not my task."

Or at night under the glory and glare of tracer bullets, looking across No Man's Land at the Somme. At the Christmas Truce, December 24, 1914, the Victors and Ruffians, all eleven killed, filed onto the field, made up a proper football squad, played against a German team. For all I knew, the Germans might also have been departed dead playing.

The Victors broke out a case of brandy, the Ruffians, wine. We drank with the Germans, toasted St. George. The Germans raised their glasses to St. Michael. Our hearts begged the saints to signal that we would not fire another shot, the war over, the peace to hold forever, all to return to homes and families. We ate sausage spread with dark mustard spread on rye bread, pickles, and roasted potatoes. We served up plum pudding with hard sauce and mince pies. That night my angel brothers reverently carried the dead and tenderly moved the wounded to aid stations.

I awoke next morning to gunfire and bombardment. My heart, filled with joy and hope the night before—last night a heavenly miracle—shriveled to a walnut-hard center of grief and regret.

At Passchendaele the battlefield had been raked with every known kind of armament since July. My crew and I arrived in muddy October. Every day the shrieks of the horribly wounded, the groans and cries of the dying, filling the interstices of quiet between the explosions of the bombs, the clatter of machine gun and rifle fire across No Man's Land. I was wounded, spent the night huddled in a cold muddy bunker. My dear Lieutenant Dease came to me. He told me that the Golden Arrows of God went about their duties, some escorting the souls of the fallen to the gates of Judgment and pleading for redemption for the souls of those who died sin-stained, curses in their dying mouths. Nancarrew and Jessop and Sage brought succor to those in pain. Catchpole and Palmer entered the minds of those despondent and fearful, inspiring them with courage and hope. The rest, Hardy and Lang, Paul Carmichael, Sergeant Sanders, were perpetual mourners. Angel Lieutenant Dease tenderly tended my wounds. They healed at his ministering touch.

The Angle of Mons

Marching Northwest into Belgium
October, 1918

Somewhere in the last weeks of October of 1918–military historians would refer to these as the One Hundred Days–we fought through places where I had fought four years before. After all I had been through, all the places I had been, all the fighting I had done, all I had seen and suffered, I would not have guessed that I would tread the same roads, fighting westward and north instead of east and south. Le Cateau, the Forest of Mormal again. Mons again. The same places again, but vastly different, mightily altered. Wreckage and destruction everywhere. In place of fields lush with the bounty of the earth, and freshly harvested fields, and centers of industry, mining—desolation. Crops harvested to feed the Germans. Coal, mined for Germany. Iron smelted into German rails and weapons and ammunition. No hearty natives and their smiling children. Now the dispirited, abused, insulted. The aged, the crippled, the ill, old women, emaciated widows and children. The fit men dead, in prison, war camps, or enslaved, working for the Germans. Devastation. The people barely survived on the little food the enemy allowed. The German occupation of four years drained the life from the people.

Then, splendid Mons again. Burned out shells of buildings on both sides of the Rue de Nimy. Years of rain and snow and heat and cold turned them into menacing skeletons, bones of the dead. City of St. George, of whose Golden Arrow of God I am the last and only. His care in battle my shield. In the cold of winter, my warmth. In the heat of summer, my shade. How many I killed to his honor, I cannot count. The soldiers the bullets reach too far to make out. Bullets from many rifles, shells and shrapnel from artillery.

The twin guns–one died, one lived, at least in name. Vixen, long ago dead and scrap along with the Ruffians and Victors who served her.

The war's end in sight. We felt it coming, heard it was on its way. Rumor. The German army falling to ruins. I had a good sense for it, having been in since the beginning. Something of an expert. Signs everywhere.

By now I was little more than a ghost of myself. Vicki, and me, Tommy Atkins, trudging toward victory. New cells replace old ones many times in our bodies over a lifetime. Though I am Tommy Atkins

224

with all his memories, experiences, beliefs, not a shred of me is the Tommy Atkins that I began with in jolly old, good year of our Lord, 1914. All the bully beef and plum jam and tea and grog and iron rations that have passed through me changed me.

It is true for Vicki as well. No part of the gun original. A new barrel every twenty thousand rounds. Every part repaired till worn useless, finally replaced. Even the tripod base is new. I kept the original reciprocating key, worn and useless. Strung it on the chain about my neck with my identity number disk. Scratched the names of my original five brothers-in-arms with a steel stylus. Where they are I'll never know. But their names are here with me, close to my heart, graven in my memory as deeply as an inscription on a gravestone. I cannot count the number of gunners Two, Three, Four, Five, Six who fed Vickers thereafter. Dozens in the course of the war. Their names and faces, a blur.

The future lay before me. What to do? Stay in the army? Return to ordinary life? I would not know what to do. Prepared for no profession, no trade. I stink of blood and gore, death.

November 11, 1918 time: 10:40 a.m., Greenwich Mean Time. Armistice to be proclaimed at 11:00 a.m., we've been told. But here, far from working telegraph lines, we knew nothing certain.

I am in sight of Nimy bridge once more. The Germans run across the bridge. They leave behind the grieving Belgian people. We in chase. I stand at the same abutment where the Ruffians fought those years ago. Where Lieutenant Dease met death, transfiguration, apotheosis. He comes to me in visions, dreams, and visitations still. He speaks to me now. "Yes, the end is near, brother Golden Arrow of God." I touch the golden arrow on the back of my lapel again, many times touched as a talisman, an amulet.

The last German soldiers, bedraggled, slovenly, scurry toward home. Old men, mere children–now taking a final stand across the Nimy bridge.

November 11, 1918 10:50. Few bullets come in our direction. A few feeble mortar shells, most of them squibs, duds, the German factories producing defective ammunition. No miners now to dig saltpeter. Few to smelt brass for cartridges. Yet, here and there an explosion.

The brown water in the canal seemed the same brown water that flowed along the canal four years ago.

Me and Vickers, Victoria, Vicki–victorious. After Ypres in 1914 I was made Gunner One, later promoted to Sergeant. No promotion beyond that ever came. Any chance, though hinted at, lost in the miasma of bureaucracy. It didn't matter to me. I came to manhood in the war's first months. In the years since I came to something vastly different from the boy I had been. I had absorbed the spirits and personalities of those who had taken me in hand–the sarcasm and wit of William Catchpole and Ziggy Palmer, the common sense of Carrew Nancarrew, Paul Carmichael's intelligence, and the saintliness of my beloved Lieutenant, Maurice Dease. Qualities also of the Victors, Sergeant Sanders, the clever soldiers, Hardy and Lang, and the rest.

But now I was little more than a ghost.

Winters. Freezing in the trenches, benumbed with cold. Summers sweltering in the sun. The inescapable stench of the trenches. My brain now seared with pictures from which it will never be free.

November 11, 1918: Nimy Bridge, 10:55. Five minutes to the final "Last Post", the last "cease fire,"

A bullet, without aim or intention, more a salute in parting than a salvo, pierced my heart.

I had died before, so knew of Life after life.

Dease's voice rang out. "Tommy Atkins, it was not your time the first time, my brother. You had to live to bear witness."

Tommy Atkins, His Ascension

I ascended from my body. Below, I saw my corpse growing smaller as Dease and my brothers-in-arms carried me aloft. At first my body the size of a dog, than a mouse, now a bee, an ant, then lost to sight in the depths of the land. Then billows of golden cloud enwrapped me. My ears rang with the whine of wind tearing through trees, the baying of hounds, lions roaring, the shrill groan of bagpipes, and penny whistle shrieks. As if struck by vertigo, I spun into the darkness of night, enshrouded in the cloud of gold.

Angels swarmed about me, like humming birds around nectar-filled lilies. Certain angels revealed themselves to me in voice. Their names blossomed in my mind: Ananyal sang, "I am blessed by God; I have plenty, more than enough, rose branches in bloom." I saw the angel Piel teaching Jacob, bringing home his lessons with resounding slaps. Then, the apocryphal angels presented themselves. Before each I bowed as low as I could bend. Jehudial shouted, "Praise the Lord." His right hand cradled the crown of acceptance, the left gripped a three-stranded whip. The apocryphal angel Barakiel was a statue of gold. Angel Salathiel declaimed, "Your soul belongs to God." And next to God–Mittaron–once Enoch, son of Jared, father of Methuselah, Noah's great-grandfather–in the flesh, a living man. He sat on a flaming column beside God's Throne. Before the apocryphal angels, each the size of Leviathan, I prostrated myself. I see the angel Uriel wrapped in smoke. I see the angel Gabriel, himself fire. I watch them bury Adam in the ground when his life had circled through his days, again, here as they did on earth. And now by my side, in a swirl of drops of molten lead, as if falling from a shot tower, a statue shaped itself, became St. George incarnate.

Angel St. George proclaimed, "Tommy Atkins, God's Golden Arrow, you are the alpha and the omega, the beginning and the end, tied end to end, the ouroboros, the snake circled, its tail clasped in its mouth."
In that instant, I saw all the souls of all the soldiers who died through those terrible years. I saw their tears a torrent, a river spilling from end to end–Le Havre to Luxembourg, three hundred and fifty miles long, a fifty-mile wide swath. I suffered the agony, terror, pain, suffering of every soldier, every refugee, every citizen of every ravaged and occupied town and village, each city. A scourge from which there was no surcease.

My ears ring with the devil's laughter. No greater joy, no greater triumph has he tasted since his fall from Heaven.

Tommy Atkins:
Angel of Grief, Memory, and Tears

All who claim authority from God, God curses for their arrogance and stupidity, their fraud, lies, lack of trust in his Word. Next time, and there shall be a next time, the shrieks of pain, the cries of grief that shall arise from the soldier, refugee, and citizen shall deafen God himself. I tell you, this very ground will reek again with the stench of dead men's flesh. Disease shall desolate the ground. Millions, I say truly, millions will fall, destroyed in ways not yet formed in fiendish vapors in the minds of men. There shall be factories whose fuel is the bodies of the dead, whose product shall be misery and tears, ash and bone. There shall be clouds, monstrous mushrooms exploding out of the ground, the heat of the sun blooming forth. Men shall turn into thin air, and buildings disintegrate in an instant. The earth shall feed on flesh and drink blood, as in days of old when the gods needed them for food and drink.

These prophesies surpass what you can believe. Nonetheless they are true. You shall see this come to pass. Write it in your log, journal, your diary, commonplace book.

Dear Reader

And at the end, I, Tommy Atkins, the angel of grief and memory, shall roll the Heavens together, and with them, the realm of Hell. I will call on the angel Dease and my brother Golden Arrows of God. Other angels shall help us–some no bigger than fleas whose wings beat loud as thunder, some the size of men and women, robust and smelling of work and long flight, some big as stars, showering the dark sky with threads of light. Then, like one skilled in knots and cloth, a sail-maker, or one who coils baskets from plaited straw, I will wind and furl the air, shall twist the universe. Others will grind the demons we conquered as in a mill press. I shall call the angel St. George and the angel Jeanne d'Arc and name God from the least name to the most secret. When I say the last the universe shall be born anew, Eden again a blooming garden, man and woman, innocent once again.

About the Author

Jerred Metz has written six books of poetry and three of non-fiction prose. He teaches writing at Strayer University. Aside from short stories, this is his first full length novel. He lives in Columbia, South Carolina with his wife, Sarah Barker. His grown children are successful in their endeavors and have children of their own.

WORKS CONSULTED

Begbie, Harold, *On the Side of the Angels*

Booth, Martin, *The Doctor and the Detective*

Campbell, Phyllis, "The Angelic Leaders", *The Occult Review*

Chinn, George M., *The Machine Gun: History*

Clarke, David, *The Angel of Mons: Phantom Soldiers and Ghostly Guardians*

Coppard, George, *With a Machine Gun to Cambrai*

Foster, R.F., *W. B. Yeats: A Life I: The Apprentice Magus 1865-1914*

Galet, Lieutenant-General, *Albert King of the Belgians in the Great War*

History of the First Royal Fusiliers

Haithrnthwaite, Philip, J., *The World War One Source Book*

Machen, Arthur, "The Bowmen"

Lomas, David, *The Battle of Mons*

Lycett, Andrew, *The Man Who Created Sherlock Holmes*

Nicolle, David, *Crecy 1346, Triumph of the Long Bow*

Silver, Carole, *Strangers and Secret People*

Spears, E. L., Brigadier-General, *Liaison 1914: A Narrative of the Great Retreat*

Stashower, David, *Aurthur Conan Dolye, Teller of Tales*

Whitehouse, Arch, *Heroes and Legends of World War I*

Made in the USA
Coppell, TX
22 March 2022